BEAUTIFUL BROKEN THINGS

Stories

BY ROSE BLACKTHORN

Yarrow noticed the shadowy figure near the lilacs many times, but always from the corner of her eye. Whenever she turned her head, it would be gone; a frustrating game of hide and seek. After Grandma's reaction to Yarrow's worries during the storm, she didn't bring up these fleeting visitations to either of her grandparents. Instead she tried to come up with a way to get a better look at it.

She tried sidling toward the bushes without turning her head, she tried looking away and then back quickly, she even tried lying on the grass beneath the graceful drape of flowers. Nothing worked, although she often got the overpowering feeling that the shadow was watching her, as it had done through the downpour. Finally she'd had enough. "If you won't play fair, I won't play at all."

Surprisingly, that did the trick. The center bush trembled, then shivered, and Yarrow jumped back. A face, thin and angular, appeared between the heart-shaped leaves and heavy flower clusters. It was a boy, perhaps a year or two older than she, with unruly black hair and lilac colored eyes. And he was smiling.

"Who are you?" she asked, then flushed at the rudeness of her tone. He had startled her, though.

"I am Irial," he said, with a strange fluid lilt to his words. His voice was deeper than she had expected, and the teeth his smile revealed were very white and sharp. "I wondered how long before you'd speak to me."

DEDICATION

To all of you: friends, family, and everyone in between, who have supported me, believed in me, cared about me, and let me know you were always there.

Thanks to Mom, Grandma and Grandpa, Geno, my (claimed) dad Sam, my other mom and dad Shirley and Ralph, to the Harding/Arthur clan who read all my stuff, and to so many people who I've only ever met on the internet but are still my true and loving friends.

Special thanks to Christopher Jones who did *everything* but write the stories in this collection, you are awesome.

Last, but not least, to my fur-kids Shadow and Malibu who keep me entertained, irritated, often cuddled, sometimes sleepless, but always thoroughly loved.

INTRODUCTION

When school was out during the summer months we were regularly kicked out of the house, told to go play outside, and out of the front doors we poured, dozens of kids, left to our own design.

Outside we learned about good neighbors and bad, how some of the older kids were safe to play with, while others proved to be dangerous tricksters. We learned which neighborhood dogs would bite with minimal provocation, and occasionally we'd come across adults bearing inexplicable auras of menace whom we'd avoid at all costs.

There were secrets to be uncovered everywhere, protected by locked gates or walls prohibitively topped with broken glass that we'd still risk climbing, just so we could see what lay on the other side. There was the factory across from Grandma's house that opened its doors in the summer to let the weavers cool off. The movement, the dust, and the deafening wall of sound, drew us inexorably until we stood mesmerized at the doorway, gazing in, our imaginations on fire.

There was the path through the bluebell wood—not the real path, the secret one—where we'd hide if we heard someone coming and who knows, maybe *we* frightened *them* into thinking they were being observed by hobgoblins peeping from behind trees.

We were running recklessly along the sharp edge of life, spurred on and protected by a finely tuned sense of fear and wonder—an instinctive knowledge that opened us to infinite possibilities and hidden realms, where things were not always what they seemed.

Some say these fanciful senses disappear when we grow older, as we become world-weary and prone to reason. Personally, I think they stay with us, dormant, like an eye waiting to open, or a second heart waiting to beat. They kick in during the stories we read, the art we admire and the films we watch. They send us gloriously aloft whenever we take a walk by the seashore. They ignite instantly when we're walking home in the dead of night on a country road and we hear the rumbling breath of some strange beast. *What was that—a dragon or worse—a werewolf?* A smile appears when we acknowledge the herd of cattle over the other side of the hedge, but just for a moment we're right back there, our imaginations running riot, and the smile is one of remembrance and not just an admission of foolishness.

I first came across Rose's literary works a few years ago. We both had tales in *Eulogies 2: Tales from the Cellar,* edited by Christopher Jones, Nanci Kalanta, and Tony Tremblay, and her story "The Lilac Hedge" beautifully rounded off the anthology with a traditional, quite menacing, tale of the Fae. I'd also enjoyed some of her flash fiction, and especially her superb short story "What We Do For Love" that warns of the dangers of naivety and presumption, so when I was asked to write an introduction for her forthcoming collection I jumped at the opportunity.

One of the main themes in the collection is the sea and its shores, and why not? We've been fascinated by that boundary between two worlds ever since we first crawled out onto the rocks. Year after year, we risk drowning in our thousands and yet, despite the sea's indifferent hostility we continue to float, fish, swim, and occasionally dive into its prodigious depths in order to determine the mysteries of it. In "A Cache of Pearls" a girl is swept beneath the water, presumably never to be seen again. Elsewhere, in "Before The First Day Of Winter" and the aforementioned "What We Do For Love" the reverse happens and creatures of the deep slither forth onto our blissfully ignorant shores.

Shape-changing is another significant theme, where the boundaries between the self and the world we inhabit become blurred, aptly illustrated in the tense, fear-laden "Skraelings" and the weird and delightful think-you-know-where-this-is-going "A Thing Of Beauty."

There are tales of the afterlife, of body horror and murder; of soul-stealing, and terrors lurking in the dark. The tales are lyrical, magical, but nonetheless well-grounded. They're the kind of stories you might come across in the collections of Neil Gaiman, Angela Carter, and Tanith Lee. Some bear the nastiest of twists, others turn out all right in the end. All wander off the well worn path and into the variegated instability of the unknown, where danger and magic lurk around every corner. And yet, now our senses have awakened and we're equipped with the beating of the clandestine heart, stories such as these are undoubtedly survivable. Forewarned is forearmed, as they say, and who knows? On a particular night, on that dark country road, it may well be a dragon lurking beyond that hedge, after all.

Janet Joyce Holden
January 2018

CONTENTS

A CHILD NAMED SORROW

He was small, appearing younger than his age. Pale blond hair topped a high forehead and snub nose. His eyes, when he let her see them, were dark and deep, a non-descript color. He was polite and quiet, very well-behaved. How any parent could have abandoned such a child, Penny would never understand.

As though he felt the weight of her gaze, he turned from contemplating the dandelion stem he held. The yellow flower was gone, replaced by a fuzzy round seed head.

"Come in and wash up," Penny said with a reassuring smile.

He looked back at the stem he held and blew to free the multitude of fluffy parachutes. Dandelion seeds drifted across the yard, settling in the dry thinning grass, and Penny sighed.

When he crossed the yard to her, Penny smiled again and held out her hand, hoping he would smile back. Instead, his somber expression did not change and he dropped his eyes. But he took her hand and walked with her into the house.

"Are you hungry?"

"Yes," he said, but didn't seem enthused.

She turned him toward the hall. "The bathroom is the first door on the right. Wash your hands, and when you come back lunch will be ready."

Without another word he followed her directions, disappearing into the half-bath. A moment later, Penny heard the water turn on.

She went back to the counter to finish the sandwiches she was making for lunch. Faded ginger hair fell across her tired eyes as she thought about the boy.

She'd found him on the side of the road. When she stopped

her car, he'd solemnly answered her questions, dark eyes hidden after the first soul-searching look he'd given her. He was clean and well-nourished, but alone. When she asked where his parents were, he'd shrugged in a matter-of-fact way that brought a lump to her throat.

"They're gone," he'd said evenly. "They didn't want me anymore. Nobody wants me."

Remembering his forthright words made tears sting, and she blinked as she carried two plates to the table. Her eyes sought the framed photos on the wall. Penny herself, younger and happier, holding her daughter as she leaned against her husband's side. She blinked hard.

"Where are they?" the boy asked, and she nearly dropped their lunch.

"What?"

He pointed to the grouping of pictures.

Penny cleared her throat. "My daughter passed away. Tom— Tom left after that."

"It makes you sad," he said, meeting her eyes now. His were dark, as black and empty as the hollow space that had grown in her since she lost her family.

"Yes," she said, uneasy. "Didn't you say you're hungry?"

"Very hungry," he agreed.

Then Penny was on the floor, not knowing how she'd gotten there, with the boy perched above her. His mouth gaped, revealing sharp pointed teeth. When he darted forward, she couldn't even scream.

She remembered hearing once that sorrow gnaws at your heart. She had never expected it to be so literal.

A ROOM WITH NO VIEW

Lilia has been here for so long, she remembers nothing else. On bright days, light comes through the upper arched window sash. Because it faces north, no sunlight ever slips inside. The bottom pane has been painted black so she cannot see anything outside except the high curved slice of unreachable sky. By mutual exclusion, no one outside can see her, either.

She has a secret though, for even with her crippled limbs she can climb. When she is left alone, she scales the tiled sill and pulls herself above the obscured glass to perch on the narrow rail. For long hours Lilia crouches there, her thin arms wrapped around her knees. She hums softly, but cannot sing the words. Long ago in the time known as *before* a woman had held her, kept her warm, and sang in a sweet voice. Now, Lilia hums the tune and traces the map of her scars. She looks out upon a world that does not know she exists.

When the key clatters in the lock, she scurries down like a spider with half its limbs removed. Dr. Heidrich comes in, unannounced as always. "Come now, Lilia. It is time."

There is no place to run, nowhere to hide. The lock on the bathroom door was removed long ago, for Lilia has no privacy. She cowers in the corner beneath the distant arch of summer sky.

The orderlies bring her back to where Nurse Absinthe waits with the needle. There is a sting, and the cobwebbed ceiling fades along with the scent of licorice.

She wakes to darkness in the echoing silence of her room. Touches her face, where bandages obscure the contours of brow and orbit. It will hurt, it always does; but she has to know.

The tape and gauze come off with little effort, for she has become dexterous despite the missing digits. Stitches sew her lids together over nothing, and now she cannot even cry.

Lilia turns to the window she cannot see. Dr. Heidrich has taken her one piece at a time—fingers, bones, bits and pieces of her healthy organs—and now she is a patchwork horror. The climb up the sash is terrifying, but less so than the alternative.

She crouches on the rail, mutilated hands and eyeless face against the glass. When it breaks she will fly, and be seen by the world at last.

DRAGON BOUND

Kieran Wynn entered Leicia, the crown city of Briarand, through the imposing main gates. He was required to pay a silver coin for his entrance, and state his business before being allowed to continue.

"I've come to make my name," he said evenly, "And volunteer to save the Princess." To his credit, he did not flinch when the guardsmen burst into guffaws of derisive laughter.

"You are no knight," the guard who'd taken his coin stated. "You may be strong and able-bodied, but you haven't even a sword or a spear. How do you expect to save the Princess?"

Kieran shrugged. "You have sword and spear both, and you haven't saved her," was his reply.

The guard bristled, face turning red as his mirth left him. "Get on your way then, peasant," he said as his fellows shooed Kieran into the city. "Next time I see you, you'll be on your back, for sure."

Kieran ducked his head and hid his smile. "On your back" meant ready for burial, but he was in no hurry to die. The proclamations heralded throughout the kingdom had stated quite plainly that any man who would risk his own life to save the Princess would be richly rewarded. There would be land, titles, and an undisclosed amount of gold. Kieran had two younger sisters for whom he must provide. He was no knight, nor schooled in weaponry and war. But he was intelligent and even-tempered. He was willing to risk his life—not for the Princess, but for his sisters. They waited for him in the care of their spinster aunt. He had promised to return with a new life for all of them.

With the city wall behind him, he strode with purpose along the cobblestoned main road. In the distance, atop a modest hill at the center of the city, stood the royal castle. It was built from grey and white stones, with its own protective wall around it, and a slender spire standing tall from the center. Pennants of deep red with a white quatrefoil flower in the center flapped in the light breeze. The sun shone down, bright and hot in a cloudless sky. But there seemed a pall of despair over the bustling city. The Princess, only daughter of the King and Queen, had been taken from her kingdom almost seven years before. Rumors abounded that she would never be returned, but the royal family continued to offer rewards for those who would attempt it.

Kieran followed the wide thoroughfare up the gentle incline until he came to the gates of the castle's outer wall. Here were stationed more guards, but these seemed much more serious about their duties than the lot down below. When Kieran approached, the two guards standing in the entrance crossed their spears, blocking any further progress. From an alcove within the shade of the wide gateway came another man. According to the colors attached to the shoulder of his tunic, he was the captain.

"What is your business at the castle?" he asked. He was neither rude nor friendly, but went straight to the point.

"I have come to volunteer. I am here to save the Princess," Kieran returned just as directly, and the captain sighed.

"Yes, of course," he said, and gestured for Kieran to follow him. The other two guards straightened their spears, opening the way.

The shadow beneath the gate was dense and much cooler than the air outside. The small alcove to one side served as an office of sorts, with a small table and two chairs placed against the wall. The captain sat in one, and gestured perfunctorily to the other. After a momentary hesitation, Kieran also sat.

"What's your name, lad?"

"Kieran Wynn, sir. I come from the north, from the village of Croí-adhmaid."

The captain used a quill to write on a piece of parchment

already lying on the table top. "Have you any next of kin?"

Kieran hesitated, mouth open.

The captain glanced up, and a tight smile touched his mouth. "In case you don't return, Master Wynn. The King and Queen have set up a fund from which they send a small amount to the families of the men who die trying to fulfill this quest."

Kieran felt his cheeks warm with embarrassment, but he only said, "I have twin sisters, Kiri and Kami. They are with my aunt Eilwen, on a small farm just outside Croí-adhmaid."

The captain simply nodded, and wrote down the additional information. When he was done, he rang a small metal bell that sat on the corner of the table. In response, a boy appeared, dressed in the livery of the castle. "Take Master Wynn to the castle, to the Steward. Tell him this young man is here to make his attempt."

"Yes sir," the page replied, taking the piece of parchment with Kieran's information and bowing quickly. Then he led the way through the gate, and back out into the hot sun between the wall and the castle itself.

Kieran gazed around, his blue eyes sharp, not wanting to miss anything though he was sure he appeared the country bumpkin. He'd never had the opportunity to travel to Leicia before, and wanted to be able to relate everything he saw to his sisters when he went back home. If, he reminded himself, he went back home.

In a moment the page led him into the castle proper, past more guards and servant women replacing the straw on the stone floors. Kieran had a brief glimpse of tall hand-made tapestries covering the stone walls with artful renditions of old tales, complete with dragons, unicorns and men dressed in golden armor. Then the page led him out of the great hall into a narrow passage. The boy had said nothing to him so far, and now in the confines of this hallway Kieran could do little but keep up. When they reached an arched doorway, the page stepped inside and halted with a deep bow. Not knowing the proper etiquette, Kieran bowed as well.

"Yes, what is it?" asked a low voice.

"Lord Steward," the page said, stepping forward with the

parchment, "Captain Warin instructed me to bring this man to you, and state that he is here to make his attempt."

"Very well. Back to your duties," and the man seated behind the heavy carved desk waved his hand as though to shoo the boy away. He looked down at the paper and said, "This says your name is Kieran Wynn, is that right?"

"Yes, sir," Kieran replied, trying not to stare. The Steward, dressed in rich clothing and with hair and beard painstakingly curled in long ringlets carefully arranged, was horribly disfigured. One eye was brown, the other cloudy white; the right side of his face from which the white eye shone was rent with deep scars that extended from forehead to jawbone.

"You needn't look so terrified, Master Wynn. It's not contagious."

Kieran caught his breath and squared his shoulders. "My apologies, sir. I didn't mean to be rude."

The older man shrugged and got to his feet. "So you've come to volunteer, have you? Going to save the Princess and make a name for yourself? You're not attempting this to impress some girl, I hope."

Kieran shook his head firmly. "No, sir. I am a single man, with no land or household. But I have two sisters for whom I must provide. The reward offered for saving the Princess would be enough to take care of my sisters until they find husbands and have children of their own, and even after that."

"What do your parents think of this plan?"

Kieran shook his head just once. "Our father died when my sisters were still babes. Mother fell ill, and never fully recovered. She died only a year after Father. My mother's aunt took us in, but she is aged and frail and needs to be looked after now."

The Steward nodded, seeming to sympathize with Kieran's plight, but his scarred face made it hard to read his expression. "Well, I see you have plenty of reason to succeed, Master Wynn. If you're ready, I will take to you meet the King and Queen."

Kieran cleared his throat nervously. He had not expected to meet the royal family.

The older man came around his desk, walking with a pronounced limp, and put a hand on Kieran's shoulder.

"Kieran—may I call you that?—King Rordan and Queen Fiera speak with every man who would attempt to rescue the Princess." He squeezed Kieran's shoulder, then turned the younger man to accompany him back down the narrow hallway. "It is they who will give you the information you require if you are to have a chance at success."

"Of course," Kieran said, following the limping man. "I just was surprised, sir."

When they reached the great hall again, the Steward waited for Kieran to walk beside him. "This is their daughter. Of course they want to meet any man who is willing to take on this terrible challenge. And for future reference, you may call me Aristide. I am Steward to the royal family, but no knight or landed lord."

"Thank you, sir—Aristide," Kieran said and ducked his head in a gesture of respect. Then he shortened his steps to keep stride with the other man.

As they passed through the great hall, moving at a slower pace than the page had kept, Kieran had the opportunity to study the tapestries and furnishings more fully. The needlework and coloring on the wall hangings was exquisite, the tables and chairs made by a master craftsman. Even the wrought iron sconces attached to the walls that held torches or lanterns were graceful, much more than just serviceable.

"Do you approve?" Aristide asked with a wry lilt in his tone.

"Forgive me, but I promised my sisters an account... of, well, everything," Kieran explained, his face warming again.

The Steward nodded, keeping his smile to himself. Many men had come to the castle seeking their fortune by fulfilling the royal quest, and he had met them all. Most had been proud, bragging of their exploits and their expertise. None of them had succeeded, and in truth Aristide had not mourned their loss. He found himself feeling quite differently about this young man.

At the other end of the large central hall was a wide curving staircase that led to the right. The Steward started up the steps, his labored stride slowing a bit, but Kieran simply kept pace with him. Tall narrow windows were cut into the curving outer wall, and he glanced out at the view each time they passed one. By the time they'd reached the top of the spiral, he was looking

back toward the main city gates he'd entered less than an hour
before. The streets and buildings dropped away in measured
steps that showed more organization than had been apparent as
he'd travelled those streets.

"Come now Kieran, we're nearly there," the Steward said,
sounding a little out of breath. He walked along a wide hallway
toward a large arched doorway. The doors were already thrown
open, and the Steward passed inside without announcing
himself.

Within was a large chamber walled in stone and floored in
dark glossy wood. More tapestries and hangings filled the room
with color. At the far end of the room on an ornate pedestal stood
two grand claw-footed chairs. They were covered with gold
and gems, the cushions made of blood-red velvet. The thrones
however were vacant.

"Your Highness," Aristide said, looking to the side were two
people sat on a low couch. "I've brought someone I'd like you to
meet."

The man remained seated, but the woman stood gracefully.
"Of course. Please, bring him in."

King Rordan seemed to be in his late forties, still slender and
physically capable. But there were lines on his face, dark smudges
beneath his brown eyes, and a liberal sprinkling of grey in his
dark hair. His wife, Queen Fiera was still strikingly beautiful.
She appeared at least a decade younger than her husband, with
rich auburn hair and exquisite green eyes. But her face was pale,
and she seemed not to have smiled in a very long time.

"King Rordan, Queen Fiera, this is Master Kieran Wynn. He
has come to volunteer to attempt to save your daughter."

The King nodded once but said nothing, and the bleak
expression on his face did not change.

"You are certain?" the Queen said. Her voice was cool but
kind, and she seemed genuinely interested in his answer. "If
you have any doubt at all, Master Wynn, you would be wise to
reconsider now, before we go any further."

Kieran squared his shoulders and nodded. "I'm certain,
Your Highness. I was certain before I ever left my home in
Croí-adhmaid."

"You are from the north, then," the King said softly, his voice as dark and dour as his expression.

"Yes, Your Highness."

Rordan nodded again, and returned to his silence.

"Please, Master Wynn. Sit down," the Queen said, gesturing to another low couch across from the one where the King was sitting. "Aristide, would you have some food brought up? This young man looks hungry, and food and wine might ease the telling of this tale."

"Of course," the Steward said graciously, then limped back across the room to the open doors.

"Don't drag it out, Fiera," the King said, as morose as before. "The chances are he'll fail like all those before. And we're running out of time."

"Enough," she said curtly, then pressed her lips together as though to hold back any more sharp words. She sat, putting her hand over the King's. "Rordan, we can't give up hope. Not now. Not after all these years."

The King sighed, turning his hand to clasp hers, but he only shook his head and said nothing.

Kieran sat stiff and uncomfortable on the other couch, keeping his eyes downcast. He was embarrassed to have witnessed this exchange, and did not know what to do. He would never presume to offer advice to those of a higher station, and he certainly did not want to offend. But although he was young and poor, and without any power or social status, he did know something of grief.

"When I was twelve years old," he said softly, still looking down at the floor, "and my sisters were still babes, my father went hunting. We had no money, just a small farm and a sturdy house. Father thought to bring home a deer, some to sell and the rest to feed us."

Rordan and Fiera were silent, both listening to the young man who had come to rescue their lost daughter as so many had before. Aristide, coming back from sending for food, waited just inside the doorway to hear what he would say.

"I wanted to go with him," Kieran went on, keeping his eyes down. "I begged him to let me go. But he told me that my job, when he wasn't there, was to take care of my mother and sisters. That without him, I was to be the man of the house, so to speak. So I sulked and frowned, but stayed at home. When he didn't come back, Mother sent me to the village, to ask for men to help search for Father."

"Did they find him?" Fiera asked.

Kieran nodded. "He met bandits in the forest. They killed him for his bow and his dagger, and the silver ring he wore on his left hand. The men of the village tracked them, and brought them back to the elders for judgment. They were hung in the village square, for murder and thievery."

The King had raised his head now, his weary eyes resting on Kieran's face.

"Father's bow and dagger were returned to us, and the silver ring he'd worn," Kieran continued. He held up his left hand, showing a simple silver band worn on the first finger. "But without him, my mother lost her strength. Sometimes I think she gave too much of her heart to him, and when he died her heart died too. Within a year she was gone as well."

The Queen had closed her eyes, as though unable or unwilling to witness his remembered pain. The King however looked on directly, recognizing perhaps a kindred spirit.

"My mother's aunt took us in," Kieran went on evenly. "She was and is a kind and gentle woman, rich in love if nothing else. She tells my sisters stories of before we were all born, of how our mother and father met and fell in love. How happy they were just to be together. I have tried very hard to do as Father told me, to be the man of the house, and protect my family. But I feel the loss of them, my parents, every day. There is no way to bring them back, to heal my broken family. But as long as your daughter lives, there is hope. There is still time to bring her home. I couldn't save my father, or my mother. But I want to try to save your daughter."

"So speaks a noble heart," Aristide said when Kieran fell silent. He limped back into the room, servants with trays of food and drink following him.

When the servants had placed their trays on low tables, and filled goblets with wine and water, they retreated, closing the chamber doors behind them. Rordan, still bleak and weary, held a goblet of wine toward Kieran.

"You may come of peasant past, but you have a noble heart, as Aristide said. Eat, and drink your fill. Then my Queen and I will tell you what you must do, to save our precious Meriel."

Kieran walked slowly, trying to ignore his aching legs; he was not much used to riding. The horse that had been provided to him paced along behind. To the west, the sun sank low on the horizon, bright flashes in glittering reflection from the unending sweep of water. Before him, due south, the rocky land was descending. He knew from his map, and the instructions given to him by the King, that he was close to his goal. A last rocky precipice hid view of the solitary tower where the Princess was confined.

"This is as good a place as any to sleep," he said aloud. The horse, as though it understood him, stopped and dropped its head, searching for something to eat. Kieran tugged the reins, and the horse obligingly followed him a few feet more to a tiny streamlet of water. While the horse drank, Kieran pulled down the packs and then stripped off the saddle. There was no grass for the horse to graze, so Kieran opened one of the packs. Inside was a small compacted bale of hay. He cut the cords binding it, and dropped the feed on the rocks for the horse to eat.

This close to the tower, he didn't dare light a fire, even if there had been an abundance of wood to burn. Instead, he drank water from the stream and ate bread and cheese from his pack. When the horse was settled, and the sun had dropped below the edge of the sea, he lay down on the ground and pillowed his head on his pack. He stared up at the sky, waiting for the first star to appear, and listened to the sound of distant surf. From the south he heard a strange cry, long and full of defiance or pain. The horse neighed, tossing its head nervously as it sidestepped. When the far-off bellow drew out to silence, his mount calmed again. Kieran kept waiting for the stars.

While he slept, he returned in dreams to the castle. Once again he sat on a couch covered in velvet and brocade, eating rich food and drinking the finest wine. While he ate and drank, he listened to the Queen tell their story. From time to time the King added something, but for the most part he was silent.

The Queen had been unable to conceive. So she sent for Melainyx, a sea-witch who lived at the southern border of the kingdom. Melainyx came and worked her magic, and soon the Queen was with child. When asked the price of this spell, she had simply said the cost would be known when the time was right. The sea-witch had gone, leaving the King and Queen with plans for the child to come.

Meriel had been born to great wealth and power, and to parents who wanted her more than anything else. The Princess had her mother's extraordinary green eyes and her father's jet-black hair. She was a lovely child, full of laughter and charm, and the entire kingdom had rejoiced with her parents.

But on the eve of her twelfth birthday, Melainyx returned. With her she brought her own son, a boy with black eyes and cold heart named Taranis. She came to claim her reward for the spell that brought Meriel to the King and Queen. The Princess would marry Taranis, so that when King Rordan died he should become King of Briarand.

Meriel was distraught; the King and Queen adamant that their beloved daughter should never wed a boy so cold and cruel. They refused to pay Melainyx's price. But at dawn the next day, they found the Princess gone, spirited away in the night. Melainyx left a note; either King and Queen betrothed their daughter to Taranis, or on Meriel's nineteenth birthday the wedding would take place without their blessing.

The King and his knights rode south, to the place near the sea where Melainyx lived. There, they found the solitary tower on the forbidding rocky headland. There, they met the black dragon that the sea-witch had summoned to protect her hostage and herself.

The knights attacked, to kill the dragon and rescue the Princess. The dragon killed them all, seemingly invulnerable to their weapons, and at last the King had fallen back. Besides the King, the only survivor was a page, a boy only a few years older than the Princess, and he was badly wounded.

Since that time, men had come from all over the

kingdom—warriors and thieves, mercenaries and would-be knights. All to save the Princess and reap the reward offered by the royal family for her rescue. None of them had succeeded. None of them had survived.

Kieran woke, unrested and still weary. He felt he had dreamed that terrible story over and over all through the night. What chance that he would succeed where all else had failed? Yet, he wanted to try.

He drank more water, and ate some more bread. Then he mounted his borrowed horse, and rode south. In a short time he crested the last rocky escarpment and finally saw the legendary tower. It was tall and slender, blank rock walls except for a heavy wooden door at the base and large square windows that circled the top. There was no wall surrounding it, no guards in evidence. Just dry rocky ground leading to the tower, and beyond it a tumbled expanse of boulders dropping to the sea.

Kieran got off the horse, and removed its saddle and bridle, dropping all his possessions onto the ground. He stroked the horse's head, leaning against its solid warmth for a moment. Then he stepped back and slapped it on the flank sharply. The horse started, rearing a bit before lunging forward.

Kieran crouched, half hidden in the rocks, and watched.

From the tumbled boulders beyond the tower rose the dragon. Black scales and claws glistened in the morning sunlight, and the huge wings nearly swept the ground as the beast drove upward. Again came the blood-chilling scream that he'd heard the night before, only much louder now at close quarters. The horse screamed as well, rearing again and nearly falling as it struggled to change direction. The poor creature scrambled on loose stone and turned to race toward the sea. The dragon, a thing made of shadow and grace fell upon it with talons outstretched. It plucked the squealing horse from the ground as lightly as a maiden picking a flower, and flew back to its nesting place among the boulders.

Kieran clenched his teeth against the agonized shrieks from his late steed, and raced across the open ground to the base of the tower. The heavy wooden door opened easily at his touch, and he slipped into the shadowed interior without being seen.

Inside the thick stone walls it was quiet. He could not hear the ocean waves, or the feasting dragon. Thankfully, the horse had finally fallen silent. With his father's dagger in one hand, and the sword given to him by the Queen in the other, he cautiously crept up the dusty stairs that spiraled up the interior of the tower.

The higher he climbed, the more he could hear the waves on the beach below, and the wind soughing through the open windows at the top of the tower. He heard no voice, no other movement on the wooden floor of the room above him. When he reached the trap door that opened upward into the top of the tower, he hesitated for a long moment. His heart was pounding, his throat dry as he gasped for breath. He felt as though he'd been running for miles. He couldn't remember ever being more afraid. What would he find when he opened this last door?

Finally he sheathed his father's dagger and grasped the metal handle on the door. Before he could change his mind, he pushed the door up into the room above, running up the last few steps with the sword held at the ready.

The room was large and open, taking up the entire top of the tower. Three heavy pillars supported the weight of the slate roof and richly detailed tapestries had been strung between them to enclose the center of the room. All of the windows encircling the room were open, with no glass or shutters to cover them. The floor was spread with thick carpets and furs, and rich furnishings were scattered throughout. Hanging on the stonework between the windows were paintings, all of the same subject. A girl with long black hair and vibrant green eyes. In some her hair was intricately styled in braids and curls, held back from her slender face with ivory combs and jeweled pins. In others her hair hung loose down her back or over her shoulders. Her clothing in the paintings ran the gamut as well, from decorous bejeweled ball gowns to a simple shift of white cloth that only hung to her knees. The girl was the only person in any of the paintings, and in all of them her jade colored eyes wore the same expression. Lonely, weary, trapped.

Kieran cautiously circled the room, seeing no sign of the girl herself. Only the space between the three pillars, curtained as they were, could possibly hide her. He approached the center of the room, pausing to listen for a long moment. Was the girl still sleeping? He reached out to pull the tapestry aside, and let the sword drop.

Obviously this was where the girl slept; there was a large bed draped in silk and brocade, with pillows heaped at one end. The bed was unoccupied. There was nowhere else for the Princess to hide. She was not here.

Sunset was a wild cascade of color and sound. The tide was coming in, and waves crashed against the rocky shore with breathtaking sprays of white water. The sun was molten gold descending into clouds of copper, bronze and blood-stained steel. Kieran sat against the stone wall, gazing out at the dazzling yet desolate view. He had spent the day, after searching the tower for any trace of the Princess, watching out the windows. Quite a bit of that time had been spent observing the dragon. It was huge, but certainly not ungainly. In flight it had the grace and control of a hawk. On the ground, it moved with the strength and muscular weight of a lion. Surprising him, it had even taken to the water for a while. It swam and dove, spending minutes at a time below the surface, and even then it moved as though in its favored element. Kieran found himself wondering if it could move through soil and stone as easily. At this point, he would not have been surprised.

The gaudy sunset glanced off the dragon's ebony scales, glittering in an almost blinding progression of refracted light. As the sun began to flatten against the edge of the sea, he saw something moving down below. It wasn't the dragon; that magnificent beast still crouched at the edge of the water, wings spread wide as though waiting for a gust of wind powerful enough to lift it. Something smaller, little more than a shadow in the last blinding rays of sunlight, was moving toward the base of the tower.

Kieran sat up, risking a glance over the window sill, but only caught a glimpse of the figure entering the tower through the single wooden door. He looked around quickly, but truly the only place to hide in this open room was within the curtained confines between the stone pillars. As quietly as he could, he slipped to the center of the room and crouched against one of the heavy round supports.

Out of sight, the wind blew through the open windows, sighing against the stonework. The sea rumbled and boomed over the rocky beach, surging forward and then falling back in ancient rhythm. An odd crooning sound came from the same direction, and Kieran guessed it was the dragon. Had it spotted the intruder entering the tower?

For a long moment there was silence. The light in the tower abruptly dimmed, plunging the curtained chamber into near darkness. Kieran held his breath, the sword unsheathed and held before him at the ready. A rending, agonizing bellow sounded, close enough to almost be in the room, and Kieran forced himself not to move, to stay in his hiding place.

"Enough, already," a soft sinewy voice said, "I don't need to suffer your screeching."

There was a muffled sound, as though something had been dropped heavily onto the carpeted floor. Light appeared, flickering in the sea wind, and Kieran saw two silhouettes on the tapestry.

"Your suffering means nothing to me," said a soft feminine voice.

Kieran saw the larger shadow shrug. "Why should it? I brought you wine, and more paints."

"You can leave them there." The more slender shadow crossed the cast light, and then more candles or lanterns were lit, diffusing and multiplying the silhouettes. It was dizzying.

"What, not in the mood for company?" There was a coldness to the voice, and yet amusement as well. Kieran did not like the sound of it.

"Taranis, if it was in my power, I would kill you right now. Better your blood on my hands, than listening to your surly attempts at manners."

There came a heavy sigh, and Taranis dropped something on the floor. "But it is not in your power. I didn't choose this either, Princess. I want you no more than you want me. Yet your birthday swiftly approaches." With no farewell, he turned and went down the steps, pausing only to pull the trap door shut behind him.

"You can come out," Meriel said, and Kieran started. "I saw you in the window earlier. Taranis might not know you are here, although surely he wonders why the trap door was open."

Taking a deep breath, Kieran stood and held aside the draped tapestry. Standing near the windows was the Princess he'd come so far to rescue. Her black hair fell free down her back, stirring in the wind that came off the water. Her eyes were as extraordinary as the Queen's, a rich shade of green like flawless jade. Her face was slender and lovely, and she wore a long white tunic belted with moonstone links.

"What is your name?" As she spoke, she bent to pick up the bottle of wine Taranis had dropped on the floor. Beside it was a box filled with paints. She was the artist who'd painted all the portraits.

"I am Kieran Wynn, m'lady. I've come to rescue you."

She smiled, the expression seeming unfamiliar to her. "You are no shining knight, Kieran Wynn. Though I see you have the requisite sword."

He turned his head just slightly, as though listening for a sound that was almost out of range. "Have you spoken with so many knights, that you can recognize one on sight?"

She knelt, opening the box to check that the containers inside were still intact. When she was satisfied, she looked at him where he stood, sword still to hand. "I knew many knights in my childhood. Lately, I haven't known anyone, except the oaf who just left."

Kieran let the sword-point rest on the floor, his brows drawn together. "Where is the witch, Princess?"

She laughed softly, the sound lovely and marrow-freezing. "Melainyx? Dead and gone, these many years. How many? Let me think," and she got gracefully to her bare feet to carry the box of paints to the empty easel. "Five; yes, she died five years ago, almost to the day."

"How?"

"The dragon, of course." Meriel turned back to him, her expression empty, eyes predatory. "She lost control of her own magic. It ate her, just like it ate your horse."

"Then why is the dragon still here?"

She walked back to the table where she had left the bottle of wine. "Taranis—he was the one who was here, the witch's ill-favored son, you heard him? Taranis says that when a sorceress makes a spell, especially one that is very powerful and dangerous, if that sorceress dies the magic just keeps going. There's nothing to stop it, or control it any longer." She gripped the leather-wrapped cork with one pale slender hand, and pulled it from the bottle with little effort. "Her magic, now, could go on until the end of the world. At least, that's what Taranis says."

"I don't understand," Kieran said softly, watching as she poured the wine into two graceful cups. "The witch is dead, yet you and her son are both still here."

"There are two ways to break the spell, and end the magic," Meriel said, coming to him with a cup in each hand. "You just have to decide which will bring the happy ending that you're hoping for." She handed him one cup, and lifted the other to her lips.

"I'm listening," he said, tasting the wine.

"The magic is a living thing now, after so long," the Princess said, taking a seat on the nearest chair. "It's changed me, you know. I'm not what I used to be. Neither is Taranis, for that matter."

Kieran sat when she gestured, but said nothing.

"I know my mother and father sent you," she went on, dropping her gaze when she said this, as though unwilling to see his expression. "They've sent so many over the years. Mother promised she would never forget me, and Melainyx counted on that."

"They're your parents," Kieran said. "Of course they wouldn't forget."

Meriel lifted her hand as though brushing that away. "The magic that binds me here, binds me to Taranis. I have no love for him, nor he for me. And, if she had ever bothered to ask, Taranis would have told his own mother he had no desire to be king. She took both our choices from us, and changed us forever from what we would have been."

"So, how can I break that binding?" Kieran asked, already knowing what her answer would be.

"You'll have to kill him. Or the dragon." She met his eyes now, her gaze so cold like deep water. She hardly seemed human. "Which will be easier to kill?"

"I'm not a murderer," he whispered.

There was frost in her voice when she said, "Killing a dragon isn't murder? That beast could live a thousand years. The sea-witch's changeling son has no more right to live than the dragon."

"Then why don't you kill him," Kieran asked, shocked to hear the words come from his own mouth.

She looked at the cup in her hand, then drained it. "I can't. I am bound." She stood, setting the cup aside, and walked toward her makeshift bedchamber. "You have until sunset tomorrow to decide, peasant knight. To help with your decision, I give you my word—if you choose to kill the witch's bastard, the dragon will give you leave to depart."

Kieran sat long into the night, listening to the song of open water and restless wind. The Princess was silent. The full moon rose and shone down upon the desolate headland. There was no sign of movement anywhere. The witch's son had gone to ground somewhere. And the dragon was already in the tower.

By dawn, he had made his choice.

More than a week later, on the Princess's nineteenth birthday, Kieran passed once more through the gates of Leicia. He was grimy and worn from his travels, and from the weight he carried on his back. Yet the heaviest load he bore was the knowledge of what he must tell the King and Queen.

As soon as he gave his name, he was whisked by carriage to the castle gates, and ushered inside with all haste and hope. In a very short time, he found himself once again in the large open room where he'd first met Rordan and Fiera.

Queen Fiera stood with hands clenched and tears trembling in her deep eyes. But it was the King who spoke, his deep voice gentle as he took in Kieran's appearance.

"Are you injured?" he asked, before anything else. Kieran

felt tears sting his own eyes at this.

"No, I am not. Just hungry, and foot-sore," he replied.

"Aristide, send for food," the King said, and the Steward nodded.

"It's already on its way, Your Highness."

"Please, Master Wynn, sit," Rordan said, coming to take Kieran's elbow and help him to a seat. "Did you... What did you find?"

Kieran allowed his pack to slide down to the floor. "I am no minstrel, and I have no heart to draw out my tale," he said, looking at the Queen as she sat across from him. "So I'll tell you as simply as I can. I found the tower you told me of. I found a dragon and a girl. But the sea-witch died years ago, and her son was trapped there as much as your daughter."

Fiera put her hands over her mouth. Rordan sat beside her, silently. Aristide, once a page and now a Steward, closed his eyes and listened.

"The dragon that guarded that tower, and killed so many men over the years, was once your Meriel," Kieran said simply. "She gave me a choice, a way to break the spell and save her. So I released her from her prison."

Fiera covered her face, unable to hold back her tears any longer.

"Where is she?" Rordan asked. He seemed numb, unable to fathom what had happened.

"Meriel is gone," Kieran said, opening the pack at his feet. "The dragon is free, and will trouble your shores no longer. She asked me to bring these to you." From his pack he pulled out all the portraits that the Princess had painted and hung upon her walls. Unrolling them, her distinctive green eyes gazed out at the parents who had lost her long before.

"And the witch's son?" Rordan asked.

Kieran pulled his father's dagger from the pack, still stained with blood. "The dragon took his body, when the deed was done. I asked no more of it."

The King stood and crossed the space between them, kneeling down on one knee to match Kieran's height. He took the young man's hands in his own, and for the first time there was light in his dark eyes. "You have earned your reward, and more Kieran Wynn. You freed our daughter, and returned."

"I didn't bring her back to you," Kieran whispered, throat burning with unshed tears. He had not saved her; he had only set her free.

"But you did," Fiera said, gazing at the paintings.

"Yes," Aristide agreed, "You did."

WHAT WE DO FOR LOVE

L'thyros lay quietly, listening to the incoming surf. The rhythmic pounding of the waves was almost hypnotic, reminiscent of listening to his heartbeats. He had laid his great head against the sand and stones of the beach, the better to appreciate the nearby surges of water. His one great eye looked downward. He was strong and brave, ancient and learned, but the dome of the sky stretching above him was just short of infinite, and it crushed him beneath its weight.

"Oh my God! Look what the storm washed up!" came a high-pitched chirping sound. A human's voice. L'thyros had heard them before, understood their limited infantile language, but winced minutely in discomfort. Their voices were never pleasant, but at least beneath the water they were somewhat softened.

"Holy shit, it's huge!" another human, slightly deeper tone, but still irritating. "I didn't know they could grow so big."

"We should call someone!" the first human again. It spoke as though everything it said was of the utmost importance. L'thyros shuddered, and one of the humans screamed. "It's still alive! Hurry, Larry, call the Coast Guard!"

There were soft chiming tones, then the deeper voice said, "We're at the beach, south of the Ponsler Wayside about half a mile. There's a—shit, what is it?"

"It's a giant octopus!" the higher voice exclaimed.

"Yeah, it's a squid or octopus or something. I've never seen one so big. It's washed up on the beach, a good fifteen or twenty feet from the surf."

There was another voice speaking, so tinny and

far-away L'thyros couldn't make it out in the thin medium of the atmosphere.

"Yeah I know, but it's still alive," the human went on, arguing. "It's still moving. Can it be saved?"

More words into the human's ear that L'thyros didn't attempt to understand. He could sense more approaching, these from the south rather than the north as the first two had come.

"Okay, we'll wait for you here." A musical tone sounded at the end of the conversation, making L'thyros groan; it could not compare, but was vaguely reminiscent of the sounds of deep water through his mate's gills when they swam in tandem. "The Coast Guard is sending help, someone should be here in half an hour."

"Can it live that long outside the water?" the first human shrieked, moving closer. "Should we dump water on it, like they do with beached whales?"

"What happened?" came a new voice. This one was deeper still, barely painful at all to L'thyros. He listened to the waves, to the sound of his hearts beating. He couldn't wait much longer.

"The storm last night!" the first one, screeching again, "It must've washed up and got beached in the high waves!"

"That's something you don't see every day," the last one said, moving closer. "Take a good look, Danny. You'll never see one that big at the aquarium."

"Is it a sea-monster, Grandpa?" This voice was high-pitched as well, but young and timid. The tone was not painful, and it drew L'thyros.

"No, Danny. Just an animal. But a big one, that's for sure." This human was circling now, trying to get a better view of L'thyros. "It's been a while, but I'll bet you it's a squid."

"How can you tell?" the other low-toned human asked, seeming very interested in what the other human was saying.

"Octopi have eight arms. Squids have eight arms too, but they also have two extra tentacles that are used to hunt with. From what I can see, this big fella has more than eight all together."

"How can you tell, Grandpa?" asked the young one, following the deep-voiced one closely. They had almost moved far enough for L'thyros to see them. "It's all raggedy looking, like shredded kinda."

"That's just because it's out of the water, Danny. They're not meant to be out in the air, like we are."

L'thyros lay perfectly still, his eye still looking down at the rocks on which he lay. But he could see them approaching. So small, with their stiff jointed limbs. They balanced seemingly without effort, swimming through the air as he might skim the ocean floor. They had strangely colored and textured skins, and fine seaweed dangled from their domed tops. But the small one, the timid one—he was exactly right.

"Is it going to die?" the small one asked, slipping his appendage free of the larger human, and moving closer. Almost close enough to touch.

When the sneaker wave hit, L'thyros was ready. The humans were not. The wave wasn't deep, maybe two feet when it reached him, but that was deep enough. L'thyros took a deep grateful breath of saltwater, his gills gaping open in relief, his heartbeats increasing. The first two humans fell, unbalanced by the wave. The older human stumbled, reaching toward the small one. The small one, mouth gaping as though it too would gasp in a cleansing breath of the sea, fell into L'thyros.

He used his two smaller tentacles to catch the little human. As the wave slowed and began to rush back out across the beach, he pushed with all his strength, lifting his heavy head. In only three beats of his three hearts, he was out far enough to drop beneath the surface. The small human struggled weakly, but L'thyros did not let go. He had put in too much effort to lose his prize now.

His mate, N'garya would be pleased. None of her friends had ever sampled such a delicacy.

LEAVES

Leaves cover the ground, brightly colored and crunchy, crackling with cool fire. Jacob, dark-haired and dark-eyed, uses the wooden and plastic rake to scrape them up in piles. The air is cool, sky painfully blue, and everything seems crisp as a ripe apple.

Bony fingers protrude from beneath the largest pile. Jacob pauses, contemplating the pale, curled digits; they seem to be beckoning. The leaves are just a temporary blanket.

"Afternoon, Jacob," Mr. Jenkins the neighbor calls from his yard. "How's your mother?"

"Time will tell," he replies, moving leaves. "Funny how beautiful dead things can be."

SOMETHING SAVORY

Frogs were croaking, and the sun had dropped behind the trees, leaving everything in that clear delicate light just before nightfall. Jeren sat in his car, parked beneath the overhanging branches and trailing leaves of an old weeping willow. He sat with the engine off, windows rolled down, smoking a cigarette in silence. Across the road, half obscured by dense shrubs and two mature pine trees, was the house he was watching. Front windows glowed golden through the encroaching shadows, and he could hear just the softest hint of music escaping through one of those open windows. It would be full dark soon, and then he would have to head home. If he stayed out all night again, his parents would likely take the car away from him.

He put the cigarette to his lips, inhaling deeply of the acrid smoke, eyes drawn for a moment to the bright red ember at the end. When he exhaled and looked back across the road, he saw something moving. Already the shadows beneath the trees were becoming too heavy to see through, but he caught a glimpse of a figure moving furtively away from the house and farther into the woods.

Jeren paused for a moment, fingers trembling as he crushed the half-smoked cigarette into the ashtray. Before he lost his nerve, he grabbed the two objects off the passenger seat beside him. The car keys were already stashed in his front jeans pocket, so he got out of the car without rolling up the windows and closed the door as quietly as he could. When he turned back, there was no sign of the elusive figure, but he'd seen the direction it was moving. Jeren ducked out from under the willow, checking the road in both directions before loping across the cooling blacktop and into deeper shadows.

Ahead of him, slipping between the trees, he saw glimmers of pale grey as his quarry went on. In his left hand he held the flashlight that he'd taken from the car, but hesitated to turn it on. It was becoming more and more difficult to see his way, but once he used the light she would know he was following. In his right hand, he held a knife. The blade was ten inches long and gleamed even now along its sharp edges.

Jeren crouched, grimacing as a twig snapped under his foot, and peeked around the trunk he skulked behind. Along a slight widening of the path, he could see her albeit dimly. She had stopped where the trees crowded close once more, and seemed to be looking back the way she'd come. Had she heard him?

"You can come out," she said, just loud enough for him to hear.

He stayed hidden, ducking down in hopes she was only guessing he was there.

"If you're going to follow me, you might as well just walk with me."

Jeren held his breath, trying to make himself small.

When her narrow hand touched his shoulder he screamed and fell back into the bushes, dropping both knife and flashlight in his fright. Twisting onto his back, he searched frantically for his weapon, finding the light first. He thumbed the switch, shining a beam of brilliant white into her pale face.

She stared down at him as though the light weren't blinding her at all, and her lips curved into a small unnerving smile. "Come with me, Jeren," she said, her voice smooth and lilting, and held her hand out to him. Her fall of dark hair was like shadows around her pale face, and he took her hand as if hypnotized.

"Rune," he whispered, letting her help him to his feet.

"I want to show you something," she said, pulling him away from his hiding place.

He left the flashlight, its beam bright in the tangle of undergrowth; it shone on the length of steel blade still lying on the ground.

Rune Amsel came to Miller's Ford halfway through the
summer break. She moved into the old Transom two-story
house standing alone on Mill Hollow Road, along with an older
man and woman that everyone assumed were her parents. It
was a month and a half before school would start, but it didn't
take long for most people in town to recognize her. She had
remarkably fair skin and dark hair, and secret eyes which gave
nothing away, not even a glimmer of light. When she went
shopping in town with the older couple, picking out organic
fruit or tender cuts of meat from the grocery store, most people
stopped what they were doing to watch for a moment.

"She doesn't get her looks from her mother," Mrs. Brandon
said to Shelly Marks at the Post Office after buying new stamps.

The Amsel's had just passed the broad front windows.
Mrs. Amsel was pale, but not like her daughter; she was pale
as though just recovering from a lingering illness. Her mousy
brown hair was liberally touched with grey, and she dressed
without any regard for fashion.

"Or from her father," Shelly replied. The man was tall but
stooped with rounded shoulders, and thinning blond hair hung
over his jug-handle ears and poked over his rumpled collar.

"Did they use a moving company?" Jack Howard asked
as the newest residents of Miller's Ford walked through the
hardware store picking out new deadbolt locks and garden
tools.

"I never saw any big trucks coming through," Ray Kendal
of Kendal's Hardware replied. "None of 'em look strong enough
to move furniture."

Nancy Straight who had handled the paperwork for the sale
of the property made a point of never gossiping, but in this case
she had to say something. Everyone was *so* curious. At lunch
with her three closest friends, she mentioned, "It was a little
odd. They bought the place sight-unseen for the asking price.
No haggling at all." She took a sip of sangria, allowing that since
it was after noon a little wine was fine. "I have no idea how they
got moved in so quickly. I went out the day after closing, and
they were already settled!"

"Is it just the three of them?" Jan Lensing who owned the beauty shop on the corner asked.

"I was under the impression there was a son as well, from something Mr. Amsel said. But I don't know for sure."

"Well the daughter is certainly lovely, in an unconventional way," Tracy McNamara said, twisting a strand of auburn hair through her fingers. At twenty-three she was the youngest at the table, and used to being the prettiest girl in town. "What did you say her name was again?"

"Rune." Nancy almost seemed to taste the name. "Her name is rather unconventional, too."

"Maybe we should go on out there to the Transom's—I mean, the Amsel's," Patsy Evars said. She was married to Bob Evars, who currently served as mayor of Miller's Ford, and fancied herself the matriarch of the town. "Take them a casserole or a pie, and welcome them officially. It would be the neighborly thing to do."

When they did so the next afternoon, Nancy and Jan driving out in Nancy's gold realtor-mobile and Patsy meeting them there, they found the house locked up and quiet. There was no answer to their knocks, and Jan saw nothing inside when she cupped her hands around her face to gaze in the front windows.

"Should we just leave the food on the step?" Nancy asked when it was clear no one was home.

"Can I help you?"

The soft voice startled all three women, and Patsy nearly dropped the plastic container she held. They turned to find the Amsel's pretty daughter standing between the two parked vehicles.

"Oh dear, you scared us!" Nancy held her hand against her chest as though soothing her rapid heartbeat, and smiled. "We just came out to bring some food and welcome your family to town."

Rune tilted her head to the left, her dark eyes expressionless. When she blinked slowly, long lashes brushed her cheeks like moth's wings. "They're not here right now. They had some business in the city." Her voice was light and gentle, her stance relaxed, but Jan felt a chill ripple up her spine, and Patsy gritted her teeth against the urge to groan. "You can leave the food if you like. I'll let them know you stopped by."

When the girl began to approach, Patsy stepped back involuntarily, nostrils flared like a horse that's been spooked.

"Yes, that would be fine," Nancy agreed, still guarding her heart with one hand. "Just tell your parents that I brought Jan Lensing and Pat Evars—the *Mayor's* wife—by to say hello. If they, I mean if any of you need anything, we are here to help."

Jan said nothing, just nodded her head quickly as she set the pie pan she held on a chair resting on the covered porch.

"I'll do that," Rune said, a sly smile touching her lips. She was close enough now for all three women to see that she wore no make-up, almost unheard of for a teenage girl in this day and age. "You are welcome to stay for a while, if you'd like. I can bring you something to drink."

"No, no, thank you dear," Nancy said, forcing her sales smile onto her face. Her pulse pounded in her temples. "We'll come back another time."

When Rune reached for the container Patsy held, the Mayor's wife flinched and nearly dropped it. "Are you feeling quite well, Mrs. Evars?"

"Yes, fine," Patsy said quickly, letting the girl take the casserole. She went down the three steps so fast she almost tripped, but just let her own momentum carry her back to her car.

"Please come again," Rune said, watching as the other two women returned to the gold Cadillac. Her smile never wavered as they hurriedly backed out of the drive.

"Did you see?" Jan asked once they were on Mill Hollow Road headed back for town.

"See what?" Nancy asked, frowning as Patsy floored her little Mercedes and fairly vanished on the road ahead of them.

"The car. That big sedan they drove into town yesterday," Jan replied. "It was parked back behind the house. I saw it as you pulled away."

Nancy swallowed, but made herself shrug and put on her sales face again. "Most people these days own more than one car."

"There's something not right about that girl," Jan whispered, rubbing the gooseflesh on her forearms.

"Don't be silly," Nancy scoffed, but then fell silent as she too stepped a little harder on the accelerator.

As the season moved into the hottest days of the year, Rune was seen often in town. She had made no friends, was polite when spoken to but not at all chatty, and seemed content to wander through the different shops alone. Occasionally she might buy something—a sequined scarf and a pair of black strappy heels from the ladies boutique, a lacey headband and rhinestone-studded hair clips from Jan's salon, or a couple of paperbacks from the general store—but mostly she just browsed. Her parents were seen only rarely; usually grocery shopping, and then they always had Rune in tow.

It was no secret that most of the high school age boys had noticed Rune as well. She was often approached by those who would be starting their junior or senior years in September, but no one in particular seemed to catch her eye.

Rick Saunders, the quarterback for the school's varsity team, was determined he would be the one to break through her cool façade. His best friend Jeren Henning was interested as well, but deferred to Rick out of years of habit.

On a Saturday afternoon Rick and Jeren were hanging out in front of the Double-Dip Ice Cream shop when Rune came into town. She always walked unless she came in with her parents in the car, and even though it was already over ninety degrees and sultry, she seemed as cool and composed as a queen in winter.

"Hey, Rune," Rick said, flashing his dimpled smile at her, the smile that worked on all the girls in town, even those years older like Tracy McNamara. "How about I buy you a milkshake?"

Her lightless eyes gazed at him as though weighing his worth, and her lips curved just the slightest bit. "Thank you Rick, but I don't like ice cream." She continued her pace, not hurried but purposeful.

"Aw c'mon," he said, pushing away from the wall and matching her gait. "You don't have anywhere you have to be, do you? I'll buy you a soda then, and we can hang out for a while."

He turned up the wattage on his smile, practically shining with All-American charm.

She kept walking, glossy hair sliding over her shoulders as she shook her head. "I do have some things to take care of," she said, her smile maybe getting just a bit wider. "But you could come by the house tonight, after it cools down. We could have a glass of iced tea on the porch, and talk."

"It's a date." Rick emphasized *date* and took her hand, pulling her to a stop on the sunbaked sidewalk. "I'll see you tonight."

Rune looked down at his tanned fingers enfolding her own fair hand, the smile vanishing from her face. When she looked up at him again, her black eyes seemed icy, or maybe just calculating. "Tonight," she agreed, and slipped her hand free of his grip. Without any flirting or follow-up she continued down the street, hips swaying as she walked and dark hair flicking back and forth across her shoulder blades.

"Wonder how far she'll go on a first date?" Rick mused, coming back to lean beside Jeren.

"You're not going to get anywhere with her," Jeren predicted, grinning at the affronted look he received.

"We'll see," Rick said, confidence in every line of his body.

When his car was found Sunday morning, wrecked off the sharp curve a half-mile outside of town, the consensus was that the popular boy had been speeding. Wet pavement and narrow roads were a bad combination for a cocky young man.

Jeren told Chief Williams that Rick had made plans to see Rune Saturday evening. When the chief went out to speak to her, she was composed but somber.

"I wondered why he never showed up," she said, standing on the porch with her morose parents behind her. "I waited until much later than I should have, before simply going to bed. I thought maybe he'd meant it as a joke."

Chief Williams nodded, making a note in the little pad of paper he carried. "Sorry to be the bearer of bad news, Ms. Amsel." He stuck his pen in his shirt pocket along with the pad of paper and nodded at the older couple who had until now said nothing. "I can assure you that most of our young people are cautious and well behaved. We figure there must have been a mechanical failing with Rick's car, or maybe an animal darted across the road. Anyway, don't have any worry about your daughter. I'm just glad she wasn't with him when it happened."

"Yes, we're very grateful," Mrs. Amsel said, not looking at the chief or Rune. She kept her gaze low and nodded slowly. "Wouldn't know what to do without our girl."

The next time Jeren saw Rune she was walking down Mill Hollow Road with a bag from the nursery in her arms. At first he intended to just keep driving. He was attracted to her, but his best friend had died going to meet her, and how could he just pretend that hadn't happened?

Before he realized what he was doing, he had pulled over onto the shoulder of the road and got out of his car. Rune was a few yards away, still walking toward him and she hadn't slowed her step.

"Hello, Jeren," she said as she came closer.

"Hi," he replied, feeling unaccountably shy now that they were alone together. "Would you like a ride home?"

"Sure you want to associate with me?" she asked, halting a couple yards away from him. "People might talk softly, but I still heard them."

Jeren flushed, embarrassed and mortified, although he hadn't said anything. When Rune had appeared at Rick's funeral, most everyone thought it was in bad taste, even if she'd done nothing wrong. "I don't care what anyone thinks."

She tilted her head, her secret eyes taking in his abashed expression. Then she shifted the bag so she could offer it to him. "I'd appreciate a ride. This is heavy."

Jeren nodded and took the brown paper sack from her, surprised at its weight. "What have you got in here?" he asked, popping the trunk to put it inside.

"Potting soil, a package of pea gravel and some seeds." She got into the passenger side without waiting for him.

"You should have driven your parents' car," he suggested and got back behind the wheel.

"They're not my parents." Her voice was soft and level, and

when he looked at her he was surprised at how close she was.

"They're... they're not?" he said, breathless.

Her lips curved and she leaned closer. She smelled warm and kind of smoky, like sandalwood or cedar. "No. My parents died. The Amsels are just my guardians."

"I'm sorry." He wanted to lean over, see if she would let him kiss her. But they were stopped on the side of the road in broad daylight, and he'd never said more than a dozen words to her before this.

She shrugged and sat back, turning to face front. "It happened a long time ago."

Jeren took a deep breath, then started the engine and pulled out onto the road.

When they passed the sharp curve where Rick's car had wrecked, Rune turned to look at the place where it had come to rest—violently—against the thick trunk of a tree. "Do you miss him?"

"Uh, yeah." Jeren kept both hands on the wheel and his eyes on the road. What kind of question was that?

Trees swept past them on both sides. There were few homes along this stretch of Mill Hollow Road. A lot of this area was national parkland, and most of what was privately owned had never been developed. When the gravel driveway of the old Transom house appeared on the left, Jeren turned between the untrimmed bushes.

"So, do you miss your parents?" he asked as he put the car in park.

Rune looked at him, her gaze almost tactile, and he wished he hadn't asked. "I can remember the way my mother used to brush my hair, and how Daddy always smelled of Old Spice cologne. My brother ate too much and was jealous of me." She tipped her head again to the left, as he'd seen her do before. Her face was serious; her voice as soft as he imagined her skin must feel when she said, "No. I don't miss them. Not anymore."

He could hear his heart thumping, and the breath wheezing through his tight throat. Then Rune turned away and opened her door. Jeren got out, opening the trunk to retrieve her bag for her.

She took the heavy package from him as though it weighed nothing. "Thank you, Jeren."

Behind her the old two-story appeared deserted with shadows already gathering on the covered porch. He thought he saw someone standing at the screened door, but it did not open and it might have just been a trick of the light. "You're welcome," he finally managed to say, torn and undecided. He wanted to stay, to ask her out, to get closer to her... And yet at the same time some distant voice in the back of his mind screamed for him to get away, to run and never look back.

Something moved behind her, like a disembodied shadow detaching itself from the deepest corner of the covered porch, and Rune turned her head. When she moved, the shadow froze. As it halted, Jeren had to wonder if his eyes were playing tricks on him; the shade beneath the porch roof looked completely natural.

"I have to go now," Rune said, a slight undercurrent of irritation beneath her smooth voice. "Thanks again."

"Yeah, no problem." Jeren went around the car to the driver's door which he'd left open. Before he got in, he looked across the car to where Rune was stepping up onto the shaded porch.

Something dark and formless shuddered and hunched away from her, as though the shadows cowered from her presence. She held out one hand, and hesitantly the indistinct darkness curled around her, drawn to her the way smoke was drawn to a flue.

Before she could glance back and see him staring at her, Jeren slid into his seat and started the engine. He threw it into reverse and nearly spun his tires when he reversed out of the driveway. Just as he turned the wheel to back onto Mill Hollow Road, he looked toward the house one last time.

Rune stood on the top step of the porch, feet primly together and arms crossed. Hunched over her was something dark but undefined, curled around her as though holding her in a ghostly embrace. Her pale features were composed, her eyes absolutely black beneath her level brows.

Jeren caught his breath, heart pounding once more. Above, in the window on the second floor, he saw Mr. and Mrs. Amsel,

Rune's guardians. They stood with mouths open as though calling for help, their splayed hands pressed against the glass. The expressions on their grey, faded faces were of abject horror. Jeren looked back at Rune and she was smiling now, although she hadn't moved.

He put the car in gear and floored it, not caring if he smoked the tires. In seconds the house with its strange occupants was far behind. When Jeren passed the spot where his best friend had died, he whispered, "Rick, did you really die on the way out there? Or were you trying to get home?"

Several hours later found him back on Mill Hollow Road. Jeren's parents had gone to their weekly bridge night, leaving him to fend for himself. Usually he would hang out with Rick, but that was no longer an option. Instead he found himself brooding about Rune Amsel, and what had happened to his best friend. He kept seeing Rune's discomforting smile, and the strange sentient shadow that had alternately avoided and then clung to her. He kept remembering the terrified expressions on the faces of the adults who were supposed to take care of her.

Finally, too restless to stay at home, he got in his car and went for a drive. Consciously or subconsciously, when he ended up back at Rune's house he wasn't surprised. He parked the car across the road, beneath the trailing branches of a mature weeping willow, and crept across the pavement to the untrimmed bushes along the front of the yard.

By this time it was full dark. As he hadn't planned to return, he hadn't bothered to prepare. He had no source of light, and nothing to protect himself. For a long time he stayed hidden near the tangle of shrubs, watching the house. Both front windows were lit from within and the soft sounds of music escaped occasionally along with the trailing ends of threadbare sheer curtains. Other than the flutter of the draperies in the breeze, there was no movement he could see inside.

Jeren started to move closer to the house just as something flitted across the light. It seemed a shadow of a shadow, and if he'd blinked he would have missed it. He dropped back into a crouch and waited.

When the front door opened, Jeren saw the tall gangly figure of Mr. Amsel, shoulders hunched and head held low. He stepped out onto the porch, turning to look back inside where his wife stood. Her face was ghastly, jaw clenched as though to hold back a scream and her hands were knotted together at her stomach. Standing relaxed and pretty beside her was Rune.

"I warned you," Rune said, looking from one adult to the other, her face composed. "I only have so much strength. I can't keep fighting both of you. If you won't behave, then you have to be punished."

"Please," Mr. Amsel said, his voice hoarse but low, as if he knew raising his tone would help nothing. "We'll stop. We'll do whatever you want."

Rune shook her head, putting on a sorrowful expression. But her black eyes never changed. "After all these years we've been together, it's too late for that. Controlling you, keeping you from doing something that you'd only regret, takes its toll on me. Even though I ate just two weeks ago, you have worn at me until I'm hungry again."

"No," Mr. Amsel said, holding up his hands to ward her off.

"Don't play innocent with me, Henry. You really brought this on yourself." Rune looked at her ersatz mother, tipping her head to one side. "Go upstairs now, Abigail. Be a good girl."

Tears streaked the woman's face. She had dug her nails into her own hands until blood dripped from the cuts. She wasn't looking at Rune. She stared at her husband, fear and desperation in her tormented eyes.

Hidden in the shadows across the yard, Jeren held his breath. He didn't know what was going to happen, but he knew it would be awful.

"Don't cry for him. He had terrible, dirty fantasies about me. Some might say he's getting what he deserves." Rune smiled, an edge to her voice now.

Mrs. Amsel sobbed, and Mr. Amsel's shoulders shook as though he were crying, too.

"Everyone eventually gets what they deserve," Rune said, her smile vanishing. "Time to go, Henry."

"But we l—love you," Mrs. Amsel stuttered and flinched when Rune looked at her.

"Upstairs, Abigail. Don't make me tell you a third time."

Terror-stricken, the woman gave her husband an anguished look, then turned and disappeared. The sound of her feet rushing up the stairs could be heard even by Jeren.

"Let's go for a walk, shan't we?" Rune stepped forward, her pale long-fingered hands closing on his arm. "Just you and me, in the dark. It'll be romantic."

"Have pity," Mr. Amsel begged, then cried out for no reason Jeren could see.

"Don't ruin it, Henry." Rune came down the shallow porch stairs, the trembling man at her side. She didn't bother to close the front door, leaving golden light spilling down the steps. She took him with her across the too-long grass and beneath the shaggy pine tree. Following close behind was something black and impossibly fluid, an errant shadow with no source.

Jeren waited in his hiding spot. He thought of following, but was afraid of getting lost. He stared at the house, with its open front door that should have felt welcoming. After eavesdropping on what had been said, he expected to see bars, and wondered what kind of power Rune had to force Abigail Amsel to hide upstairs while something obviously unpleasant was about to happen to her husband.

He awoke hours later, dazed and covered in cold dew. He was lying beneath the old hedge, still hidden from the house, but early morning songbirds were beginning to sing. Stiff from sleeping on the ground, Jeren groaned when he sat up. The sky was just getting light although the sun had not yet risen. The front windows and door of the old house were closed and dark, and he had no idea if Rune and her guardian had returned. Muscles protested when he got up, still crouched under the heavy foliage, and he glanced up at the second floor.

Someone stood in one of the bedroom windows, face pale in the early morning glow. Jeren moved back slowly, afraid that Rune had known he was there all along. The woman in the window moved, leaning her forehead against the glass. Growing light revealed grey-streaked hair and a pallid complexion.

Abigail Amsel gazed at him with no hope at all.

When he got home, his parents went from angry to relieved and back. In the end though, he got away without punishment because of Rick's death.

"I know you miss him," his mom said gently, giving him a warm hug. "But just remember how much we'd miss you if anything happened to you."

"Don't worry us like that again," his dad said, and nestled inside the ire of his voice was a note of pleading.

"I'm sorry," Jeren said for at least the dozenth time. They let him off the hook after that, sending him to bed without grilling him for his whereabouts. For that he was glad; he didn't want to lie to them. Instead of sleeping, he made plans.

He didn't know why Mrs. Amsel was so frightened of Rune, and he didn't know what had happened to Mr. Amsel last night. But of one thing he was very sure. Rune had something to do with Rick's death, somehow. She'd fed on him in some strange esoteric way. She might as well have admitted it to him. *Even though I ate just two weeks ago,* she had said. Two weeks ago, when his best friend had died.

In the darkness of full night, Jeren followed Rune along a path she seemed to know well. There was no moon, only a scattering of stars twinkling in the narrow slices of sky between the trees. Ahead he could hear running water and the sounds of night creatures chirping, clicking, or rustling. He walked in a fog, his hand enclosed by her slender fingers. He wondered if Mr. Amsel had come this way with her. He wondered if Rick had.

"I know you've been very curious about me," Rune said, leading him between the trees and through the pathless undergrowth. "I could feel it, every time your eyes sought me out, like a blind dog scenting for something... savory."

Jeren's throat was locked, his tongue felt swollen. All he could do was pant for breath and follow her.

"This isn't what I planned," she went on, her voice silken in the darkness. "But it isn't the first time I've had to improvise, either." She stopped in a clearing where the trees fell back and revealed a huge swath of cloudless dazzling sky. A creek burbled through the opening in the trees, mossy stones making a natural step bridge across the cold water. Lying beside the brook was Mr. Amsel.

Jeren wanted to pretend that the man looked as though sleeping, but he couldn't. Rune's guardian lay grotesquely flattened, his neck twisted sharply and limbs canted in unnatural angles.

"We're friends now, aren't we?" she asked, turning to put her hand on his chest over his thundering heart. "I like you ever so much more than Rick. You're smarter than he was, more attuned to the warning of your senses."

Jeren looked down into her secret eyes, unable to do anything else. As dark as it was here, he could see her very clearly.

"So as a friend, I'm asking for your help." Rune moved closer, pressing herself against him in a way that he once might have found exciting, but now only alarming. "No one must ever find his body, Jeren. So you're going to bury him for me. Right here, in this lovely spot." She reached up, her cool fingers playing over his sweating face and tracing the lower curve of his eyelid. "And I'm going to take a little bit of you—just a tiny bit. You won't even miss it." She pinched the tender skin below his eye, making tears well. "And from now on, forever in fact, we'll keep each other's secrets. Do you understand, Jeren?"

She pulled her hand away from his face slowly, trailing something from below and behind his left eye. Something that squirmed and fought yet caused him no pain as it went. It simply left behind an aching emptiness, like a hunger that would never be sated.

"What is it?" he asked, feeling tears streak his face. "What are you?"

Rune smiled, a genuinely happy smile that was ill-suited to her porcelain features. "It's your soul, Jeren. It will be safe with me." The wriggling thing spread and thinned, becoming a sentient shadow like the one he'd seen last night, curling around her like a shawl. "As for me? I am the most important thing in your world." She pointed, directing him to the shovel leaning against a nearby tree. "Better get started. Your parents will be angry if you come home late again tonight."

He turned to take up the shovel. Mr. Amsel didn't matter anymore. Rick didn't matter. His own suspicions about Rune, and the horror and fear in Mrs. Amsel's face, were of no consequence anymore. He started to dig. He could no longer think of anything else he'd rather do.

FOR SOME PEACE

Carlisle's wife was a nag. Jessamine never stopped complaining, so he went out to the shed for some peace. She followed him and watched frowning from the doorway.

"What are you doin'?" she finally asked, hands on hips and the jut in her jaw that meant trouble.

"What's it look like?" he returned question for question.

"It looks like you're makin' a coffin!"

He nodded, using a planer to square an edge. "You ain't wrong."

"Who you makin' a coffin for?"

"My first wife."

"*I'm* your first wife."

"Yep." The coffin was done; the time had come to fill it.

A CACHE OF PEARLS

Pearls could be found, sometimes, at the edge of the waves. Cast up, cast off, and left like offerings from the sea. There was no accounting for it, no scientific explanation. Studies had been done, pH levels, measurements taken and depths sounded. But still, there was no reason.

"Magic," Nila breathed, crouched barefoot in the sand. It wasn't sugar white sand, or the soft red sand from their records. This sand was black as deep night, and the pearls glowed like scattered stars.

"No such thing," Sayd argued. Dark hair curled over his warm brown eyes, and he carried a canvas bag with which to collect the treasures they found.

"How do you know?" Nila tossed red-gold braids behind her shoulders. The moons hung low above the horizon, tiny things that barely stirred the water. They were misty orbs in the deepening red sky, reminding her of the pearls in the sand.

"It's just fairy tales." He bent, plucking a pearl the size of his thumbnail from the high tide line.

"There are no fairies, here." Leaving the search for pearls or other treasures, Nila skipped toward the sea. Waves, shallow and long, stretched in both directions out of sight.

"Stay out of the water!" Sayd called after her, but kept his eyes down. Thalos had promised him a silver knife if he brought back a dozen pearls.

Up to her ankles in cool dark water, Nila gazed out to the distant horizon. "No fairies. But mermaids, surely." Her voice carried over the perfectly smooth sand, and then there was a splash, and then silence.

Something glinted, half buried in the sooty sand. Sayd knelt, knees pressing divots into the beach, and teased the object out. An iridescent swirl of calcium was revealed, the spiral shell of some long dead sea creature, and Sayd cried out. "Nila! Look at this!"

There was no response, just the soft susurration of water sliding over black sand.

"How could you let this happen?" Sela's face was twisted, half anger, half sorrow. The large golden pearl she wore at her throat had been brought to her by Nila. "You go together, so you can watch each other!"

Sayd kept his eyes low, although not as low as his heart. Nila had disappeared less than a dozen yards from him, in water only four inches deep.

"We'll search," Thalos said, his voice so deep it seemed the waves of sound could be seen and felt, as well as heard.

"It's too late, and you know it," Sela accused, but she didn't try to stop them. "All this for trinkets," she whispered.

Sayd lifted his eyes, glancing at the necklace she wore, and she caught him at it.

"Trinkets," she hissed, and pulled the pearl from her neck. When it dropped to the floor, she turned her back to them.

Silently, Sayd retrieved the pearl, dropping it into the canvas bag he still carried.

The area where Nila disappeared was searched. The beach in both directions, and the water out two hundred yards where the sand beneath finally fell away into the depths. There was no sign of her, or of anything else. The sea was still as lifeless and empty as they had always found it to be. Whatever might hide in its depths remained unknown. Whatever creature produced the pearls was still an enigma. And Nila was gone.

Sayd spent hours with the search parties, tied together with lengths of rope so that none would be lost. They walked out to the shelf were the drop-off began. They launched the ancient boats, so long disused. When the search was called off, Sayd kept looking. He did not gather pearls to bring back anymore.

He no longer cared about the silver knife. He told no one about the strange spiral shell he had found when Nila went missing. Each evening he watched as the moons lifted above the black sea, and he waited for Nila to return.

Five years passed. Sayd hid his cache of pearls and went to work in the greenhouses. He studied the legends of Earth, the world from which his people had come. He went through all the old files and photos of the oceans from that lush blue planet. They had come here because of the sea, their ancestors expecting a bounty of life. But they had been disappointed, and there had been no going back. The black ocean that covered most of this world was empty and useless to them. They pulled water from the cloudy skies, and grew their crops in the protected greenhouses, and they survived if did not thrive.

He found the oldest records, the satellite images and recordings of this world, their home. There were topographical photos that teased an understanding of the terrain beneath the water. Those before him had long since found the information useless, and filed it away. But Sayd wondered. He saw a place far from home, far out into the deepest water, where an odd design seemed built upon the ocean floor. It teased him, the feeling of something half recognized. He knew what others would say, if he showed them. Sela had never forgiven him the loss of her daughter, and Thalos had distanced himself. But no one was as harsh with him, as he himself.

The ancient boat sat light on the water, and Sayd kept a close eye for leaks. The low waves and lack of storms made his travel easier, but he was hard pressed to find what he sought. Even in the brightest day, it was hard to see down into the depths. But he was sure it was the right place. The spiral shell that he'd kept glimmered between his fingers, then sank without a sound into the sea.

"Magic," Nila said, and Sayd turned to see her at his bow. Pearls circled her throat and wrists, and red-gold hair hung wet over her shoulders. "And mermaids, Sayd. Come see!"

"Fairytales," he breathed, and then joined her.

ROOMMATES

Jack had been living in the basement apartment for less than a week when he realized he was being watched. The pervasive feeling became more and more obvious as time went on. He didn't have much in the way of possessions, but when he came to the conclusion that he really was being observed, he went through it all. There were no hidden cameras, and no holes in the walls, floor, or ceiling that he could find. But the sensation persisted, becoming so strong it was almost like a physical touch, until he found himself looking over his shoulder regularly.

He told his best friend about it. Matt, true to form, made fun of him.

"Dude, get over it. This isn't some conspiracy movie, and you have nothing anyone would spy on you for." Matt stuffed another cluster of greasy French fries into his mouth, and reached for his soda. "I mean, look around."

Jack sighed, but he got the point. He owned nothing of value, and he wasn't some closet genius with the secret of turning lead into gold, or making girls' panties magically drop. There was no reason that anyone would have enough interest in him to go to the trouble of spying.

But the feeling continued, and kept getting worse. He was becoming paranoid, and the hairs on the back of his neck were getting stronger from all the sit-ups they were doing. He was starting to develop a shy bladder, because he just *knew* someone was watching when he went in to take a piss. He even gave up masturbating. Lights off, pitch dark, under the covers—still no good. What if the asshole had night-vision goggles? And it had to be a guy, right? What woman in the world would spend her time covertly ogling him?

On the day he actually caught a glimpse of his peeping tom, he screamed like a little girl. He was in the bathroom preparing to shave before heading off to work at the reprographics shop where he ran a copy machine. He'd slathered his narrow jaw with canned shaving cream and held the disposable razor in one hand. With the other, he reached to turn on the faucet. He glanced into the sink as he did so—and saw the eye inside the drain hole, gazing up at him.

For a split second, his brain tried to tell him it was just a reflection of the light over the mirror reflecting in standing water at the bottom of the drain… And then it blinked. Eyelid, lashes and all, and then the big blue eye was staring up at him again. That was when he screamed, dropping the razor as he cranked the hot water full blast.

A while later, he didn't know how long although the mirror was now fogged over by the hot water, he peeled his bare back off the bathroom wall and cautiously approached the sink. He turned off the faucet, and watched as the water descended into the drain, finally emptying the sink again. Gingerly, he snatched the razor out of the porcelain bowl, and gazed into the black drain hole. There was nothing there.

He pushed the little stopper on its chain into the opening, filled the sink with water, and shaved quickly, ignoring the sting as his shaking hand caused several nicks. Then he got dressed and left the apartment, trying to ignore the palsy in his hands, and the strange looks from people on the bus. When he got to work, he realized he'd forgotten to take the little shreds of toilet paper off his shaving cuts.

He came home armed with a bucket, a long screwdriver, and several wrenches in varying size. He started in the bathroom, checking the drain in the sink and the tub. Both were empty. He put the business end of the screwdriver into each drain and stirred it around, just to check. With the bucket under the p-trap to catch any water, he carefully took it apart with the wrenches. He found nothing but a hairball covered in toothpaste residue. Next was the kitchen sink. It was a double basin with a disposal in one side, which he left alone. Screwdriver inserted into the drain, bucket below the p-trap, and pipes taken apart. Again, there was nothing. What did he think he was going to find?

"I am losin' my mind," Jack said, and put the trap back together.

The next day was Saturday, and Jack slept in. For breakfast, he settled on a couple slices of toast with jam cups he'd swiped from the diner down the street. When he set the knife on the edge of the sink, it overbalanced and slid down into the opening for the disposal.

Something moved, and the knife *tink*ed against the edge. He reached for the switch to turn on the disposal, but couldn't run it with the knife in there. Slowly, he grasped the handle of the knife. When he tried to pull it out, something came out of the hole. It had tentacles with little round suckers that rapidly slid up the knife and wrapped around his hand. It was cold and slimy, but burned his skin where it gripped. He yanked, but whatever held him was stronger. The knife bent and disappeared into the disposal. In the darkness, Jack saw a big blue eye staring lovingly up at him. Then his hand was pulled into the opening. He braced himself, breath rasping in a high-pitched wheeze, but his arm steadily disappeared into the disposal.

When Matt showed up for their Saturday night video game challenge, he found the door unlocked but the apartment empty. Everything seemed to be in the usual state of messy disorder, but three things struck him as odd. First, Jack's keys and cellphone were on the floor by the futon. Second, one of Jack's faded red sneakers was in the kitchen sink. And third, he had the distinct feeling he was being watched.

DOG DAYS

The sky is a parched, brittle dome, the sun a smear of molten light. Every footstep churns dust into the air, and each breath becomes a furnace draught. It's late August, the hottest days of the year. Not a good time to be running, but you do what you must.

"Hurry, Chance," Grace calls, face a flash of white amidst flyaway hair. She's ahead of me now.

I had a dog once, named Gracie. That was before; and no one has pets now.

The belling is close. The pack has almost caught up.

Dog days once had a different meaning.

LANGUISHING

The house at the end of the overgrown lane wasn't just haunted, she was aware.

Currently, her ghostly apparitions were in the back garden, playing croquet with a spider's egg-sack. The skeleton in her closet was quite mad, and had a bad sense of humor. He kept calling out in a sing-song voice, "I'm not coming out! You can't make me come out of the closet!" and then giggling shrilly.

The house sighed, front door gaping open in invitation. Such a long time she'd waited for new visitors. Last year's Halloween guests languished beneath the floorboards, refusing to be sociable.

GRAMPY'S
END OF THE WORLD PREDICTION

Grampy always said, "When the world ends, it won't go out with a bang. It'll go with a whimper."

A'course he died a decade back, so he never knew.

I been thinkin' on him a lot lately. Cantankerous old man who always had to prove hisself right.

Most of our kin are hidin' in their root cellars, clutchin' their bibles or their rifles, whichever they put more stock in.

Me? I'm sittin' here in the yard, listenin'. As the sun goes nova, the sky burns. Sounds more like a tea-kettle shriekin' than a whimper. But it's definitely not a bang.

WE WERE WOLVES

The smoke still rises, thin and acrid from the bonfires built in the fallow fields. It colors the sky brown and yellow, like old fading bruises. In the village, women wail and rub ashes into their hair, trailing long and tangled down their backs. Soot lines their mourning faces, and children hide within their grey-streaked arms.

Those who are left, the survivors—cursed or blessed, depending upon who is asked—lie beneath the tattered thatch. We wait, wounds staining our bandages with rust, pain gnawing at exposed nerves as a starving dog worries a bone. They'll be back. The words were not spoken, but the promise writ in blood.

This is the reward we've earned, not sacrificing our children to those ancient gods and devils who once walked the world. They are jealous of our lives and loves, the bounty drawn from fertile ground. So now as the season winds down they come, to harvest their own crops of blood and bone.

The fires crackle, rustling, whispering their secrets to the wind, and the sun slips low behind the mantle of the coming night. They're coming again, striding across the stubbled fields, umbrae with scythes and wicked blades to hand. This time will be the last.

We were wolves once, wild and wary, standing fierce in defense of our mates and young. Now we are but the reaping, and no tardy prayers will save even the chaff.

STORY TIME

Night had fallen on Hallow's Eve, and the crows winged their way to the gathering place. It was tradition; birds of carrion and death spent the night of the dead in the old church tower. They flew through the glassless windows, and up to the cobwebby rafters. Pinion to tail-feather they packed the upper spaces, waiting with muttered croaks and muted caws for the Storyteller to arrive.

When he did, he was given the space of honor. In the belfry, where the church bell once tolled, he took his place. Dark gaze upon the flock, quoth the Raven, "Nevermore."

LET ME ENTERTAIN YOU

The dog was a mutt, maybe fifteen pounds, with sad dark eyes. It was dressed in a blue ruffled tutu just above the hips, and when the music began it stood on back legs and danced in circles. Tongue dangled, and dirty feet did the flamenco on the bar. The customers clapped and jeered, cruel really. They tossed coins at the dog's owner.

After closing time, I caught the jerk out back. The dog gave up its tutu without a fight. At gunpoint, we both watched as the dog's owner danced in circles, tongue dangling, tutu tight round his neck.

RAMBLE ON

Winter approaches; leaves of every hue fall about me. It is the time of ending. Darkness gathers and moves in frosted shadows along every road, kissing every window with feathered decorations.

Inside I see warm rooms, fires lit and families gathered, sharing their love against the cold and dark outside. I am cold and dark, outside. But my purpose never changes. I am a nomad, a wanderer that so few welcome.

Cowled, with shepherd's crook to hand, I travel my own lonely road. My package of souls nestles close beneath my cloak. They comfort me, as their mourners lament.

OUTSIDE THE GATES

She was too big for her skin. She felt enclosed, tied, shackled by her own dermis, nearly to the point of being unable to move. This feeling had come over her three times before, so she wasn't frightened by it now; rather a fatalistic kind of apathy fell over her. She'd have to go to her secret place to hide, to shed her old self, where no one would see. Other people would not understand, of that she was very sure.

She remembered a time before—before everything had changed. She remembered when she'd fit inside herself comfortably, with room to spare. There had been a time when she'd been like everyone else. She wanted to cry for the loss of that time, that comfort; but she'd also lost her tears when everything changed.

"What are you doing?" Romo asked, watching her as she slowly shuffled across the yard. "Where are you going?"

"For a walk," she replied, turning her head only enough to see him from the corner of her eye. "I'll be back soon."

"Can I go too, Manda?" he asked, starting after her. His dark hair stuck up in wild snarls, and there was a smudge of dirt on his chin. At thirteen, he considered himself too old to play with the children, but was still treated as a child by the adults. Manda at fourteen was his closest age-mate, and lived in the same limbo of not-child/not-adult.

"Next time," she said, trying to quicken her pace. She couldn't push too hard. She was afraid it would start, here in view of everyone.

"But, I'm done with my chores—" he called, still taking hesitant steps toward her.

"Next time," she repeated, her voice more harsh than she intended. She lengthened her stride, wincing as she felt something tear.

Romo stopped, bottom lip protruding a bit in an unconscious pout. He watched until she was out of sight, arms crossed over his narrow chest. She'd been walking funny, like she was in pain, or was in fear of breaking something.

He glanced around the garden. He could hear voices on the other side of the corn rows, but the tall stalks with their glossy rustling leaves hid the speakers from his sight. He looked back at the notch in the wall where Manda had disappeared, over across the garden, and then to the longhouse where everyone in the main camp lived. Making up his mind, he darted to the wall, checking back one last time to be sure no one was watching, then followed her tracks in the dirt.

Her head ached, heart pounding in her chest, and Manda had to force her heavy feet to keep plodding along. Her people lived in a long narrow valley flanked on both sides by high barren hills. There were two main reasons they had settled here; partly this was due to the weather, for the hills diverted the worst of the storms and protected their settlements. The other reason was security; in fifteen years, they'd had no skirmishes with outsiders, and had been able to live peacefully.

Manda followed the path she knew so well. Unlike most of the girls in the settlement, she was an avowed tomboy. She had spent years slipping away to explore these hills, enjoying the feeling of self-sufficiency her solitary journeys gave her. During those jaunts she had discovered a small cave south and west of the longhouse and cultivated fields, where no one else ever came. She had gone there the previous three times this feeling had come upon her, and stayed hidden and safe from both predators and prying eyes.

Carefully, cautiously she climbed the steepening incline. Her skin felt like leather that had been soaked and then left in the sun to dry; it tightened around her limbs constricting movement, corset-like it hindered her breathing. She was running out of time, but could not force her body to move any faster.

When she finally reached the low opening of the cave mouth she was shuddering from exertion and the pain of her condition. She should not have waited so long to go.

A couple of hundred yards behind, Romo watched as she disappeared into a fold of stone. He crouched in the shadow of a gnarled tree, waiting for her to come back out. He was worried about her. Manda could run as fast as any boy, and she stepped lightly when she walked. But on this trek she had trudged, forcing her legs to move beneath her; and the farther she'd gone, the more obvious her discomfort had been.

After a while, he realized the shadow of the tree had shifted away from him, and though he'd watched the place where she'd gone, he had seen no further sign of her. Maybe she was sick? Maybe she was laying on the rock up there, trying to call out for help, but no one could hear her?

Finally, he moved closer. As quietly as he could, pausing often to listen, he climbed up the steep hill. When he could clearly see the cave mouth, he stopped again, biting his bottom lip. There was a rustling sound and soft whimpers coming from the dark interior. In the still-bright sunlight outside, Romo could see nothing within the cave.

He waited a little longer, but nothing else happened. The sun blazed down from the west, the rustling and quiet cries came from inside the low stone arch, and he could still see nothing in the dark interior. His worry for his friend became more overpowering than his fear at being rebuffed, and he crossed the last few feet to the cave mouth.

The opening was low, so low that he couldn't enter erect. Instead, he scooted beneath the arch on hands and knees, instinctively moving to one side so that he wouldn't block the sunlight. It still took several moments for his eyes to adjust. And even when they did, he was not sure what he was seeing. And when he realized what he was seeing, his eyes widened in shock and fear. He scrambled backward out of the cave and promptly fell off the stone ledge, rolling down the steep hill. Unconscious, he lay at the bottom of the incline, a thin stream of blood running across his forehead to soak his tangled dark hair.

Romo awoke with a soft damp cloth on his forehead, lying on a cloth pallet stuffed with dried grass. The curved wooden roof of the longhouse was dark above him, brightened only by the flickering light of an oil lamp on the squat table beside his bed.

He turned his head, and gasped sharply when he saw the fine mop of reddish-gold hair resting on the edge of his pallet.

Manda jerked up at the sound, her face pale and angular, her skin smooth and untouched by the sun. Her summer tan seemed to have faded overnight. "Romo," she breathed, reaching one hand toward him, but he shied backward. The movement reminded him of the head injury he'd sustained, and he groaned at the pain. "Romo, please hold still."

"What are you doing here?" he asked through gritted teeth, eyes squinted so he didn't have to look at her straight on.

"I found you this morning," she said, pulling her hand back. "You were unconscious. I brought you back to the longhouse. Senna said it's not serious, you'll be fine in a few days."

He said nothing, didn't move, just looking at her between his lashes.

She sighed. "I—I know what you saw, Romo. I'm sorry..." She trailed off, unable to say what she was sorry for. "You should have stayed here, instead of following me."

"What are you?" he asked, his voice little more than a hiss.

Her head dropped, disheveled hair covering her face so he could no longer see her eyes. "I'm still your friend," she whispered.

"I saw you!" he said, louder than he'd intended, tone accusing.

She put her face in her hands, and he wondered if she was crying. She wasn't like other girls; he couldn't remember the last time he'd seen her cry. Finally, she looked up again, her eyes dry, her face unmarked. "I won't bother you anymore," she said, getting to her feet. "Just, please—" She seemed to be fighting with herself, before finishing, "Please don't tell anyone."

He didn't say anything, didn't even nod or shake his head, just stared at her. When she turned and left, he still remained silent.

It took two days for Senna to release him from the infirmary and let him go back to his own living space. Romo didn't see Manda at all during those two days, although more than one person told him how lucky he was that she'd found him before a coyote or mountain lion. He just nodded at them, not trusting himself to say anything. Manda was his best friend, but she wasn't who he'd thought she was, and he didn't know what to do about it.

Because he was avoiding Manda, it was a few more days before he found out that she wasn't even at the main camp.

"I worry about her," Cora said to Romo's mother Liene while fixing the evening meal. "I know she can take care of herself. And she's grown so much in the last few months. But she's still my daughter, and I don't like her being out in the wilds at night."

"So tell Dall to send her home," Liene replied, pushing stray hair out of her eyes with the back of one hand. "She's still a child; you've a mother's right to keep her close."

Cora shook her head, eyes on the vegetables she was slicing for the pot. "She really isn't, though," she said softly. "She's been training with the other students the last few days, and Dall said she's got a gift. She can already out-fight and out-track most of them; even some of the young men."

Liene nodded, her eyes full of sympathy for the other woman. "It's been years since we've had any trouble, Cora. I'm sure there's nothing to worry about. In fact, it's good to know she'll be prepared if anything ever does happen."

"Manda's in training?" Romo asked incredulously, breaking into the women's conversation. "She's not old enough!"

"Romo," his mother admonished. Children in the settlement were loved and well cared for, but never spoiled. Self-control was taught from a young age, and there was little tolerance for rudeness. "You know better."

He bit his tongue, forcing himself to bow his head to the women. "My apologies Mother, Cora. But no one told me Manda was in training."

"It was… sudden," Cora said hesitantly. "Manda asked Dall, and offered to challenge one of the other students for a chance." She swept slices of carrot into the pot before her, then took some stalks of celery to cut up. "He agreed, thinking to prove she wasn't ready. But she won the challenge, so he took her to the outer camp."

Romo just stared at the women for a moment, not knowing what to say. It should have been two more years before Manda went to the outer camp, if then. Now she was gone, and he would only see her if she chose to come back on Dall's leave. He forgot that he'd been avoiding her. He forgot that he was angry at her.

"We'll be sending supplies out to them in a couple of weeks," Liene said, knowing how much her son had always liked Manda. "If you're feeling up to it, you can go out and back with the wagon."

He nodded without much conviction, and excused himself.

Romo stood at the bottom of the hill, looking up the steep incline to the little shelf of rock from which he'd fallen a week before. He chewed on his bottom lip, trying to make up his mind. Finally, knowing it would eat at him until he did something about it, he climbed up the steep rocky path to the opening of the little cave. He crouched beneath the arch, suddenly afraid of what he might find inside. But the need to know was greater than his fear. With a deep breath, he entered the cave for the second time.

Inside it was dark, and the dust raised from his movements made him cough. He waited until his eyes adjusted to the dim light and moved slowly forward, trying not to kick any more dust up into the air. The cave was only about six feet across, about the same in height. He moved to the back wall of the cave, seeing something odd crumpled on the floor. He reached out slowly, touching it lightly with his fingertips. It was dry and stiff, hollow and crackling a little under his touch. He felt his gorge rise as he realized what it was, but forced himself to lift it with both hands. He hadn't dreamed what he'd seen, he held the proof of it in his hands. But what should he do with it?

Manda finished her cup of water and debated going back for another. She knew she was drinking more than any of the other students, but she always became extremely thirsty before her skin began to tighten; it was the first sign that it was about to happen again. What was she going to do? She was far enough from the settlement that she couldn't go to her little cave. She hadn't been given enough time or freedom since coming to the outer camp to explore the surrounding area for a protected place to hide.

"You want more?" Daved asked, holding up a water skin. "You finished the first one pretty fast."

"Yes," she said, holding her cup out for him to fill. She remembered Daved, although he'd changed since he'd left the main settlement. He was five years older than she, very tall and strong from his years at the outer camp. Before he'd left to begin training as a warrior and defender of their people, he'd been shy and bookish. Now he was self-possessed and sure of himself, one of the best warriors at the outer camp. He'd taken it upon himself to teach her the fine points of hand-to-hand and knife-play. He hadn't said much, but she was sure she had impressed him.

"A few weeks, and you seem to have been here a year," he commented, dropping the depleted water skin on the rock beside her. "Dall says you've grown a foot in height in the last year. Did you find some magic beans?"

She took a moment to swallow her mouthful of water; she didn't want to choke on it. She knew her rapid growth had not gone unnoticed, but what was she to say? "No beans, magic or otherwise," she replied quietly.

"Well," he said, possibly unsure of how to continue. He sat on the rock, the water skin between them, and looked down at his hands. "I've heard the captains talking. They're all pleased with your abilities."

Manda shrugged. She wasn't embarrassed, just uncomfortable. Coming to the outer camp had seemed the best solution, to get away from Romo and his accusing eyes. She'd thought if she got away from him, maybe he would just forget what had happened, and her secret would be safe. But she was under closer scrutiny now than she'd been with her friend, and the probability of getting caught had gone up.

"If you want, you'll probably have your pick of assignments

when your training is done," Daved continued, still looking at his hands. "Trainer, get your own squad, out-land scout..."

"Outside the gates?" she asked. The gates blocked the only easy way into the valley settlement. Every other route involved near vertical cliffs of rock and treacherous shale deadfalls.

He nodded, lips curving in a bare smile. "Yeah. We send regular patrols to the out-lands. Here we've got arable land, clean water, and a protected area that's easily defensible. Plenty that out-landers would be willing to take. We've got seed crops, livestock, and fertile women. That's more than a lot of places have."

"How do you know?" she asked, her amazement at his words making her forget her own worries for the moment.

"I'm a scout," he replied; not bragging, just stating the obvious. "I'm back in for my break, but in a couple weeks I'll go back out." He didn't miss the speculative gleam in her green eyes, or the tale-tell way her mouth tightened, as though she were biting back words she wanted to, but didn't dare, say.

"What's it like?" she finally asked, looking back down at her cup.

Daved shrugged. "We've got it pretty good here. Enough to eat, and it's safe to walk around. But outside..." He thought for a moment, cool eyes distant in his oddly angular face. "The old cities are still standing even though they're gutted, and there's a lot of people living there. But it's nothing like what we have here. No families, no cooperatives. It's dangerous. There are things out there our people know nothing about. Things they have never seen, and never will."

"I'd like to see," she said softly.

Daved looked at her, waited until she met his level gaze, and nodded just once. "I think maybe you will."

Manda nodded back.

Just over a week later, Manda knew she couldn't wait any longer. Her skin had tightened to the point it was interfering with her breathing. She'd still never had the chance to search for a suitable place to hide until she had gone through her change and recovered, but now she was out of time. After sundown she quietly crept from the barracks, and made her way through the outer camp. She knew where the students and regular soldiers patrolled, and planned to head a couple of miles beyond the furthest regular patrols. In the short time she'd been in the camp, she'd learned to move silently and leave little in the way of a trail. It was more difficult now, because of her growing stiffness; but she took her time and was cautious of her surroundings.

It took her half the night to find a sheltering rock overhang far from the camp and the patrols' regular routes. By that time she was nearly sobbing with pain and anxiety. She carefully crawled into the little cubbyhole, too small and open to be called a cave, and shuddered as she felt the skin on her back split.

She closed her eyes, and slowly worked her shirt off over her head, then rested before expending the effort to remove her pants. Beyond the tumbled rocks and boulders in which she sheltered, the stars blazed cold and uncaring in a pristine sky.

Daved sat cross-legged on the ground only a few yards from the sheltering overhang where Manda had spent part of the night and most of the next day. When she emerged from her refuge, he nodded at her. "I brought water," he said.

She froze, staring at him. How had he found her? How long had he been there?

"And some food. You must be starved."

When she did not move, didn't say anything, he got to his feet. He was still quite a bit taller than she, but not by as much as he had been.

"Another two inches?" he asked, holding out a full water skin. "Maybe three," he amended, cocking his head to look at her.

"I…" she trailed off, not knowing what to say. He had to know her secret. Why was he smiling at her?

"You're not the first, Manda," he said, still proffering the water skin. When she finally took it from him, he nodded. "I wasn't the first, either."

She stared at him, the skin held halfway to her open mouth.

"We're rare. None of us has figured out what the trigger is," he said, reaching into his knapsack to pull out a packet of bread and cheese. "You're not a monster. You're special."

She forced herself to take a sip of water; her mouth was too dry to speak without it. "How did you know?"

"About you?" he asked, and she nodded. "Dall told me about your challenge. And how much you'd grown. That's why he called me back from the out-lands, so I could test you myself."

"Dall knows, too," she said, not a question.

He laughed softly. "Of course. We're valuable."

"But I've never heard anything about anyone like me before!" she said, anger and worry and relief coloring her voice.

"Not many know about us," Daved answered calmly. "Most people would be scared, think there's something wrong with us, that we're a threat. We don't brag, we don't tell. We just do what we're best at."

"What's that?" she asked, suddenly wanting to just sit down. This conversation was as emotionally draining as last night had been physically draining.

"We're bigger, stronger, and faster than everyone else," Daved said. "We protect our people. That's what we're here for."

"Protect them from what? Nothing has threatened us in a generation!"

Daved shook his head. "That's what you've been taught. That's what most of the settlement thinks. It makes it easier for them to live their lives, thinking they're safe. We've been attacked before, and will be again. As long as we have what outsiders want, there will be a need for those like you and me."

She just stared at him.

"Come on," he said, handing her the packet of food. "We have to hide your molt. When we get back to the outer camp, Dall will fill you in. And then, I'll take you outside the gates."

"My... molt?" she asked.

Daved nodded, reaching into the cleft in the rock, and pulling out the stiff crackling shell that was her shed skin. "It's uncomfortable, I know," he said, rolling the brittle molt and crushing it into a rough ball the size of a small melon. "It'll slow down in a few months, when you reach your full growth. I stopped molting three years ago."

Romo thought about Manda all the time; he dreamed about what he'd seen in the cave that day. He remembered the way she'd sat beside him in the infirmary and the pain in her dry eyes when he was cold to her. He did not tell anyone about what she'd left in the cave. He missed her.

He did not go with the supply wagons on their next trip to the outer camp, or the one following that. It was six months before he concluded that he had to see her again. She was his age-mate, his best friend. And he had abandoned her long before she abandoned him. She had not come back on Dall's leave even once, and he did not know how she was.

He was fourteen by the time he went to the outer camp to help unload the wagons. He had grown a couple of inches, and put on some muscle, and some of the older students at the camp teased him that it was time he joined them. All he wanted was to see Manda, but she hadn't appeared to greet the supply wagons.

Finally, before they made ready to sleep, he asked about her.

"She's not here," Dall said gently. "She's out on patrol, and won't be back for a couple of weeks."

Romo nodded, biting the inside of his cheek to keep from crying. "Is she alright?" he asked, trying to talk normally past the lump in his throat. "The last time we saw each other, we had an argument."

Dall was aware that Romo had seen more than most of their people had; Manda had told him all about it months ago. He also knew that Romo had never spoken to anyone about it. "She's doing well," he replied, putting a hand on the boy's shoulder. "She has found her place. This life suits her."

Romo nodded, unable to say anything more.

"Will you come to the outer camp, when you're of age?" Dall asked.

Romo shrugged. "I don't know, yet."

The captain nodded, squeezing Romo's shoulder once, then turning away. "You have shown great restraint, Romo. You would be welcome," he said, and left the boy staring after him.

At Year End, Manda returned to the settlement with Daved. There was to be a feast and a celebration, as there was every year, for the return of the sun and the lengthening days. Cora was ecstatic to see her daughter, who'd been gone more than a year, and amazed at the young woman's appearance. For young woman she'd become. She was tall and strong, standing six feet in height and easy in her bearing. Her strawberry-blond hair had grown, and she wore it pulled back to bare her angular face. She had scars now on her browned smooth skin, earned while protecting her people, but she didn't speak of them, or of what she had experienced outside the gates. She was content, happier than she had been for months before joining the outer camp, and Cora couldn't help but notice the intense closeness between her daughter and the tall young man who stayed at her side.

Romo couldn't help but notice either, and his heart hurt from it.

"Romo," Manda said in greeting, looking down into his dark eyes.

He said nothing, just staring back at her.

"I've missed you," she said. She had thought of him often, but he was more a memory to her now than a friend. Her voice was soft, but her expression gave little away.

He nodded, feeling tears burn his eyes. She wasn't his Manda anymore.

And her eyes, as always, were dry.

CONSEQUENCES

Ember hung the hummingbird feeder from a hook on the back porch. She had filled it with simple syrup she'd made herself, not bothering to add the red food coloring always found in the store-bought nectar. She had read somewhere that the red dye wasn't necessary for the birds to find it, and no one knew if the artificial coloring had unforeseen side-effects on the tiny avians. Soon however, Red Dye #40 would be the last thing on her mind.

When the feeder was secure, she turned to look out over the low railing that bordered the covered porch. Her backyard was short, sloping to the line of shrubs that demarcated her property. Beyond that was a narrow unpaved path that wound between properties down the hill to a swath of tall sea grass and then another sharp drop to the beach. She had an unencumbered view of the ocean.

Ember sighed, closing her eyes as she breathed in the salted air. She couldn't imagine any other place she'd rather be, although it was harder now than it had once been. Since Dave had left, satisfying his mid-life crisis with a young girlfriend and a new sports car, she just scraped by. She sold framed photos and handmade jewelry at a local shop, supplementing her part-time wages filing and typing dictation for the semi-retired lawyer who had handled her divorce. Opening her eyes once more, she gazed back out at her beautiful view. "I don't know how Dave could leave this," she said aloud, turning to go back inside, "Even if he was done with me." The words were bitter, but no longer brought the requisite tears to her eyes.

Inside, the small house was bright and well-ordered.

Samples of her photography graced the walls, reflecting her love of the ocean and wildlife. In the living room, she displayed her favorites. There were prints of the jewel colored hummingbirds that frequented her back porch feeder, seagulls hovering over the beach, and long-legged sanderlings hunting along the surf-line. The largest print was of the group of crows that often perched in the old pine in her front yard. She got this beautiful shot one morning with sunlight streaming through the needles dappling their dark plumage with glints of blue and purple.

She went out to check the mail, mouth quirking down when she saw that the pine tree was empty of her resident murder. Inside once more, she sat at the kitchen table and went through the envelopes. Most were bills addressed to "September Edwards", or flyers and ads addressed to "Resident". In the divorce, she had opted to return to her maiden name of Fields, but none of these billers had updated their records as of yet.

High-pitched squeaks and a flutter of activity brought her attention to the big back window. Diving and darting beneath the overhang, several hummingbirds had found the freshly refilled feeder and vied for a spot at one of the four apertures. She got herself a cup of coffee and sat again at the table, turned so she could observe the tiny gem bright birds.

"...it's awful, really. Have you been down on the beach this morning?"

Ember caught the tail end of Jan's comment when she walked into The Sand Dollar Gallery the next day with two frames under her arm.

"No, but there isn't anything on the news, either," Randall answered, turning when the little bell above the front door chimed. "Oh, good morning, Ember."

"Morning." She smiled at the thirty-something bespectacled man who operated the gallery, and took her photography and jewelry on consignment. "I brought you those two pictures I was telling you about."

"Wonderful, let's take a look."

"Hi, Mrs. Edwards," Jan said, glancing back down at her smartphone.

"Fields," Ember said.

"Hmm?" The young woman, only a couple of years out of high school, was engrossed with the screen of her phone.

"It's not Edwards anymore," Ember elaborated. "I went back to my maiden name."

Jan glanced up, a puzzled expression on her face before Ember's words sunk in. Then her cheeks heated with embarrassment. "Oh—I'm sorry, Mrs.... I mean, Ms. Fields. I knew that, I just wasn't thinking."

Ember shrugged. She doubted she was much on anyone's mind, let alone this pretty popular girl. "No worries," she said, thinking that once she had been as pretty as this girl, although never popular. Shy and introverted, she'd fallen in love and never looked farther for meaning to her life. *I'm only forty years old,* she reminded herself. *It's not like my life is over. There are still good things to look forward to!*

"Yes, these are wonderful," Randall said. He had set the two frames on the counter and propped them up so he could see the photographs. One was a view looking down over the town as the houses dropped away toward the pale golden beach in the far distance. The other was a shot of a brown pelican skimming the incoming surf, curved wings outstretched and long neck crooked back. "Beautiful work, as always. I'm sure these will sell fairly quickly."

Ember nodded. He was nice, and made a point of showing her photos to the tourists who brought in most of the money in town. But even if she managed to sell a framed print a week, that was still only a small amount to add to her bank account.

"That reminds me," he went on as he set the frames aside to be hung later. "I have a check for you."

"See, this is what I was talking about," Jan piped up, returning to what she'd been saying when Ember came in. "Lane posted some pics online, even if there's nothing on the news yet." She held up her phone so Randall could see it.

He rolled his eyes for Ember's benefit, then took the phone and held it so he and Ember could both see the screen. On the website, below a tag that said, "What the f--- is going on?" was a stretch of sand that they both recognized. Littering the beach were piles of what had to be dead fish, for as far as could be seen into the distance. Wheeling above in great flocks and hopping about among the corpses were carrion birds—seagulls, eagles, and even what had to be crows or ravens.

"That's Wayfaire Beach isn't it?" Ember said, brows drawn as she gazed at the small perfectly rendered photos.

"Yeah, just north of town," Jan agreed.

"Did you notice anything on your way in this morning?" Randall asked, and Ember shook her head.

"No, but I can't see Wayfaire from my house, or on the route I took here."

"There hasn't been a tanker spill or anything, has there?" Randall handed the smartphone back to Jan. "If there's oil in the water, we need to be sure the authorities are aware. That could cause all kinds of havoc with all the wildlife, not to mention what it will do to tourist season." It might be crass to worry as much about tourist season as the widespread destruction of the local wildlife, but their small town depended on the money brought in by out-of-towners. Without it, many residents would go bankrupt.

"Lane didn't say anything about oil in his post," Jan said.

"I'm going to call Ted, and see if he's heard anything."

As Randall picked up the phone to call the Sheriff, Ember said, "I'm going to go down to Wayfaire and take a look myself. I'll be back later to get that check."

Randall nodded while dialing, his expression worried while he waited for the call to go through.

Ember got into her ten year old Oldsmobile, checked behind her, then backed out and pulled onto 3rd Street heading toward Ocean View Drive. The winding residential road ran parallel to the beach for a couple miles before curving back to the main highway. Just before the curve, there was a parking area for the coast trail. A dozen vehicles filled the small lot, but Ember maneuvered her car into a shallow space and parked.

When she got out, she was assaulted simultaneously with the harsh cries of the birds gathering, and the stench of dead fish that littered the sand. There were more people than could be accounted for by the cars in the lot, including a news crew from the local station in Newport. A reporter stood before her cameraman attempting to keep her blond hair from blowing in her face as she fought not to grimace at the stench.

The deposit of dead animals seemed to have started a couple of hundred feet south of the trailhead, and continued north out of sight. Ember put her hands over her mouth and blinked rapidly against stinging tears. There were more kinds of fish than she could identify, although she saw several sharks near her vantage point. There were also dolphins, a swarm of jellyfish strewn amongst the other dead, and more than a dozen sea lions. She couldn't see any whales, but wouldn't have been surprised if there was one blanketed by the multi-species flock of feasting birds.

A few feet away, with her high heels sinking into the sand, the reporter was speaking into her microphone, "...waiting to hear from the NOAA and experts from the Newport Aquarium, but at this time it seems clear that there has been no industrial accident on land or sea that could account for this scene of destruction. All tankers in the area have been accounted for, so there are no obvious answers. Authorities are asking that people stay at home and don't come down to the affected areas, as these narrow access roads can't handle the traffic, and will simply slow down emergency personnel. Also, we ask that everyone please stay out of the water, until a determination has been made as to the source of the contamination..."

Ember walked away, moving south to where a large log had been deposited at high tide. She sat, her watering eyes following the ripples of feasting birds. Gulls, sea eagles, and terns shared space with vultures, several species of hawks, and large numbers of crows and ravens. She witnessed as the birds tore into the carcasses, enjoying a feast like they'd never before attended, and a disquieting thought occurred to her. What had killed all these animals the birds now gorged on?

Having seen enough, Ember lurched to her feet and hurried back to her car, hoping to make it out of her illegal parking spot before she was blocked in by the line of vehicles moving toward the trail. With tears still welling in her eyes, and memories of what she'd seen making her stomach roil, she drove straight home without stopping by the gallery for her check. When she crossed the bridge before turning onto the street that would take her home, she saw the first corpses of fish and seals being pushed up onto the previously pristine beach.

Over the next three days, Ember stayed at home. She had a stack of paperwork from Mr. Thomas, Esq. to keep her busy with transcribing. After seeing the carnage washing up on the beaches south of the river, she didn't even care to sit on her back porch to enjoy the view. Instead, she kept the blinds drawn, and lit a fire in the fireplace to try and lay the awful stench blowing inland on the ocean breeze. Most of all, she shied away from the thought that had occurred to her at Wayfaire Beach.

She turned the TV on occasionally, just to hear if there was any new information regarding the mass die-off. There were so many conflicting theories and viewpoints, she invariably just turned it off again. At one point her phone rang. A glance at the caller ID showed her ex-husband's number, so she didn't answer. Knowing him as she did, she was sure he wasn't calling to check on her wellbeing, but to determine what he could get out of the situation.

On the second day, when she went out to check the mailbox, she frowned again at her empty pine tree. The crows hadn't roosted there *every* day, but often enough she'd become used to their garrulous presence. More than missing their noisy company, she wondered if the whole murder had been down on the beach, joining in on the easy pickins'. The thought made her shudder.

On the third day, she went out onto the back porch to check the hummingbird feeder. Ember couldn't turn her eyes away from the beach. There were crews of people on the strand, picking up dead animals and putting them on trucks that had been driven onto the packed sand. They appeared to have made quite an effort, for there weren't many corpses left in sight. She couldn't imagine how many trucks had been needed to clear off the beaches from south of town clear up toward Newport where the heaviest depredation had occurred. Her bottom lip twinged, and she realized she'd been chewing on it nervously.

There weren't any birds down there now; in fact, she couldn't remember seeing any birds at all the last couple of days. Even the hummingbirds had been absent, leaving the feeder almost half full.

With a sigh, she took the feeder down and into the house. Mechanically she emptied and washed it, then refilled it with fresh nectar stored in the refrigerator. Her teeth found her lip again, and reluctantly she used the remote to turn on the small television above the kitchen counter.

"...the preliminary reports from NOAA suggest that the combination of chemical waste that has found its way to our oceans by the ton, and the radioactive waste water which has been slowly dispersing into the Pacific from the nuclear plant in Japan, has caused the mutation of certain strains of algae and phytoplankton. It's not yet clear what kind of unforeseen consequences this might cause, but authorities are stating there is no indication of danger to human beings or land animals." The reporter on the screen was calm and unworried while he read from his note cards. "What kind of mutation are they talking about?" the news anchor, a grey-haired and distinguished looking man asked, and the camera angle changed to show him at his news desk.

The reporter glanced back down at his notes. "The mutations they've observed show a parasitic element. Since the host animals did not survive, it's hoped this will be the end of it."

"Okay, thank you Gary for your report," the anchor said, and turned back to face his own camera with a carefully cultivated smile. "Next up, we'll hear from—" Ember switched off the TV.

She went into the bathroom to splash some water on her face. She felt flushed and anxious, and didn't know why. "You need to get out of the house," she told her reflection, noting the hectic patches on her cheeks. "You've been cooped up for days, and the only one who's even called is the jerk who left you for another woman!" Tears wanted to well up, but she forced them back and used the hand towel to blot her face.

"I can go down to the Gallery, and pick up that check Randall promised me," she said aloud. The longer she was alone, the more she found herself talking to the empty house as though it might answer. "Then, maybe I'll stop at Luna's for dinner." Feeling better now that she was going to go out and do something, she picked up her purse and keys, and went out to her car.

Her drive into town was unremarkable, with only a few other vehicles on the road. She glanced at the beach while crossing the bridge to find it empty except for leftover tire tracks and the prints of many feet marked deep into the sand. She forced her eyes back to the road, determined not to dwell on the odd foreboding that had haunted her since watching the birds on the beach.

After picking up her check and chatting with Randall for a few minutes, she went to the bank to deposit the money. Then it was a rare evening out at Luna's for a dinner of salmon and baked potato, fresh bread and green salad with house vinaigrette. She visited with the family at the table behind her, and found just being out in public was an emotional lift that she'd been needing.

Finally, in better spirits than she'd been since maybe the divorce, Ember drove home. The sky above was pristine blue, the smell of death had been scrubbed away by the sea wind, and it seemed everything was clean and lovely once more.

When she turned onto her street, the first thing she noticed was the sleek convertible parked in front of her house. Ember pulled into the driveway and parked, gazing for a moment at the black sports car in her side mirror. She knew she was scowling, but couldn't help it. Her renewed good mood was gone as though it had never existed, and she got out of her Olds slowly. Something moved in the front window, and she gritted her teeth. She had never changed her locks, but now she wished she had.

As she came up the front walk, the door opened and her ex-husband Dave stood there with his fake white smile and hair freshly dyed to cover the grey. "September! You look great, sweetheart. I've been trying to get in touch with you—."

"You called once," she said and brushed past him into the house. "What do you want?"

"Honey, don't be like that," he said, still standing in the open door as she dropped her purse beside the couch. "I heard about all the hullabaloo going on here, and naturally I wanted to make sure you're alright."

"What happened to Bambi, or Brandi, or whatever your girlfriend's name is?" she asked, hearing the bitterness in her tone without being able to control it. "Did she dump you?"

"Her name is Candace and you know it."

"Oh, right—Candy." Her own sarcastic tone made her grimace, and Ember took a deep breath to calm down. "Whatever. That still doesn't explain what you're doing here, uninvited."

"I've been thinking about you—about us, actually." He composed his features into an expression of regret and held his hands toward her, palms up and open. "I made a terrible mistake. I know that now. When I think of the pain I put you through—"

Ember found that her head was shaking back and forth emphatically, even while her heart was pounding. There was a sound in her ears, growing loud and cacophonous, reminding her of the greedy hungry birds on the smorgasbord beach. "Out," she said, barely able to manage any volume. She was furious with his nerve, to think he could just walk back into her life and she would take him back. She was furious with herself, at how much that thought had appealed, for just a moment...

"I've missed you, and I know I don't deserve a second chance," he began, but she didn't let him continue.

"Get out," she said louder, forcing the words. "Now. And don't come back."

"Honey," he said, when she screamed.

"Get out!" Her hands were clenched into fists, and the clamoring harsh noise in her ears seemed to increase in volume.

Dave raised his hands again, his palms toward her now as though to ward her off. "Okay, okay, I can tell you're not ready to discuss this," he said as he backed through the open front door. "I'll give you some time to calm down—"

"Don't make me tell you again."

He stepped back again, stumbling as he missed the doorstep,

but caught his balance before falling. When he looked back up at her, framed in the open door, his expression was severe, and there was no sign of that patented salesman's smile. "I'll call you in a couple of days, when you've had some time."

She shook her head again, and stepped back far enough to close the door and lock it. Through the front window, she watched him grimace at the closed door, making an angry gesture with one hand that might have been obscene, then turned to walk across her front lawn. As he crossed beneath the lowest limbs of the huge old pine, something dropped on him. There was a flurry of black feathers and sharp talons, and Dave lost his footing and fell to the grass.

The screeching, croaking calls that Ember had been hearing grew louder even with the door closed, and she stared wide eyed and motionless with her hands over her mouth as her resident murder pecked and slashed at the man she had given her heart and her youth to, the man who had taken everything she had to give and set it aside as worthless. The day had become surreal, and it wasn't until she realized Dave was no longer moving beneath the blanket of black feathers and sharp beaks, that she was able to break her paralysis.

Surprisingly, her first reaction was neither sorrow nor fear. Even when a couple of the crows flew to perch on the front railing before the window, displaying blood covered beaks and gore-spattered feathers, all she did was gaze at them for a long moment. Their eyes, as they looked back at her through the glass, were not the same glistening black orbs they had been previously. Their eyes were clouded, and rimmed with red as though they wept bloody tears, and there was an odd greenish tinge to their usually blue-black feathers not covered with blood or viscera.

"You were at the beach, feasting with all your friends, weren't you?" Ember whispered, talking to herself as much as the birds. "Are you the new hosts for those mutated parasites the news people were so quick to dismiss?"

Finally, she went into the kitchen to call the police. Regardless of her feelings for the man, she couldn't let Dave lie dead on her lawn. Waiting on the kitchen counter, sparkling in the last long rays of evening sunlight, was the hummingbird feeder that she'd refilled before going to dinner. Ember's hands trembled just a little when she picked it up, but she crossed to the back door and went out to hang the feeder on its waiting hook.

Standing on the covered porch, she closed her eyes to the warmth of the setting sun, and took a deep breath of the fresh ocean air. When she heard the familiar buzzing sound of hummingbird wings, she smiled. At least that hadn't changed.

She turned her head, still smiling as the first two hummers reached the feeder and began to drink. The smile faded a bit when she got a good look at them. Their dark glossy eyes were clouded and rimmed with red, and Ember remembered then that hummingbirds ate insects. There had been a lot of insects on the beach, taking their share of the carrion feast.

Several more hummingbirds zipped through the yard, making for the feeder that she kept filled for them year round. Not all of them stopped at the feeder this time.

The tiny jewel-bright birds that had often brought her joy and amazement, zoomed around her, between Ember and the half open back door. Before she could do more than raise her hands, they attacked. Their blurred wings rasped and burred like a swarm of bees or angry buzz saws. They darted in and back, easily evading her uncoordinated attempts to swat them away, tiny claws scratching and long beaks stabbing.

She turned, stumbling toward the door, waving her hands wildly in front of her face. Blood dripped from lacerations on her face and arms. When one of the tainted hummingbirds dipped past her guard and sunk its needle-like beak into her right eye, she fell into the door and landed hard on the floor. Her temple struck the peach colored tile, and Ember didn't move again.

Following the sounds of screams and the high-pitched chirping of aggressive hungry hummingbirds, the murder came around the back of the house. The crows, sure of their place in the hierarchy of predation, moved in and began to feed. The hummingbirds, having sated their initial thirst for protein, went back to the sweet nectar they had come to expect.

TOTALLY SCARY

I was sitting on the couch, with my dog in my lap, a blanket wrapped around my shoulders.

The news was full of it—not just the Weather Channel, but every TV channel and radio station was babbling on and on about the coming storm. It was supposedly the largest chain of storm systems in recorded history. And the worst of it, so far anyway, was supposed to hit our little neck of the woods within the hour.

The wind had risen, gusts shaking my house as though it was built of cardboard. The lights had been flickering for the last half hour, and I expected them to go at any time. Really, I was surprised they hadn't gone out already.

My cell phone rang. I glanced at the screen. Jimmy, my on-again off-again currently ex-boyfriend was calling. Miko, my terrier mix, looked up at me with button-bright eyes, as if to say, "Are you going to answer that?"

Sigh. "Yeah?" I said into the phone.

"Are you okay?" he asked, sounding breathless. The microphone of his cell was picking up blasts of air, so he must've been outside.

"Yeah, I'm fine. Just sitting on the couch watching the news."

"Things are getting really bad out here, babe," he said, shouting into his phone. I might have yelled at him about that, but really, if he hadn't been shouting I wouldn't have been able to hear him. "I'm on my way over."

"Jimmy, why don't you just stay home?" I replied, raising my voice to be sure he could hear me. "Channel 4 says there's like hurricane-force winds out there. I'm safe in my house, you shouldn't be driving in this."

"Sorry, sweetheart, I can't hear you!" he yelled, "Just stay put and I'll be there quick as I can. Stay away from the windows!" Then the call ended. He might have hung up, or the call might have been dropped. Hard to tell.

"Shit," I sighed, setting the phone down. After our last argument and break-up, I really wasn't in the mood to spend a power-out huddled-in-the-corner scared-shitless evening with him.

Miko whined, cocking his head to one side as he did when he was concerned.

"It's okay, little guy," I said, rubbing his ears. "Jimmy's coming over to save us." He was only a dog, but I'm pretty sure he got my sarcasm.

The drive from Jimmy's place to mine wasn't far, and usually only took about ten minutes. He showed up almost 45 minutes later. He was drenched to the skin, windblown and shivering. The gym bag he'd brought with him was dripping.

"What took so long?" I asked, doing my best to keep the irritation out of my voice. I hadn't wanted him to come over, but I'd still been worried when it took so long, and I couldn't get hold of him on the cell. "The power went out 20 minutes ago, but it's still warm in the house."

His teeth were chattering so hard I could barely understand his reply. "Had-d-d-d t-t-t-to l-l-l-leav-v-v-ve the c-c-c-car t-t-t-two b-b-b-b-blocks b-b-b-back-k-k-k," he stuttered, stripping off his soaking wet coat and taking the towel I handed him.

Miko barked and barked, bouncing around like a furry little Mexican jumping bean. The blast of wind when I'd opened the door had blown everything off the table in the entryway, and pieces of paper littered the floor like huge rectangular snowflakes.

"Get in here and warm up," I ordered, pushing him toward the living room while I scooped up the papers off the floor.

I looked out the sidelight once, before joining him in the interior room. The color of the sky was grey and green and sickly yellow, and there was more than one tree down on my street.

Candles flickered on the coffee table and the tops of my

bookshelves, dancing a little at some draft of outside air. The gusts had gotten worse, and there occasionally came the ripping sound of shingles peeling off the roof. If I'd had a basement, instead of a crawlspace, I'd have been down there already.

Jimmy stripped off his wet clothes, dropping them in a pile on the tiled hearth, dried off with the towel, and redressed from some of the clothes he'd packed. They were a little damp. As he changed, he talked, ignoring Miko's little whimpers and growls. "There are trees down everywhere, and 3rd East is completely flooded," he said, his voice muffled as he pulled a shirt over his head. "I saw a bunch of windows blown out, a couple newer houses over on Statice had lost their roofs! It's totally scary out there!"

"I still don't know why you decided to come over," I said, grumbling, as I cuddled Miko on the couch. "You could've gotten hurt. You should've stayed at home where it was safe."

"Gotta take care of my girl," he said with the grin that I used to adore. When he sat down next to me, Miko growled, baring his sharp little teeth.

"Before the power went out, they said there were some weird things going on in the storm," I commented, rubbing Miko's ears. "Not just meteorological stuff. Creepy, like science fiction kind of weird stuff."

"What, aliens? Asteroids heading for earth? The end of the world as we know it?" he asked, seemingly recovered from his trip over here."

"Something like that," I answered, watching the tentacles rise up behind the couch, behind Jimmy. "You ever read any H. P. Lovecraft, Jimmy?"

His brow drew down in puzzlement. "H. P. who?"

Miko's button-bright eyes were watching our new guest as well, his little pink tongue showing as he panted. He seemed to be smiling.

When the appendages closed around him, pulling him off the couch, Jimmy started screaming, drowning out other less-appealing sounds. Miko just wagged his little tail. I watched the nearest candle flame, ignoring the wet noises from behind me, while I rubbed my dog's ears.

COMING OF AGE

Cody was small, much smaller than his brothers. They all topped him by inches and outweighed him by pounds. His eyes were large in his narrow face, and his elbows and knees always seemed in the way. His brothers made fun of him.

"When it comes time for you to shift," they would taunt as they pinched his thin arms or pulled his black hair, "You won't be a crow like us. Not even a jackdaw or a rook. You'll probably change into a cricket!" Then they would laugh raucously, sounding like crows even when they wore their human shapes.

Cody didn't cry, and he no longer tried to fight back. They were bigger, and there were six of them, and he never won. So instead, he stole away and hid where they were too big to fit.

"I won't be a cricket," Cody vowed to himself fiercely. But no one could say what anyone would become on the eve of their thirteenth year, when their first change occurred. His brothers all became crows, like their father. Their mother had not been a crow, although Cody did not know what she had been. She died when he was a baby, and Father did not speak of her.

As his birthday neared, Cody avoided his brothers. "When you become a cricket, be sure to hide," they would call to him. "Crows like to eat crickets, you know."

Finally his birthday arrived, and the change was upon him. His brothers waited in crow-shape, to further torment the cricket they expected. Cody stretched, still thin and large-eyed, but no longer were his knees and elbows in the way. He was strong and sleek, a hungry black cat.

"I don't mind eating crow," he said with sharp teeth, "How about you?"

THE IMPORTANCE
OF GOOD GROOMING

Tom leaned close, eyebrows raised and eyes wide as he attempted to peer up his right nostril. The light-bar above the mirror flickered, and shadows fluttered across the bathroom wall behind him.

"Damn moths."

Chin tipped up, neck straining and eyes beginning to sting in anticipation, he inserted the end of the tweezers into his nose. Carefully, he clamped the slanted metal tips onto the offending black filament.

"Disgusting."

He took a deep breath, and before he could change his mind, yanked hard.

The moth dragged from his sinus cavity flailed until he released it to join the rest.

THE LILAC HEDGE

Yarrow grew up surrounded by flowers. She was named for a flower, as was her mother Viola and grandmother Lily. Her most intense memories were of hours spent in the garden with her grandmother. But not all of her memories were happy.

She was an only child, and although she loved her mother Viola intensely, they had never spent much time together. Yarrow's father left when she was too young to remember him, and she never knew why or what happened to him. Her mother met another man, and married him. Viola then spent most of her time doing what she supposed would please him. She kept her hair long and full, make-up flawless, and wardrobe stylish—at least as much as she could afford. She was kind to her quiet, intense daughter; but in an absentminded way. Whenever possible, she traveled with her new husband, a long-haul truck driver who owned his own rig.

"The only way to make money," he always said, "is to keep this rig a'rollin'." He lived by that creed, and booked his runs back to back whenever possible.

"For better or for worse," Viola would say to Yarrow, "That's what marriage is, Ladybug." Then she would pack up Yarrow's clothes and toiletries, and drive her daughter over to her parents' place to stay for a while.

Grandma and Grandpa never seemed to mind. They were very fond of Yarrow, always happy to see her, and willing to keep her for as long as their wandering daughter asked. Grandpa would take Yarrow's battered suitcase filled with clothes for the next few days or weeks, and Grandma would take Yarrow's hand and lead her into the kitchen, where invariably home-made bread had just come out of the oven.

In the summer, Yarrow spent her time in the fields, helping with the weeding and watering of Grandpa's vegetable garden. She caught pollywogs or water-snakes in the cattail-rimmed pond in the far pasture, and played with the kittens that lived and hunted mice in the hay barn. If it was autumn, she would help bring in the harvest, and then wash and prepare the vegetables for bottling. She would use the old cane rake to scrape yellow and brown leaves into piles, and stand with her hands out for warmth as Grandpa used a pitchfork to toss them in the old barrel he used to burn them. In winter, she built snowmen and forts in the front yard, or used an old broom to break off the glistening spikes of icicles that clung to the eaves. But the spring was her favorite time of year at her grandparents' place. In the springtime, in the evenings, they would sit out on the back lawn near Grandma's rose garden. Grandpa would light a couple of candles to draw any biters, as he called mosquitoes. Grandma would bring her crocheting, which she could do in the deepening darkness by touch alone, and the elderly couple would take turns reminiscing about the old days.

In the spring of the year that Yarrow would turn thirteen, Grandma inherited some old china, an antique wooden rocker, and five stunted lilac bushes from her only brother. Emery had died a widower estranged from his children, and had lived all his life in the house where he and Lily had been born. The items he left to his sister had been left to him by their parents. As soon as the ground was soft enough, Yarrow helped dig the holes to plant the old crooked lilacs. Grandma had in mind a kind of hedge, so placed the bushes a few feet apart along the edge of the back lawn.

"Emery always cut them back every year," she said, using the garden hose to water the newly-transplanted bushes. "But I think I'll let them grow a bit. The blooms on these bushes were always the sweetest smelling; but I imagine it'll be a year or two before they start putting out flowers again."

"Why is that?" Yarrow asked curiously. She sat on the grass, picking dirt out from under her nails.

"It's the shock of it," Grandma answered, dropping the hose

on the ground and walking over to turn off the water. "These bushes are so old, older than I am, older than my mother was. They came from Ireland with my grandfather, and they've been planted in the same ground for decades. Moving to a new place, putting down new roots, you have to expect them to take a while to recover."

Yarrow nodded thoughtfully, gazing at the stunted tangles of limbs. There were a few new leaves beginning to open on the twig-ends, but all in all, the bushes looked rather sad.

"We'll just make sure to keep them watered," Grandma said, pausing to tuck an errant strand of pale hair behind Yarrow's ear. "And keep the weeds out. In no time, these lilacs will be happy as ever."

Over the course of that spring and into the summer, Yarrow took special care of the lilacs. As Grandma had supposed, they didn't put out any buds; but they were soon covered in heart-shaped healthy leaves. Yarrow built little earthen dams around each bush, so that the water would stay near the roots rather than running off into the lawn. She carefully removed any other plants, either grass or weed, that sprouted too close, so that nothing would take away nutrients from the transplants.

In the summer, Grandpa took her fishing up in the hills. Between them with their simple bamboo poles they caught three trout and three carp. In years past, Grandpa had always thrown the carp back. "Not good eatin'," he would say, and leave it at that. But this time he kept them. When she asked him why, he just smiled, his hazel eyes twinkling behind his black-rimmed glasses. "You'll see. It's a surprise for your Grandma."

Grandma came out to meet them when they pulled into the yard, and to compliment them on their catch, whatever it might be. When Grandpa revealed the newspaper-wrapped carp with a flourish, she raised one eyebrow. "Since when do you like carp?"

Grandpa shook his head. "Not for me, Lily. They're for your lilacs."

It was the strangest thing Yarrow had seen in her life. With a solemn feeling of ceremony, Grandpa cut two of the carp in half, then dug holes next to each lilac bush being extra careful not to hit any roots. He put a portion of carp in each hole, an entire fish for the center bush, and filled them back in with dirt.

"Is it a funeral?" Yarrow finally asked when all was done. She'd had a goldfish when she was five, but when it died her mother had flushed it down the toilet.

"It'll feed the roots," Grandpa said, nodding his head sagely. "Used to do that with your Grandma's roses, if they were lookin' sickly. Turns the trick every time. You'll see, those lilacs will grow like gangbusters now."

Grandpa was right. By the end of summer, the bushes were lush and healthy, and reached out to each other as though to embrace. They'd all grown at least a foot in height, and the center bush more like two feet. When Viola came to take her daughter home, back again from a long stint on the road, Yarrow looked wistfully at the lilacs.

"I'm a transplant, too," she whispered to them before getting in the car, "But every time I get roots down, I'm dug back up again."

Fall and early winter were spent with her mother that year, but not long after Christmas Yarrow began to notice the telltale signs. Viola checked the mailbox every day, sometimes two or three times, to be sure she hadn't missed a letter from her husband. She rarely left the house, waiting for a phone call from him. She was kind and patient as she always was to Yarrow, but it was obvious her mind was elsewhere. On a cool blustery day in March, Yarrow came home from school to find her suitcase packed and ready to go.

Viola dropped her off with a kiss and a squeeze, and spoke to Grandma for a few minutes while Grandpa helped Yarrow with her suitcase, then was gone. After putting her clothes away in the old painted dresser, Yarrow went out to check on the lilacs.

The bushes were covered in bright new leaves, and they seemed taller and fuller than she remembered. Going up on tiptoe, she noted tiny little round bumps circling most of the twig-ends. Yarrow smiled to herself; there would be flowers this year, she was sure of it.

She quickly settled into her old routine. It was late enough in the year that the snow was mostly done, but before most of Grandma's garden had put out any flowers. Cheerful purple crocus had opened beneath the kitchen windows, and daffodils and tulips were beginning to push skyward, their stiff sword-like leaves already standing proud. The peonies had produced large round tightly-closed buds the size of a baby's fist. In the weeks to come they would open into multi-petaled flowers of a deep burgundy red.

In April, the weather warmed, and it rained. Sometimes the rain was soft and whispering, gently falling to the thirsty ground. Other times the wind blew, thrashing the trees and bushes wildly, while the rain hammered down from a thundering sky. Yarrow loved the soft spring rain, but was anxious and uneasy in the angry spring storms. It was during such a thunderstorm that she first saw the shadowy figure crouched beneath the lilacs.

"Grandma?" she asked after staring out the window for a while. Lightning arced, a hard brittle crash following only a second later, and the thunder rolled for what felt like forever. Outside the back window, water fell from the roof in a miniature flood, and for a moment Yarrow felt as though the house was underwater. Everything outside rippled and flowed, making it impossible to be sure of what she was seeing. But still, a shadow nestled beneath the lilacs, and she just knew it was looking back at her.

"What is it, dear?" Grandma asked rather absentmindedly. Grandpa had gone into the bedroom to take an early afternoon nap, and she was crocheting lace onto the edge of a pillowcase, the small silver hook darting in and out of the threads like a hummingbird's beak.

"There's someone in the back yard," Yarrow replied, and her voice shook just a little.

"In this weather?" Grandma said, looking up now, her hands falling still. "Who is it?"

Yarrow shook her head, turning back to gaze out the window. "I don't know."

Grandma set her handwork aside and got to her feet. She

crossed to the window where Yarrow perched, and leaned forward until her nose almost touched the glass. "Where?"

Yarrow pointed, and said, "Beneath the lilacs."

Grandma searched the yard intently, then stepped back. "I can't tell anything with this rain. Stay here." She left the girl at the window, and went around the old secretary and the bookshelf to the back door. When she opened it, the sound of falling water swelled. Yarrow imagined this was what it would sound like at Niagara Falls.

Thunder boomed and rolled, and the rain actually increased, making its own attempt at thunder across the shingled roof. Grandma called something through the screen door, which she had not opened, but the world outside was so noisy Yarrow couldn't tell what. She looked back out the window, just in time to see the shadow crouch lower into a kind of misshapen bow, then it turned and seemed to melt into the center lilac bush.

When Grandma came back into the family room, Yarrow asked breathlessly, "Who was it?"

Grandma shook her head and smiled gently. "No one there, dear; just a trick of the wind and the rain. Don't you worry about it." She sat in her chair again, going back to her lace-making, and hummed softly under her breath.

Yarrow stared at her for a moment, then looked back outside again. The shadow was gone.

When the storm finally subsided, and the sun peeked out again, Yarrow went outside to check the lilacs. If there had been any tracks in the soil, the heavy rains had eradicated them. It was just a muddy soup now. Every leaf and twig in the yard glittered as sunlight sparkled off the raindrops clinging to everything, and Yarrow smiled when a rainbow began to form east of the house. Her anxious foreboding was allayed by the beauty of the late afternoon, but she didn't forget about the shadow that had stared back at her.

As the days and weeks passed, the weather got warmer and the spring rains subsided. Flowers bloomed everywhere. Grandma's wild-roses were covered in bright yellow blooms from near the ground to the top of the arching canes that reached seven feet before dropping back down to the earth. Her heirloom roses were blooming as well, planted in even rows behind the house and kept weed free as a matter of course. There were yellow roses, and white, and several shades of pink and red. Yarrow's favorite was pale lavender in color; the small bush only put out a few flowers each year, but also didn't grow many thorns. A dense row of irises followed the verge of the driveway, and the oddly shaped flowers with beards, as Grandma called them, showed pale blue and variegated gold and even some that were so dark a purple as to appear black. The snowball bush to the side of the hump-roofed cellar was weighed down with heavy blossoms, but the flowers that pleased Yarrow and Grandma the most were the fragrant pale purple lilacs. The five bushes transplanted the year before fairly drooped with the weight of them all. The scent of the flowers filled the yard, and Grandma kept her bedroom window open to let the smell into the house as well.

Yarrow noticed the shadowy figure near the lilacs many times, but always from the corner of her eye. Whenever she turned her head, it would be gone; a frustrating game of hide and seek. After Grandma's reaction to Yarrow's worries during the storm, she didn't bring up these fleeting visitations to either of her grandparents. Instead she tried to come up with a way to get a better look at it.

She tried sidling toward the bushes without turning her head, she tried looking away and then back quickly, she even tried lying on the grass beneath the graceful drape of flowers. Nothing worked, although she often got the overpowering feeling that the shadow was watching her, as it had done through the downpour. Finally she'd had enough. "If you won't play fair, I won't play at all."

Surprisingly, that did the trick. The center bush trembled, then shivered, and Yarrow jumped back. A face, thin and angular, appeared between the heart-shaped leaves and heavy flower clusters. It was a boy, perhaps a year or two older than she, with unruly black hair and lilac colored eyes. And he was smiling.

"Who are you?" she asked, then flushed at the rudeness of her tone. He had startled her, though.

"I am Irial," he said, with a strange fluid lilt to his words. His voice was deeper than she had expected, and the teeth his smile revealed were very white and sharp. "I wondered how long before you'd speak to me."

"You've been watching me," she said quietly, but it was still an accusation.

"You helped me to feel at home," he replied, moving a little closer, a little further away from the lilacs. "I wanted us to be friends."

"Where do you live?" she asked, and was not surprised by his answer.

"In the lilacs."

Feeling a little odd to still be standing while he was crouched beneath the lowest branches of the center bush, she knelt down in the grass and sat on her heels. Grandpa was out in the vegetable patch, and Grandma was kneading bread dough in the kitchen. For the moment, they would not be disturbed. "How—" she started self-consciously, and twisted a lock of her pale blond hair between her fingers, "How do you live in the lilacs?"

He moved closer still, revealing porcelain-smooth skin and slightly pointed ears that showed through his tangled black hair. His fingers and hands were unusually long and slender, like the twigs and branches of the bushes behind him. "How do you live in a house?" was his answer.

"But everyone lives in a house!"

"I don't."

Stymied, she nodded. "How long have you lived in the lilacs?"

"All of my life," he said, and reached out one long-fingered hand to her. "Where do you go, when you're not here?"

Without any thought, she put her hand in his. It was smooth and cool, like touching a sapling. "I go to live with my mother. Then, when she gets tired of me, I come back here."

"You're so pretty—how could she get tired of you?" he asked, tugging gently, and she moved closer to him.

"She's married. She likes to go on the road with her husband." She ducked her head, trying to keep her long hair from tangling in the heart-shaped leaves.

"If you lived with me," he whispered, his cool breath against her cheek, "I would never send you away. I would keep you with me, always." He smelled like the lilac flowers.

"I can't live with you," she said, closing her eyes when he put his thin strong arms around her. His kiss was sweet but sharp, and she felt dizzy.

"You could live with me forever," he said, pulling her even closer.

"Yarrow! What are you doing in the dirt?" Grandma called, and there might have been fear mixed with the anger in her voice.

Yarrow pulled back from Irial, her hair tangling in the branches above her, as though the twigs were trying to hold her there. Grandma grasped her shoulders and pulled her back away from the bush. Yarrow caught a glimpse of her new friend still crouched beneath the leaves, holding long strands of her blond hair between his slender fingers.

"Go back in the house and get cleaned up," Grandma said, her voice low. "You've got grass and dirt stains on your pants."

One look at her face, and Yarrow didn't bother to argue. She turned and ran back to the house to change her clothes. Grandma stayed in the garden.

After she'd cleaned up, Yarrow went into the kitchen. Grandma was punching down and kneading a fresh batch of bread dough, and flour floated in the sunlit air like pollen on a breezy spring day. Without looking up from what she was doing, Grandma said, "I want you to stay away from the lilacs, sweetheart. They don't need the constant attention now like they did last year."

"You want me to stay away from Irial?" Yarrow asked, and Grandma flinched as though she'd been stuck with a pin. "Did you know he was here?"

Grandma stopped what she was doing, her hands still buried in smooth dough. She sighed, and turned to place the lump of dough in a bowl and spread a towel over it so it could rise. She rinsed her hands in the sink, and finally turned back to her granddaughter as she dried her hands on her apron. "I didn't think he was still with the lilacs."

"Still?" Yarrow asked. She sat on the little stool at the end of the counter and waited.

"I met Irial when I was just a little younger than you are now," Grandma confessed. "When my brother Emery found out about him, he started cutting the bushes back. When he did that, Irial went away. After all these years, I thought he was long gone."

"What is he?" Yarrow asked, remembering his cinnamon kiss.

Grandma shook her head, her faded blue eyes full of a mix of emotions she couldn't convey. "I don't know, sweetheart. But I know he can be dangerous. I want you to stay away from him. Promise me?"

Yarrow nodded, remembering his smooth long-fingered hand holding her own.

Late that night, Yarrow got out of bed and crept silently through the house to the back door. Because it was warming up, Grandpa left the wooden door open with only the screen latched, to allow a cooling breeze into the house. Beyond the heirloom roses at the edge of the lawn, Grandma stood near the lilacs. Bright moonlight shone off her long white hair falling unbraided and loose down her back. She wore a pale pink nightgown which clearly revealed her age-rounded shoulders, stooped back, and sagging bosom. Before her stood a dark-haired figure. He seemed taller and older than he had to Yarrow earlier in the day, as though he had aged years in just a few hours.

"...you can have me," Grandma was saying, holding out her liver-spotted hands. "But leave my girl alone."

The dark figure shook his head. "You ran away from me, Lily. Your time is done, and Yarrow's time is just beginning."

"You can't have her!"

He glanced past the old woman, and met Yarrow's eyes. "Her choice is her own, Lily. You can't make it for her."

Yarrow stealthily returned to her bed, not wanting her Grandma to catch her spying, or even worse guess at why she was out of bed so late. But she wondered what it was that he wanted, and why it would be so bad to give it to him.

At the beginning of June as the lilac blooms began to brown and wither, Yarrow helped Grandpa trim off the dead florets. As they worked their way around the five bushes, she occasionally caught glimpses of Irial through the dense leaves. He never said anything, just gazed at her solemnly. It was clear to her that Grandpa couldn't see him; but the way Grandma watched to be sure they didn't cut anything back too far, it was obvious she could.

When her mother called a couple of weeks later to say she was coming home, Yarrow did her best not to sound disappointed. She loved her mother, but preferred to stay at her grandparent's house. And she wanted to talk to Irial again, but under her grandmother's protective gaze had been unable.

In August, after Yarrow's fourteenth birthday, they got a call with bad news. Viola's father Franklin had apparently suffered a heart attack while working in the yard. By the time the ambulance had gotten there, it was too late.

Viola immediately drove to her parent's house, where her mother waited alone. When they arrived it was to find Lily sitting in her wingback chair with her current piece of handwork in her lap. Her hands rested limp in the folds of cloth and embroidery floss, and she stared vacantly out the back window at the lilac hedge.

While Viola spoke to her mother, holding her lax hands and trying to get an account of what had happened, Yarrow went out the back door to look at the lilacs. They had been butchered; Grandpa's hedge trimmers and hand clippers lay abandoned on the grass amongst a scatter of branches. The hedge itself which had grown to over seven feet in height since being transplanted had been hacked down to perhaps four feet. Lying beneath the lowest branches, appearing skeletally thin and pale, Irial gazed up at her with eyes that had changed from lilac purple to the brown of the dying florets.

She crouched down so she could see him more clearly. "What did you do?" she whispered.

"He tried to kill me," Irial breathed, reaching out for her with one bone-slender hand.

She raised her hand and touched the tips of his fingers gingerly. He still felt cool and smooth, yet somehow not as substantial. "You killed my Grandpa," she said, more statement than question, and he pulled his hand back from her as though her touch burned him.

"It was his life or mine."

Yarrow shook her head and stood up, backing away from the carnage.

"I'll be here," he said, and began to fade back into the shadows beneath the remaining leaves and branches. "When you want me, I'll be here."

Yarrow watched until she could see him no longer, then she turned and went into the house to comfort her Grandma.

No matter how many years passed, there was nothing quite like a late spring evening, with the scent of blooming flowers on the breath of dusk. Yarrow sat quietly within her enclosed garden, the light of a candle lending a muted glow to hollyhock and delphinium, corn flower and freesia, peony and rose. The tulips were nearly done with their blooming, waxy leaves still standing proud and healthy. Sweet peas were climbing the lattice she'd supplied for their use. But with all the beautiful colors and scents, it was the lilac that ruled this May eventide. She took a deep breath of the perfumed air, remembering the events of her youth that had brought her to this moment.

After Grandpa's death, she had stayed with Grandma. Lily never spoke of what had happened the day her husband died, but she spent time every day near the denuded lilac hedge. Two years later, on the anniversary of Franklin's death Lily was found unresponsive lying on the grass, a bouquet of heirloom roses she'd been cutting clutched to her chest. Since Viola was her only child, everything had been left to her. But there was a trust set up for Yarrow when she turned eighteen, and included in her bequest were the five antique lilac bushes.

Yarrow had grown up and finished school. She had had her share of suitors, but none of them could compete with the memories of that summer before she turned fourteen. Now, she had a little house with a yard of her own. She spent time planning and planting the different flowers she remembered and loved from her childhood. But her favorite part of the yard was the back corner where she'd transplanted the lilac bushes. For two years she'd let them grow untrimmed, and now they stood ten feet tall and laden with sweet smelling blooms. She had done her research, and surrounding the lilacs was a low wrought-iron fence. She didn't know exactly what Irial was, but she guessed he was some kind of Irish fey. And one thing all the books and folk-lore agreed on was that fey could not cross iron. Now that the lilacs were untamed, she wanted to make sure he stayed put, until she was ready.

Tonight, Yarrow waited until the last glow of sunlight had faded from the sky. She was wearing a pale purple silk shift, and her hair hung long and slightly wavy down to her waist, still the same pale gold shade it had been when she was thirteen. When the moon rose above the house to cast its glow into her garden, she got up from her bower and crossed the grass to the far corner.

Irial stood before the transplanted bushes, his lilac-colored eyes watching as she approached. His unruly black hair and clever smile were just as she remembered. "I've been waiting for you, Yarrow."

She nodded, stopping outside the ring of the ornamental fence. "I wanted it to be perfect."

He held out his long-fingered hand to her, as he'd done before years ago, but did not reach across the wrought-iron. There was a clear invitation in his light eyes.

Yarrow thought back to that late spring day, when she had taken his hand and been pulled into his arms. She remembered his sharp, sweet kiss and stepped over the fence.

BEAUTIFUL BROKEN THINGS

He had noticed the store-front within the first week of moving into the neighborhood. The broad window was curtained with sheer black hangings and a coral pink neon sign flickered *Open* over an array of oddities. There was no business name over the mirrored glass door, just a hand painted plaque with a large black crow holding an eyeball in one clawed foot.

The street was filled with little shops, all of them grimy and worn in the ever-present overcast. There were pawnshops, tattoo parlors, adult book stores, and little food stands with two or three tables or a narrow counter with barstools. This was not the best part of town to work in, let alone live, but Trey didn't have a lot of options. Unless a person had the money to pay for walls and security, this was the best he could get.

"Have you ever gone in?"

Trey started, glancing at the painted girl who stood near him. She had candy-pink hair and wore a white sequined dress that left little of her browned figure to the imagination. "Huh?"

The girl laughed, a tinkling sound that was decidedly out of place. "To the Morrigan's. Have you ever gone in?"

He looked back across the street, to the wooden sign displaying the crow and eyeball. "No. What did you call it?"

The girl pulled a case out of the beaded bag dangling from her wrist, opening it to reveal tiny iridescent tablets. She put one under her tongue before returning the case to her bag. "The Morrigan's."

"What is it?" Street lights made pools of dingy gold on the dirty pavements up and down the street, and vehicles skimmed past on their silent airfields, sending bits of paper and plastic wrappers scooting along the cracked sidewalks. Trey kept from asking about the tablets. He was clean now. He repeated it as a silent mantra, *clean now clean now clean now.*

"My name is Nousha," she said breaking through his inner monologue. "You're new around here. What's your name?"

"Trey," he answered, *clean now clean now* ran on in the back of his mind.

"The Morrigan is a magic shop." Her dark skin shimmered, picking up the yellow of the street lights and magnifying it.

"Like card tricks, sawing someone in half?"

She laughed, more tinkling. "No, not that fake stuff. Real magic. Spells and hexes, love potions and such."

He stared at her, half hypnotized by the glimmering shifting colors on her skin. "No such thing."

Nousha shrugged, her bright pink hair like the neon signs along the street. "You could see for yourself. Or not."

Trey looked back at the dark window with the *Open* sign stuttering against the glass. Past the glass, behind the sheer black curtains, he thought he could see someone standing there looking back at him. But it could have just been a reflection. Or maybe he'd caught a partial high off the painted girl's glittering skin.

A car pulled up and stopped, window opening to reveal a heavy-set man of middle age. He glanced at Trey, then to Nousha. "Feel like a party?" he asked, voice gravelly and low.

"If you've got the creds, I'm up for anything," she said in a sexy purr. She winked at Trey, then got into the car. Her skin picked up the blue and violet lights from the interior, glimmering hyacinth and wisteria before the window slid shut and the car's airfield whisked it away.

Across the street, the *Open* sign buzzed and flickered. If anyone had been standing behind the curtain before, they were gone now. Trey felt as though he buzzed and flickered, *clean now* repeating again and again in the back of his mind. He turned and went down the street to the barred security door, punched in his access code, and went up two flights of dingy stairs to what was now his home.

The light was dim, but the air cool. Water seeped down the near wall, pooling at the base before reaching the nearest drain. Trey noted it on the small digital map he carried, then continued walking along the tracks. Far off in another tunnel, he could hear trains running. Behind him, Jacob hummed tunelessly as he cleared debris away from the tracks.

Who'd have guessed I'd end up here? Trey thought, stopping to examine cracks in the wall and ceiling. Small chunks of concrete had broken away, revealing ancient brickwork beneath. He added additional notes to the map, checking the time when he did so. Two more hours before his shift was done. Then the requisite visit to his parents. He didn't look forward to it.

After inspecting the remainder of the tunnel, Trey went back to the hub. Jacob trailed him, still humming some unrecognizable song. They washed up and dumped their coveralls in the dirty laundry bin before lining up to swipe their ID cards through the time-clock.

"You hear they might be offering overtime?" Jacob asked, interrupting his own humming. The black geometric tattoos that nearly covered his face made it hard to recognize his expressions. This one appeared to be mild curiosity.

"No," Trey replied.

"You in, if they do?"

"Only if he passes the screen," Salah said, joining them. His caramel colored eyes were cool and judgmental, just like the tone of his voice. "Can you pass the screen, Trey?"

"I'm clean now," Trey replied, his voice matching the mental mantra for a second.

"We'll see." Salah inclined his head, then preceded them out onto the platform.

"Headin' to Alma's for dinner. You coming?" Jacob asked.

Trey shook his head. "I have to go high side. See you tomorrow."

Jacob shrugged, not bothering to ask, and they parted. Trey waited on the platform for the train, while Jacob trotted up the steps to the street above.

This time of day the train was packed, so Trey stood near the door with one hand on a pole to keep his balance. He watched as the dark walls slid past the windows, gathering speed until they were just a blur. In the reflection he could see his own indistinct figure. Behind him stood a dark shape, and it seemed to be watching him.

Trey closed his eyes. Too many bad memories, too many imagined mythologies configured by his chemically stewed brain, and now he saw flashes of them everywhere. Even though he was *clean now.*

Eventually the train exited the tunnels, coming out on the other side of the walls that kept the haves separated from the have-nots. There were white clouds in the sky, trees provided shade with wide green leaves, and the lowering sun cast an auburn light over everything. At the checkpoint, Trey showed his ID and the chip that gave him access to Apex on the first Monday of each month. After running his credentials through the system, the city guards let him pass with a reminder of curfew.

Trey could have taken a cab, there was an allowance for it. But it had been a while since he'd had the opportunity to walk in clean air, beneath the shade of real trees and without fear of being robbed or pressed into one of a dozen gangs. He could hear birds singing, and a group of children were playing tag in a broad swath of grass across the street. He took his time, knowing he should hurry—he only had until midnight to be back to the train. Spending an evening every month with his parents was mandatory to his sentence, and though he would follow the requirement he saw no reason to cut short what little bit of this monthly penance he actually enjoyed.

His path took him on a zigzag course down ever wider boulevards. The townhomes and single-family houses grew in size as did the yards surrounding them. In less than an hour, he had reached an area where the homes were mansions encompassed by elaborate grounds. The monolith he finally approached was clad in white marble, with twin fountains splashing merrily on either side of the gated walkway. Charles, the resident butler, was waiting on the front steps.

"Master Shain," he said, looking down his long aristocratic nose.

"Hello Charles," Trey said quietly, and nodded when the servant opened the front door for him.

The entryway was elegant, carpeted in a tasteful gold-chased burgundy and accented with delicate tables on which to display framed photos and small figurines. Trey knew the way, so didn't wait for Charles to guide him. Instead, he went to the curving grand staircase, up and to the left, to the room that had once been his. He didn't linger there; he didn't have time. Instead, he quickly changed into appropriate clothing from the closet, attempted to tame his unruly ginger hair, and made his way back downstairs to the formal dining room where dinner would be served.

The heavy table that took up most of the room was already set with gold-rimmed china, lead crystal glassware and the good silver. Since there were no other guests besides Trey, only three places had been set at one end of the table. Trey sat at the left of the seat of honor, letting his calloused fingertips trace the edges of the fine dishes. His nails were ragged, and dirt that he was unable to wash away was visible beneath the keratin.

A soft humming sound alerted him that his parents were coming. Trey stood, putting his hands behind his back and squaring his shoulders. He kept his eyes low, however; he didn't want to be accused of arrogance, as had happened the last time.

A motorized wheelchair appeared in the doorway, and Father sat rigidly upright in the seat with his feet firmly planted on the footplates. He was dressed in a suit, but a knitted shawl had been placed across his shoulders for extra warmth. Thick grey hair shadowed his forehead, and his dark eyes were vague and unfocused.

Mother accompanied him, one thin and veiny hand resting on Father's shoulder. She wore a dark blue dress with matching shoes, and ropes of diamonds around throat and wrists. Her Harlow-gold hair was perfectly coiffed, and as always, Trey felt completely out of place.

Father's chair wheeled around to the head of the table and stopped at his place setting. Mother waited until Charles pulled out her chair for her, then took her seat at Father's right. Only then, did Trey sit back down.

"Hello Father, Mother," he said softly, taking his heavy cloth napkin off the table to put over his lap.

Mother's eyes dropped to his hands, immediately taking in the grime beneath the nails. Her thin lips pursed, but she didn't comment.

Trey sighed silently, and waited while the first course was served.

The train ride back to low side seemed to take forever. Plenty of time for Trey to brood over the latest family visit. Memories passed like arduous vignettes before his mind's eye, and he clenched his teeth in defense.

"I realize that you're living on subsistence these days," Mother *said coolly, "but you could at least get a haircut and take the time to wash your hands."*

Father's eyes were open, but only focused on his food. He said not a word, as though he dined alone.

"And what kind of work is it you're doing?"

"I'm on the maintenance crew for the transit authority."

Mother's upper lip wrinkled a little at that. She had never used public transport in her life. "I hate to ask, but are you clean?"

Trey had sighed. "If I wasn't, I wouldn't be here."

Mother sniffed. She flicked her bony fingers, signaling for the servants to clear their plates and bring the next course.

"I know you don't want me here, Mother. But it's part of my sentence." Trey kept his voice soft and level. It did no good to show any emotion here; it never had.

"When I think of all the prospects you had, your potential," she mused, sipping her wine.

"I think of it, too," he said dutifully. Being here, in the cold company of his closest family, reminded him of why he'd started to use in the first place.

"Such a disappointment," Mother said. She could have meant his lost opportunities, but probably not.

He put his head against the window, unable to watch the tunnel wall rippling past as it was making him sick. After dinner he'd had a small reprieve. He'd gone up to his once-bedroom and changed back into his real clothes, leaving the fancy costume to be washed and returned to the closet. Instead of searching out his parents, he had gone outside into the garden that took up the space between house and garage.

"What are you doing out here?"

Trey had not bothered to turn. He knew the voice was only in his own mind.

"I've missed you." The voice was that of his sister Emilia.

"You're not here," he whispered.

"I'll always be here," she replied. But when he finally gave in and turned to look, he was alone. Emilia did not haunt the house or grounds, she only haunted him. But she only came to him here.

"I'm sorry, Emi," he said. Losing her had changed everything in his life.

Trey got off the train and trudged up the stairs to the street. After spending time in Apex, it was even harder to come back to the low side. The air here was tainted with the stench of smoke and chemicals, and the sun rarely shone. The sky was never clear enough to reveal stars or moon; instead the smog reflected back the clashing shades of neon and arc-sodium lighting. Graffiti marred every flat surface, and garbage collected in the gutters. By the time he reached the street where his apartment building stood, it was almost one a.m.

He stopped on the sidewalk, ignoring the heavy traffic. Cars skimmed bumper to bumper, and throngs of people jostled him and each other. Trey found himself gazing at the black crow holding an eyeball, and realized that the door below it was not completely closed. The *Open* sign flickered in the window, and a breath of cinnamon scented air escaped.

He hesitated, seeing in his memory the grand façade of his parents' house in his final look back.

Charles stood on the front steps, as though to be sure Trey were really leaving. Of Mother and Father there was no sign. Neither of them had bothered to see him off, but they had given up on him a long time ago. When Emilia died, he might as well have crawled into her coffin with her.

Without remembering how, he found himself standing on the other side of the mirrored door, his hand resting on the handle where he'd pulled it closed. He could see the throngs of people and vehicles through the glass, but could hear nothing from outside.

There was the soft sound of falling water, and he searched the dim room until he saw the fountain on a bottom shelf. A few candles burned in holders placed advantageously, and he moved slowly about the room looking but not touching the articles displayed in the many cases. There were tumbled stones and raw crystals, wooden boxes carved with sinuous designs, figurines and small statues carved of many substances and revealing an amazing range of colors and styles. In the farthest corner of the room, between ceiling high shelves filled with books, a wooden post with crossarms supported a large black bird. Head cocked to one side, Trey approached it. He had known people in the high side who had taxidermied trophies, but had never seen anything like this.

The bird looked like the painting on the sign out front, and its glossy black feathers and perfectly rendered eyes were so lifelike it nearly took his breath away. Trey reached out to smooth the fine feathers beneath the matte beak, and jumped when the bird blinked. Its beak opened, but it made no sound or any threatening gesture.

"Welcome." The voice that spoke was soft and rich, and Trey started again, nearly falling. The woman who had spoken stood near the door, her dark hair pulled back from her face. Her right eye was dark, yet glimmered with red eyeshine like an animal's; her left eye was obscured by a white caul, and he wondered if that eye were blind. "What can I do for you?"

"I'm sorry," he said hoarsely, "I didn't hear you come in."

She shrugged, unconcerned.

"What kind of place is this?" Trey asked.

"Hmm," she hummed, coming across the room toward him. "That is debatable. If you can tell me what you're looking for, I might be able to better answer that."

"Nousha said this is the Morrigan's. Is that you?"

"Ah." She stepped past him, reaching out toward the bird.

It opened its wings and hopped from the wooden stand to her arm, sidled up to her shoulder, then tucked its wings back and nestled against her ear. "The shop is known by many names. The name is less important than what my customers need. That is what defines us—what we need." She turned back to face him, her blank white-filmed eye making him uncomfortable. He didn't know whether to look at it or not. "I am Ciara Dubhbran."

He nodded awkwardly. "My name is Trey."

"Yes," she agreed. "I know. So I ask again. What do you need?"

He shook his head. He had no money to buy anything from her; he could barely afford rent and food after his restitution. He didn't even know why he'd come in here, except maybe from curiosity and the need to take his mind off the evening he'd just had.

"Few indeed are those who need nothing, Mr. Shain. You must consider yourself among the luckiest of men." She moved away from him then, the bird balancing effortlessly on her shoulder. Her long inky hair trailed behind her like a shadow.

"Not lucky," he said. "Unless you mean bad luck."

"A man with any luck can turn it to his advantage."

He realized then that she had called him by his surname, which he hadn't given her. "Wait, how did you—"

"All it takes is will, and a certain amount of confidence." She began to extinguish candles, one after another, the room falling into deeper gloom. The crow spread its wings, making a soft croaking noise but did not fly. "Think on it, if you like. I'm not going anywhere."

Trey felt dizzy, and put his hand out to steady himself. Something cool and heavy tipped out from under his fingertips, dislodged from its place on the shelf, and shattered on the floor. He looked down, aghast. How much would he have to pay for the broken item?

"Broken things can be useful, even beautiful, Mr. Shain." She knelt before him, her dark hair or the crow's outstretched wing brushing against his wrist. "The witching hour has come to a close, and so my shop must close as well. Think on it, as long as you'd like. And come again, when you have an answer."

She looked up, her long-fingered hands full of broken shards of stone, one eye white and inscrutable, the other glinting red. "I'll clean this up, now."

Clean now clean now, clamored in his mind, as it had not done since he'd found himself in the strange store. Trey closed his eyes, rubbed his face wearily. "I'm very sorry," he said, knowing he had to say something for the damage he'd done. Someone bumped into him, and he looked to find himself standing on the sidewalk before the Morrigan's. The neon sign was dark.

Across the street, the painted girl Nousha smiled slyly at him, her skin shimmering with her latest hit of Prizm.

Trey passed the screen as he was *clean now,* and took the overtime that was available. He didn't want to work in the dark, dirty tunnels any longer than he had to; but it was better than sitting in his tiny one-room apartment with nothing to do but think. And even that was better than hanging out on the street, waiting until his weakening will made him ask Nousha or someone else for a hit of Prizm, or his own drug of choice— Bliss. Yet even while he worked, marking his digital map with notations of dry-rot or rodent-chewed cables, he found himself remembering the strange tableau that had taken place on his return to low side. Ciara Dubhbran had asked him what he needed. It seemed such a simple question, yet there was no easy answer. Now he couldn't get that question out of his mind, and the words *What do you need?* began to run counterpoint to *clean now* in his ongoing mental mantra.

"Going to Alma's?" Jacob asked after their double shift.

Salah watched Trey with his judgmental caramel eyes, and Trey shook his head wearily.

It was strange getting off work in the middle of the night, even though the heavy smog never allowed the sun to shine in the daytime anyway. Trey walked slowly, too exhausted to quicken his step, and wasn't surprised when he looked up to see the crow and eyeball sign above him. The neon *Open* sign burned against the black curtains. He pushed on the mirrored door and stepped inside.

Everything had moved. The shelves and cases were

staggered across the center of the room, leaving the walls bare. A mural had been painted on the plaster, making the room into a forest glade. Dark tree trunks marched around the room, and delicate ferns uncurled between them. Spotted toadstools and dark hooded flowers grew among the painted boles, and in the corner where the crow's perch had been a full moon peeked between the bare branches.

"Have you come to an answer?"

Trey turned, finding Ciara standing by the door as though she'd just followed him in. "It's not material things that I need," he said without thinking, "and I don't know how you could possibly give me anything else."

"There are many hidden things, Mr. Shain, that do not lend themselves to easy discovery." She wore grey today, instead of the black she'd had on the last time, and her sooty hair fell free around her shoulders. "It is a wise man who truly knows himself, and only self-knowledge can ever lead to happiness."

"I thought ignorance is bliss," Trey said.

"Bliss is, as you know, not all it's cracked up to be."

He stared at her, sure that she somehow knew about his addiction to the drug, though he'd discussed it with no one since being sentenced to low side.

Ciara stepped past him taking a bowl carved from translucent stone and a small wooden box off a shelf. "Come with me," she said, walking to the corner where the painted moon gleamed from a star filled sky. She walked between the boles of two trees, disappearing into the darkness beyond them.

Trey stared, mouth hanging open. Before he could talk himself out of it, he followed her.

The room revealed was warm and cozy. A fire burned in a stone fireplace, and a low exposed-beam ceiling was hung with bunches of dried flowers and leaf stems. A low table and chairs were pulled up near the fire, and Ciara had already taken a seat there.

"What is this?" he asked. Even the air smelled different, fresh with hints of pine and mint.

"This is my home." She looked up, her white eye gleaming in the shadows of her hair.

"What if someone comes into the store?"

Her lips curved, and she opened the box she'd taken off the shelf. Inside were dried herbs. "No one can enter without my leave."

"I entered."

Her smile broadened. "Not without my leave." She put some of the herbs into the stone bowl and added water from a kettle on the hearth. "You came to me with great need. I felt it from across the street just as strongly as I feel it now. I am prepared to help you, Trey. But first you must tell me what you need."

He sat beside her, watching as she placed the bowl on the table before him. "What are you?" he asked.

"We are all many things," she replied, closing the box. "I am a woman, I am a soul, I am a daughter and a sister. Once I was a wife and mother, but no more. I am a dreamer, a creator and a destroyer. I am a witch."

"All I am is a disappointment," he whispered, feeling the bitterness in his heart that was all that he had left.

"You are what you choose to be," Ciara said, a predatory gleam in her dark eye. "You must let go of the negative, release the pain you carry like a stone. Unless that is all you are, all you want to be. There is magic in the world, Trey." She gestured to the bowl. "You don't have to believe in it. It's there, anyway."

"What is this?" He put his hands around the bowl, feeling the heat emanating through the thin stone.

"A magic potion," she answered. Even within reach of the fire, her face fell into shadow. The crow flew from somewhere to land on the high back of her chair, its dark eyes staring at Trey. "Or a simple cup of tea. It all depends on you."

He looked into the bowl, floating bits of green on the surface of the hot water that still wafted steam into the air. "I don't understand why you would help me. You know I have no money, nothing to pay you with."

"Perhaps it is my need, to help you."

The crow shifted, rattling its feathers, and the fire popped. Trey listened to the tangled words that scrambled his mind; his Mother's distaste and Father's disinterest, the judge's inflexible orders, the terrible guilt for things he had done and things he had not, and the soft words *I've missed you* from Emilia. Beneath it all, his own manta *clean now* went around and around without end. Nousha tinkled her laugh at him while her skin glittered, shifting through iridescent ripples of hypnotic color, and his desire for Bliss that never seemed to lessen tracked through his brain like the tickling feet of millions of insects.

"What I need," he finally whispered, unable to hear his own words over the clamor in his head, "is to be with the only person I ever loved, who ever really loved me."

"And who is that?" Ciara asked, although Trey was sure she already knew.

"Emilia."

"Then I can help you," she said, leaning forward to cup his face in her cool hands. He stared into her blank white eye, breathing the scent of clean wood smoke and nutmeg. Her lips were sweet against his, and for a brief moment all the noise in his mind fell silent. "Drink the potion," Ciara whispered, and he felt the hot bowl against his mouth.

The taste was bitter, like his many regrets.

Salah and Jacob walked along the crowded sidewalk. Salah was scanning the buildings and store-fronts, looking for the correct block number. Jacob watched the people, the tattooed designs on his slab face looking like some kind of ancient writing in the kaleidoscope lights.

A painted girl with bright pink hair winked at Jacob, licked her lips suggestively at Salah. "Looking for anything special?" she asked. Her skin twinkled with a recent hit of Prizm.

"Number 138," Salah said, jaw clenched tightly.

"You know Trey?" Jacob asked, more laid back and friendly than his companion.

"Red hair, sad eyes?" she asked.

"He missed two shifts," Jacob started, but Salah cut him off.

"He's in violation of his sentencing," the taller man said coldly. "If he doesn't want to be processed for a prison gang, he'd better have a good excuse."

The painted girl looked across the street, to the shop with the crow and eyeball sign above the door. "He's gone," she said.

"Found him lying on the sidewalk in front of that building," and she pointed. "Two days ago, in the morning."

"What happened?" Jacob asked sadly. He'd liked the young man who fought so hard to stay clean.

Nousha shrugged, wearing a wistful smile. "You should go over to the Morrigan's. She would know. She could maybe give you what you need." The painted girl reached for another iridescent tablet, and nodded just once to the shadow behind the sheer black curtains.

PROMISES, BLISS, AND LIES

She scuttled along the pipes, hunched low so as not to hit her head on the ring joints. Drab rags were gathered around her, a camouflage of sorts that allowed her to blend into her surroundings just by freezing in place. When she reached the opening, little more than a jagged weathered break in the reinforced concrete pipe, she crouched and looked cautiously out. The color of the light was burnt umber over rusted steel and rotted wood. Water sloshed and gurgled not far away, the chemical sludge of the waterfront that was the final destination of all the old underground sewers.

"Almost dark," she whispered, talking only to herself. Once, she had shared her thoughts with rats and spiders, her fellow denizens of the underground; before that she had had family and friends to talk to. They were gone now, but she'd gotten the habit and didn't bother to break it. "Should be safe."

She could wait forever on the cusp of indecision, and it would get her nowhere. So she finally ducked through the opening into the end of twilight. Lights glowed in the gloom, frowzy and smoke-tinted yet dazzling against the bland and fetid backdrop of low side.

"Arien."

The sound of her name startled her, and she flinched. A few feet away there was a dark figure leaning against a rickety old fence.

"I've been waiting for a long time." He stood straight and came toward her, holding out one long-fingered elegant hand. "I was worried."

She shook her head within the hood she wore to hide her

face. "No more. I said no more."

"Don't be silly, Arien." His voice was smooth, the tone slightly amused, but he took her elbow in a firm grip so she couldn't slip away. "We have a deal. You're not going to go back on your word now, are you?"

She closed her eyes, in weariness or to stop the stinging of tears. "Won't you let me go?"

He began to walk, heading away from the docks toward his waiting car, pulling her along with him. "You're too valuable to me, my dear. I can't let you go."

"Please, Brennus," she whispered, but did not fight his grip. She had promised him, but that was long ago and before she knew what he'd intended.

"First we'll get you cleaned up," he said, still with that slightly amused and patient note in his cultured voice, "and get you something to eat. You're thin as bird bones. Then it's back to work for both of us."

They had reached his car now, a long sleek black thing that looked like a weapon. A driver in uniform and cap opened the door for them, and Brennus ushered Arien into the dim leather and burnished-wood interior before getting in with her. When the limo rose onto its airfield, Arien lost all sense of movement, as though they were still sitting at the curb.

"I want to go home," she said, pulling the hood lower over her face. She didn't want to look at the soft seats or the dark windows that gave her back her own reflection. She didn't want to look at him.

"We'll be there shortly," Brennus said, and put his arm around her familiarly.

Once the sky had been blue, and the sun had shone golden and clear through green leaves and along wide boulevards faced with manicured lawns and lovely safe houses. Children had played in parks, chasing dogs or balls, and shrieking their laughter into the benevolent air. Arien remembered that time well, although it was more like a flickering old movie playing in the back of her mind. The lambent images were clear, but so tiny and far away. Those were the days when she was surrounded by parents and sister, friends from her neighborhood and friends from school. In those days, she had smiled without worry, skipping down the sidewalks with her pale hair bouncing behind her, dressed in bright colors and looking forward to every new tomorrow.

Sometimes she could almost make herself believe she could travel back there, to relive the innocence of that time. She knew, of course, that that time was no more innocent than any other. But she had been blissfully unaware of the darkness in the world, and the evil in the hearts of those who claimed to love.

With eyes closed, she retreated into inner darkness and emerged again as herself. She wore a blue dress with cream colored leggings beneath, and her long fair hair pulled back into a pony tail with a matching blue ribbon. At most, she was eight years old, playing hopscotch on the sidewalk with the help of a holo-display that changed the configuration to whatever she wished. Her sister Camryn waited to take a turn, dressed in a matching outfit although her dress was cream colored and leggings dark blue.

Arien tossed her marker, a piece of silver-grey slate the size of her palm that bounced then slid into the square she was aiming for. With a broad smile, she hopped into the pattern displayed on the pavement. She made her way through the grid to the end, turned and hopped back, only stopping to pick up her marker. Camryn stepped up to take her turn, the older girl at least as adept as Arien. While they played, a soft summer breeze sighed through the trees and brightly colored flowers played host to butterflies and droning bees.

"Arien."

The voice, as familiar to her as her own inner voice, brought her out of the memory and into the present. Brennus stood beside the huge marble tub with a bath sheet held out toward her.

"Time to get out, my dear. You're pruning."

She lifted her hands, turning them to note that he was right. But she didn't want to get out; she wanted to go back to the memory, where everything was beautiful and she was safe.

"Don't make me call for Jarek." It was said gently, but a threat nonetheless.

Without a word, Arien got up and stepped out of the tub, leaving behind cooling water and the grime of she didn't know how many days and nights hiding in low side. Her hair, long and fine, and still the pale champagne gold of her childhood, hung wet and dripping down her back until Brennus wrapped her in the towel. While she dried herself, he brought her soft warm clothing to wear. When she was dressed, and her damp hair combed smooth, he walked her down a wide hallway to a table set with fine china and crystal. Jarek, tall with bulky muscles disguised by the fine cut of his clothes, was bringing dinner from the kitchen.

Arien hesitated when she saw the big man, but Jarek merely inclined his head to her respectfully, and set a silver tray on the table.

"Sit, my dear. There is hot soup, your favorite creamy potato with peppers," Brennus said soothingly, handing her into a chair before sitting beside her. "Fresh bread, still warm from the oven and salted butter. You need to eat, to keep up your strength."

While he spoke, Jarek served, and it smelled so good. Tears stung her eyes again, for this was a different kind of memory, a sensory overload that made her mouth water and her stomach cramp. But most of all, it made her heart ache for things lost that could never be retrieved.

"Eat, Arien," Brennus said, and there was iron in his voice now. She would eat on her own, or he would force feed her. He had done so before.

"Where is your dinner?" she asked, picking up a spoon. "I don't like to eat alone."

He smiled, leaning back in his chair, reverting to the charm that was his most accomplished façade. "I've already eaten. While you bathed." He smoothed the crease in his pants and squared his shoulders while maintaining his air of repose. Arien wasn't sure how long it had been since she'd last seen him. It was hard to gauge, as he never seemed to change. "You were in low side for almost six months," he said, as though reading her mind. "It took that long to track you down, this time. Why do you insist on playing this game? You know I'm going to find you—I always find you. And then I bring you back, and we go through this all over again."

The spoon shook in her hand, but she leaned over the bowl so she wouldn't spill. The flavor of the soup was rich, like the memory of an embrace from someone beloved. She had those memories too, deep down and well hidden. She couldn't reach them with Brennus watching her. The silver rattled against her teeth, but she bit down and managed to swallow the mouthful.

"Every time I find you, you tell me you want to go home. But this is home," and he gestured around the grand dining room. Richly colored walls were accented with paintings and gilt-framed mirrors, and the marble floor was polished to a dull shine where it wasn't covered in thick warm hand-woven carpets.

"Not my home," she whispered, looking down at her bowl.

Jarek, dark and with all the expression of a slab of rock, looked from Arien to Brennus and back. He said nothing—it was not his place—but a glint in his eyes hinted at something hidden. When Brennus lifted his chin in signal, the bond-servant gave a slight bow and left the room.

"We've discussed this before," Brennus said softly, reached out to close his hand around her fragile left wrist. "Jarek is my man, and I trust him for his bond if nothing else. But you do not defy me before him or anyone else, Arien. I won't have it." His hand tightened, and Arien winced but made no sound, still staring down into her soup. "Do you understand me?" he pressed.

Arien kept her silence. She talked to herself all the time, but refused to give him another word.

Brennus waited until it was clear she wouldn't yield. Breaking her wrist would serve no purpose, and so he released her. "Finish eating. You need to rest, and we'll start again tomorrow."

Mechanically, she finished the hearty soup and a buttered slice of the warm bread. While she ate, Brennus busied himself with a handheld computer. When she was done, he signaled for Jarek again.

"Take her to her room. Make sure she has what she needs,

and that she stays put." His blue eyes were cold, and Brennus had given over pretending any affection.

"Yes, sir." Jarek waited until Arien got up, then escorted her down the hall and up a flight of curving stairs to her room. He didn't try to touch her, knowing from past experience that she wouldn't tolerate it, but kept close. She had a history of running away, but was still too tired and disoriented to try anything tonight, Jarek was certain.

He went into her room with her, closing the doors behind them. While she moved around the walls, reacquainting herself with trinkets and photos that decorated the place, he turned down her covers and made sure the windows were locked and shuttered. When he turned back, he was surprised to find her standing in the middle of the room staring at him.

"How long have you been here, in Apex?" she asked, her voice and question innocent, like a child's. "You were here last time, and the time before. But you weren't always here. Were you?"

"I was here last time," he said, surprised at her directness. "And many times before that. I have worked for Mr. Caul for the last fifteen years."

"Fifteen years," she whispered, looking down at the oval frame she'd taken from a shelf. The photo in the frame was of Camryn, her sister. "Little more than a heartbeat."

"It seems longer to me than that."

Arien nodded, reaching out to set the picture down. Rather than standing it up again, she laid it flat with her sister's face against the wood. "You have time. I envy you that." She walked around him, close enough to touch, but did not look at him again. "Good night, then. Guard my doors against the dragon." With no concern for his presence, she stripped off the clothes Brennus had dressed her in, dropping them on the carpeted floor, and got into bed. She pulled the covers up over her head, nesting in the fifteen-hundred thread count sheets and silk covered quilt.

Jarek left her then, turning off the lights before exiting the room and locking her doors. Alas, the dragon was the master of this house, and Jarek could protect no one from him. The bond-servant waited for a long time, head angled intently as he listened, but he heard no sound from within—neither her voice, nor the sound of crying.

Arien's father had been a doctor and a scientist. He worked at one of the best hospitals in Apex at the time when the dome was being built over the city. He was respected and fairly well-off, but not rich. He owned a house in an upscale neighborhood, and provided a good life for his wife and two daughters. In the mornings before work, he would sit on the patio with his girls and watch as new sections of the clear crys-crete dome were placed. Soon, the polluted air would be unable to harm the residents of the city and only those outside the fortified walls would suffer from it.

Arien slept, returning to that time in her dreams. She sat beside Daddy in the citrine glow of the rising sun, watching as far off hovercraft lifted the panels of crys-crete into place. Camryn sat on Daddy's other side, telling him about a boy she had met at school. He had ice-blue eyes and dark blond hair, and had asked her to the formal dance at the end of the month.

Three years younger, at thirteen Arien had yet to develop an interest in boys other than as friends. But she was fascinated by her sister's romance. Camryn had already confided in Arien that someday she would marry Brendan Caul, and Arien knew her sister's determination well enough to believe it.

When Daddy got up to go to work, Arien gave him a hug and smile. She had been innocent of what would come, only knowing that she loved him and trusted him with all her heart. As he got into his car and pulled away from the modest home, Arien put her hands over her face. She still resided in the memory, but knew what was going to happen and was helpless to stop it. She could relive these moments, but never change them. Beside her, still living out that long ago day, Camryn chattered excitedly about the dress she would buy for the dance. If she could have, Arien would have wept.

When Jarek came into her room, he found Arien already awake and dressed. She was curled into the window seat, shutters open so she could look out at the perfect curve of the dome.

"Did you sleep?" he asked.

She didn't answer, gave no indication that she had heard him. She simply put one hand up to place palm and spread fingers on the glass.

"Mr. Caul is waiting."

Arien tipped her forehead against the window. She wanted to disappear into her memories, and yet wished to block them off forever so they could not be used. The gentle touch on her shoulder made her turn her head. Jarek stood behind her, his hand soft on her skin.

"If you don't come, he will only be more cruel."

"He can be nothing else." But she got up and crossed the room with him, her dispassionate guard.

In the dining room, Brennus drank coffee and spoke on the phone. "Yes, there will be more for you starting tomorrow. I know, we're low on supplies. But that's been taken care of. I'll have the extract today."

Unwilling, Arien sat down and waited as Jarek brought her breakfast. Eggs and fried potatoes, toasted cinnamon bread and a mug of hot chocolate. She remembered breakfasts like this from her childhood, but it brought her no joy this morning. She ate slowly, not to savor but to put off what would come next. As always, dragging her feet did nothing but skin her toes.

"It's time, Arien. Finish your food, or go without."

Tears burned and her chest got tight as though all the air in the room had been sucked out and there was nothing left to breathe. She gripped the edge of the table with both hands, prepared to hold on for dear life, eyes squeezed shut to keep out the sight of Brennus' impatient expression.

"Jarek." Brennus stood, tucking his phone into a pocket, and tapped his foot while the bond-servant pried Arien's white-knuckled hands off the table. Jarek pulled her to her feet, his own expression set with distant distaste at having to do this. Brennus held his bond, and so he had no choice except to obey the orders given. But he didn't have to like it.

Arien opened her eyes then, meeting Brennus' irritated

And the drug has helped many people, when it was used the way it was intended." Her face, beside his in the reflection, was small and perfect like it was in his Bliss-induced trips. She was a goddess, a fallen angel shivering in the cold lab with bruised arms and no one to protect her. "He's made his fortune off of you. He charges whatever he wants for the *extract* as he calls it, and no one argues. No one knows where he gets it. No one can duplicate it. But everyone who has Blissed out would recognize your face. We have all dreamed your dreams."

She met his eyes when he finally turned to face her, wanting to see her as she really was and not as he remembered her from the dreams. In the cold white light she looked tired, dark smudges beneath her frost-grey eyes. She was too thin, and the sharp edges of collarbones and ribs were evident beneath her skin. Even with this, she appeared so young. By her date of birth, she was over sixty years old; because of the stasis, she had aged only thirty-five. But she looked like a girl in her early twenties, exhausted and reconciled to an uneasy fate.

"I'm off the Bliss now," he said, as though apologizing to her. "I've been off it for almost a year."

"That's why," she said, understanding. He had changed. He was no longer connected to her.

He didn't perceive her meaning, and said only, "I wish I could help you." He was trained as a body guard, physically fit and prepared to use weapons or any of half a dozen kinds of martial arts. But he was helpless, confessing his guilt to her.

Arien nodded. "Maybe you can," she said.

He did not hesitate. "How?"

She looked down, at where her hands clasped tightly together, bloodless fingers taut with the beginning of hope. "Were you Bliss-addicted when you were bonded?"

He nodded, dropping his eyes. He knew she would see the shame he held there.

"Does my uncle know that you're clean?"

Jarek had to consider. He had never hidden his addiction from Brennus; there had been no need, as his employer considered it just one more way of ensuring Jarek's loyalty. He had bought his supply from a dealer in low side, so as not to bring attention back to the mansion. Brennus Caul had no compunction against living well on the manufacture and distribution of an illegal substance, but certainly would never stand for the fine citizens of Apex finding out about it. "It's not something we've ever discussed," Jarek finally said.

Arien stepped closer, waiting until the big man looked up to meet her eyes. "If you were bonded under the influence of Bliss, now that you're free of it the bond will not hold."

He was frozen by her soft words. He had been bonded for fifteen years, and the constraints of habit had kept him from even testing the limits of his bond.

"You said you wanted to help me," she said, taking one more step, now close enough she could have reached out to touch him. "How far are you willing to go?"

Jarek closed his eyes, and imagined assaulting Brennus Caul, crushing the cold-blooded leech's throat beneath his own bare hands. The bond, made up of chemical links and nanotech implants, was fashioned to keep a bond-servant completely under control and unable to cause harm to the bond-holder. Before this moment, Jarek had been unable to even think of endangering his employer. The knowledge that his shackles were finally unlocked was like an epiphany. He stood straighter, feeling a weight of anger and resignation falling away from him. "What can I do?"

Brennus went to fetch Arien the next morning. After unlocking the doors, he went inside and found the bed untouched, the shutters latched and windows closed. Jaw clenched, he called for Jarek but got no reply.

"Jarek!" He used his phone, his computer link, and even the house system. According to the system, the bond-servant was nowhere on the grounds. A check of the surveillance recordings showed him escorting Arien to her room, locking her in, and then retiring to his own quarters. There was no indication of how he or Arien had left the house, or when. They both seemed to have vanished into thin air.

In a fury, Brennus searched the house from top to bottom, starting in his own huge suite of rooms and working his way all the way down to the smallest out of the way broom closet in the laboratory complex beneath the foundations. He found no one, not his aunt or his bond-servant, nor any of the domestic staff.

"Arien!" he screamed, racing back up to her room once more to search for any clues of her whereabouts. He could not lose her, she was too important. Nothing mattered, except bringing her back under his control. The sky grew dark, and low clouds sheathed the dome turning it into a convex crystal ball, but Brennus never stopped to look into it.

"What is it?" Jarek asked the doctor, who was going over the readouts on the monitor attached to Brennus Caul's head.

The doctor shook his head. "I've never seen anything like it. It's quite similar to Bliss overdose, but instead of calming and slowing his metabolism, this has put him into a heightened state of agitation. We can't give him any more tranquilizers. If we can't get his heart rate and brain activity to slow, we may have to put him into stasis."

"Of course, Doctor. If you think that is best," Arien said. She stood beside her uncle's bed, the picture of familial concern. Long sleeves hid the bruises on her arms.

Jarek nodded his agreement, but said nothing. In his role as trusted bond-servant, he stood guard as he always had. His face was perfectly expressionless, and the tiny wound behind his ear nearly invisible. He hoped whatever hidden nightmare the man was caught in would last forever. It was a promise he and Arien had made to each other. She had extracted his neurons, and he carefully mixed them with hers. Jarek then administered the full dose to Mr. Caul while he slept. It should be enough to ensure the man would never hurt anyone again.

As Brennus' only heir, Arien would have access to the fortune that had been bought with her soul. The manufacture of Bliss would end, and she could finally live the life that had been for so long interrupted. She looked across the bed, meeting Jarek's level gaze. She did not smile, not now. There would be time enough to smile once her uncle had been relegated to stasis. There, he could dream on in the everlasting nightmare he had built.

As for Arien, she had new memories to make.

BEFORE THE FIRST DAY OF WINTER

It was the last day of autumn, and the precious hours of warmth and plenty were over. Darker days were coming as the season slid irrevocably toward winter, and all living creatures made their preparations.

Gulls cried as they picked through the out-going surf, looking for edible tidbits. The lowering sun brought a glow to cool misty air, and everything was shaded gold, citrine, and rose. Sea stacks and cliffs were black, jagged reminders of volcanic origins, and the hard-packed sand near the water stretched virgin and unsullied in wind-rippled drifts to the rocky headland.

Naia hurried along the strand, searching for a particular boulder shaped like some bulky four-legged animal crouched on its haunches. She was sure it was close by, but couldn't remember if it rested north or south of where she'd reached the beach. Above, more gulls wheeled and called, flashing like memories through the hazy air.

The mist swirled and pulsed, and the sound of water curling forward and then drawing back was echoed in the beating of her heart. The breeze pulled at her long hair, auburn strands lifting and licking at the air like flames, and she gripped her upper arms with her hands to warm herself. It was chilly and she wasn't dressed for it, bare feet cold in the sand and legs pebbling with gooseflesh. The sun continued its graceful slide to the horizon, and soon it would be too dark to search. If she couldn't find it, she would have to go back.

"It's here, it has to be here," she whispered, eyes darting among the growing shadows.

At the edge of the tideline, the gulls watched her curiously, no longer searching the sand. It was almost as though they recognized her, knew her as a kindred spirit in this wild reach between sea and land.

"Please," she pleaded, her skirt flapping about her legs. And then, heart lifting, she spotted the boulder that so resembled a pudgy late-autumn bear curled up not far from the cliffs. "Let it be there," Naia said beneath her breath. She hurried to the boulder and knelt near the narrow head, reaching under the overhanging edge. At first her questing hands found nothing, and then something wet and soft gave beneath her fingertips.

"Naia!"

The voice was clear, but due to the breeze and the thickening fog, she couldn't tell from where it originated.

"Naia, where are you?" Jordon stood at the edge of the short basalt cliff, looking out over the beach stretching in both directions below. The sun sat on the horizon, slowly spreading wider and wider as though refusing to drop below the water. The fog blowing in over the surf was gathering along the strand, and he couldn't see anything except darker blurs in the grey. "Naia?" The last of his batteries had died, making his ancient flashlight useless, but he'd brought a lantern. Holding it against his chest with his back to the wind, he opened the hinged door and lit the stub of candle inside. Before the fitful breeze could get at the flame, he closed the door tight. Lifting it by the metal handle, he looked for a safe way down onto the beach.

There was a path down the ten foot drop of rock, carved as rude steps and handholds that Jordon took cautiously. He was terrified and wanted to rush headlong, but falling and breaking an ankle would help no one. As he reached the beach, the last roseate beams of sunlight made the fog incandesce, rendering his lantern redundant. But the brighter light hid more than it revealed, and his eyes burned and watered as he tried to find some sign of her.

Something moved to his right, and Jordon flinched. As quickly as the sun lit the fog, when it dropped below the horizon the billowing mist immediately became opaque. Shadows darted high, hunched low near the edge of incoming waves, and the sound of wings filled the air as the last gulls lifted from their foraging.

"Naia," he called, desperate now. He moved toward the thicker shadows, lantern held high again.

Crumpled on the sand, safe from all but the highest tide, were a faded red skirt and sleeveless white shirt. Bare footprints led from the discarded clothing to the sea, and Jordon hastened to follow.

"Naia, don't," he shouted, "please don't go!"

The mist shifted and thinned, giving him a clear view of maybe a dozen yards of wet sand and rushing waves. Standing knee-deep in rising water, Naia pulled something dark and heavy around her shoulders. Her hair lashed in the wind, and she looked back at him for only a moment.

"Naia—"

Then she was gone, and something dark and sleek swam away into the restless sea.

In the early spring of the year that whales were spotted migrating along the coast for the first time in fifty years, a stranger came to the town of Yurka. She was slim and pale, with long dark red hair and liquid brown eyes. She was dressed in rags, feet torn and bleeding from walking without shoes on the hard packed remnants of the road.

The first to encounter her was Aderyn, the old woman who was historian and keeper of words for the settlement. She had stepped outside to check her garden, for her earliest plantings of lettuce, peas and carrots were nearing their harvest. The chill sea wind played through Aderyn's white hair, and she tucked loose strands behind one ear when she caught movement from the corner of her eye.

The young woman walked slowly, gingerly along the rarely-used road. Although obviously in pain, her face was untouched by any expression of discomfort.

Aderyn went to meet her, blue eyes still sharp despite her age. "Child, from where have you come?" There were no permanent settlements to the north, the direction from which the girl approached.

The young woman stopped, her dark eyes taking in Aderyn and the garden, with the oddly constructed house in the background. "I have left my home," she finally replied, an odd accent to her words, "for my people dwindle and fail. I come to start a new life."

Aderyn pursed her lips in thought, then asked, "What is your name?"

"I am called Naia."

The name seemed familiar, although she couldn't think why; something to do with the sea. But there was time enough to puzzle it out later. "I am Aderyn." She held out her hand, beckoning. "Come with me, Naia. We will get you better clothes, and something to eat."

Naia followed her back to the house, built of weathered wood and sheets of rusted metal and pieces of translucent plastic that let natural light into the structure. The old woman gave her clean but much faded clothing, and tended to her wounded feet with warm water and a salve that burned. Then Aderyn wrapped the girl's feet in strips of raw cloth to protect them.

As soon as that was complete, Aderyn brought a bowl of warm stew and a piece of dark bread. "There is goat's milk or water, or I can make some tea."

Naia looked up from the small feast before her, seeming a bit bewildered. "Water," she said, then picked up the bread and touched it gingerly to her tongue.

Aderyn raised an eyebrow, watching her guest for a moment. Naia acted as though she'd never had bread before, and then picked up the metal spoon to study it curiously. The old woman fetched a cup of water and brought it back to the table. Naia was using the spoon to pick out items from the stew. A chunk of potato, thin pieces of last year's celery, and bright orange slices of carrot all went into her mouth one at a time. She chewed, thoroughly tasted, mulling over the texture and consistency before swallowing each bite. She seemed quite taken by the small cubes of meat.

"What is this?" she asked, pointing at the brown lump.

"Mutton." At Naia's blank look, Aderyn added, "It comes from sheep."

Naia nodded, and went back to the stew.

"You've never had mutton?"

She shook her head. "You don't eat fish?"

Aderyn shrugged. "We get some from the river occasionally."

"None from the sea?"

Aderyn sat. "Oysters, clams. We have no way to go out into the deep water, and catches are small from the shore. Madoc, one of our young men, wants to build a boat. He has studied all the old records we have of the times before. But the sea has been polluted for so long, many wonder if there are many fish left. It may be just a waste of time."

"There is still life in the ocean, but not what it once was," Naia said, keeping her eyes on the bowl before her.

When she had finished eating, Aderyn took bowl and spoon to the sink. A pump handle drew water from the cistern buried behind the patchwork house. When she turned to set the dishes in the draining rack, she started.

Naia stood directly behind her, looking over her shoulder. "Where does the water come from?"

"There is a tank behind the house. The pump pulls water from there," Aderyn answered, and watched as the girl pulled the pump handle back and forth once, a smile of wonder touching her lips when water gushed forth. "Your people have none of this technology?"

Slender fingers traced the lines of the pump handle, and Naia said, "No. Nothing like this."

"It's left over, from the old world." Aderyn stirred the coals in the hearth, setting her copper pot on the grate to heat. Her plans for the day had been interrupted by this strange girl, but she didn't mind. It had been years since she had spoken to anyone who didn't live in Yurka or the two settlements farther south along the coast. "We find things in the ruins, made of metal or sometimes wood or plastic. We have found books, a few here and there that were not completely destroyed in the great war. We learn from them what we can. My nephew Jordon is gifted with mechanical instinct. Many of the things we've found, he has studied and been able to work out their functions. He ran the pipes from the cistern into this house, so that I might have water without carrying it from the communal well."

Naia listened with her dark eyes full on the old woman's face, as though absorbing every word and flicker of expression. When the kettle began to hiss, Aderyn made tea for them both in heavy earthenware mugs.

"And your people? Where are they?" Aderyn asked when they were settled with tea and a crock of golden honey.

"North." Naia seemed reluctant to speak of them, but Aderyn just arched a brow at her and waited for more. "They are diminished. Once, we were strong. We lived on the bounty of the sea. But now, there are not many left."

"Such is the fate of all the world, child," Aderyn said gently. "I've found records that say this part of the world was once teeming with people, so much that there was overcrowding and not enough resources for all. That was part of the reason the war came about—people trying to take food and supplies and space from other people. Now, because of pettiness and greed, we have all been made to suffer. This is why I search for the records, and teach our children to read so they can see with their own eyes. We are so few, yet someday in the distant future we might once again grow to be too many. Spoiled and decadent, our distant descendants might make the same mistakes all over again."

"You are a Teacher, then," Naia stated.

Aderyn shrugged. "I am the keeper of words for my people. But yes, I try to teach those who would learn."

"Will you teach me?" Her eyes were intent, her question sincere.

Aderyn smiled; she was a teacher in her heart and so her great joy was to find someone who wanted to learn what she could share. "Of course, Naia. Whatever I know, I will gladly pass on to you."

Jordon came to see Aderyn the next day, carrying with him a basket of small heavy cylinders. He came in without knocking; he had spent as many hours at his aunt's house as his own growing up. He halted mid-step upon seeing the stranger.

"Ah, Jordon," Aderyn said, smiling at his surprised

expression. "I was wondering when you'd appear again."

"I—uh, I found some more batteries with a little power left," he said, and then stopped again when the girl turned to look at him. "I thought some of them might work for you," he added, a bit breathless.

"Jordon, this is Naia. She's going to be staying here for a while."

"Oh." He didn't resist when Aderyn took the small basket from him, just continued to meet the girl's deep brown eyes.

"He's usually not so rude," Aderyn said to Naia, her tone a bit sharp for Jordon's sake.

"Hello, Jordon." Naia's voice was soft, silken-smooth; but it was her eyes that still held him.

"I—I have more stuff to unload," he muttered, backing toward the door that still stood open behind him. For a moment he seemed unable to decide his next move; then with a jerk he turned and broke eye contact, hurrying back outside.

Aderyn sighed. "Don't let first impressions ruin him. He really is a talented and kind young man. But maybe he hasn't seen a girl as pretty as you since reaching adulthood."

Naia tipped her head to one side, eyes down as she thought of Jordon's hazel eyes and windblown sandy hair. He was tall with wide shoulders, sensitive hands and a mouth made for smiling. "He studies with you?"

Aderyn was going through the batteries, separating them by size. "Rarely. He's read everything I have. But he brings me what he finds in the ruins of the old cities; it's all stored in the big shed behind the house, until we can determine what their function was and if there is any way we can use them now."

A few days later, Jordon returned to Aderyn's house with a cart full of strange odds and ends. He had gone south and east looking for any buildings from the old civilization still standing, in which he might find more relics of the past. There was also the ongoing search for books that hadn't been reduced to cinders and ash, or bloated and molded over by water damage.

When he got there, after putting the cart horse in the small lean-to to eat and rest, he started pulling items out of the cart.

Rather than going into the house to announce himself, he decided to unload the cart first. That would give him time to figure out what to say to his aunt's houseguest. He yanked open one of the heavy wooden doors on the storage shed, blinking when he saw a light inside.

Naia turned to look at him. She was seated on a high stool near the central workbench with a lantern burning beside her. "Hello, Jordon."

He paused for a moment, then closed his mouth when he realized it was hanging open. "Hello." He made himself continue through the door to take the box he was carrying to the counter. "What are you doing out here?" He winced when he realized how gruff the question sounded, but she seemed unaffected.

"I offered to sort through the things you brought the last time." As she spoke, Jordon noticed the neat piles of junk that she had gone through. Strands of wire had been wound into loops, nails and screws separated by size, and pieces of machinery that she obviously didn't know what to do with were placed together. "I hope you don't mind. I restrung the chimes."

"The what?"

With a soft tinkling, Naia lifted a collection of slender metal tubes. She had strung them together with twine going through tiny holes drilled in the top edges, and hung a flat washer in the center as a clapper.

Jordon smiled, an expression of wonder crossing his face. "So that's what they're for," he said, coming closer to admire her handiwork. "How did you know?"

Naia shrugged. "I've seen something similar, a long time ago."

"Have you shown it to Aunt Adie?"

"No, not yet." She held it out to him, her fingertips brushing against his hand as he took it. "Do you think she'll like it?"

"Yes, of course." The chime seemed to have broken the ice, and he'd lost his shyness and tendency to stutter around her. Or maybe, it was the swift touch of her fingers against his. "Let me bring in the rest of what I've found, and we'll take it in to her."

As he brought in three more boxes filled with left-over

technology from before the war, Naia picked through them. Most of it was mismatched pieces of junk, as far she could tell. The last box was full of pieces of glass. Bottles, jars and colored pieces of flat glass shared space amongst rounded bulbs of frosted or clear glass with metal threaded ends. In the clear bulbs, she could see fine metal filaments. She said nothing, but saw in her mind's eye the soft glow of electric lights.

"That's all of it," Jordon said, setting the box of glass items down gently. "I'd better let Adie know I'm back."

Naia nodded agreement, and got down carefully from her seat. Her feet were still wrapped in strips of cloth to protect the healing abrasions from further damage.

Jordon watched with brows drawn as she began to pick her way across the floor. "What did you do to your feet?"

"No shoes," was her short reply.

"Huh." Without asking, he stepped forward and picked her up. "Put your arm around my neck," he said, and when she did, he carried her out of the shed and through the garden toward the house. "You should stay off your feet until they heal."

Cradled against his chest, Naia closed her eyes for a moment, breathing in the scent of him and enjoying the warmth of his body against her. "Aderyn can't carry me," she replied, and smiled at him.

"She probably could," he retorted, but grinned. Then he dipped to let her turn the doorknob, and carried her into the patchwork house.

The warm season from spring through early autumn was when Jordon did most of his exploring, traveling along the old roads that were now mostly covered in windblown debris or broken apart by weather and the passage of time. He used an old map Aderyn had given him, along with a compass, and marked off the names of those places where once had been towns or cities filled with people and all their possessions. Most of them had been destroyed in the war and the following natural disasters and climate changes, leaving nothing behind. The great forest of ancient redwood trees north of Yurka had been burned to the ground, leaving miles of charcoal and ash. The sea, corrupted with chemicals and airborne pollutants, had risen in its bed taking over miles of coastline. Jordon had tried going north more than once, when he first began his scavenging trips, but the devastation was too much and he didn't go that way anymore.

To the south were other settlements like Yurka; likeminded folk and families working together to survive in a world that had become very harsh. Traders traveled from Fortune and Kingrange and occasionally from as far south as Fort, named for Fort Bragg that had been relocated to Willits when the Pacific Ocean rose in her bed. These traders carried cloth and food, tools for woodworking or farming, and news from one small town to the next.

Because there were still permanent settlements of people to the south who had already picked clean nearby caches of ancient artifacts, Jordon spent most of his time searching inland. According to his map, there were some really big cities to the east, but they were far enough away that he had yet to reach them. A trip to places like Redding, or even farther to Sacramento, would mean journeying for the whole season. He didn't want to be gone for so long when there might not be anything to find.

He returned from his latest trip after being gone for a couple of weeks, coming straight to his aunt's with the cart full of finds. He looked forward to sharing his scavenged treasures with Aderyn, but even more he wanted to see Naia. He had thought of the young woman often while he was gone, even dreaming of her at night. No other woman had ever insinuated herself into his mind before, and he had missed her. When he came into the house, she was the first thing he sought. She was there, at the big table in the back by the bookshelves that Aderyn kept; but she was not alone.

Sitting close beside her, pointing out specific areas on an ancient schematic of a boat, was Madoc. The dark haired man, the same age as Jordon, was intent on the drawing and she seemed engrossed in whatever he was saying.

"Ah, Jordon. You're back!" Aderyn met him with a motherly embrace and an affectionate smile. "You must have found some wonders, to be gone so long."

"Yes," he replied, dragging his eyes away from the two at the table. "I wanted to let you know I was here before I started unloading."

"Jordon."

He turned from his aunt to find Naia within arm's reach, a smile on her lips and warm light in her dark eyes.

"I'm so glad you've returned," she said, and with no hesitation she stepped forward to hug him, her cheek pressed against his for a sweet moment.

Madoc had crossed the room as well, and with a grin he held out a hand to take Jordon's when Naia stepped back. "Good to see you back safe. Do you need help unloading?"

Jordon nodded curtly, trying to rein back the uncharacteristic surge of jealously that gripped him. "Thank you, yes." Before going back out, he pulled something from the inside of his jacket. "I found this in the remains of a building, and it made me think of you." As he spoke, he handed a small hardback book to Naia. "There is a little smoke damage, but otherwise it is unharmed."

Naia took the book, a puzzled slant to her brows, and then a kind of understanding touched her expression as she opened the cover. She raised her eyes to his again, and smiled. "Thank you Jordon. It's wonderful."

Then the two men went out to unload the laden cart, and Naia returned to the table to roll up the boat plans with the book tucked beneath her arm.

"What is it?" Aderyn asked curiously.

Naia smiled but made no move to give up the book. "Fairy tales," she answered. "Ancient legends of the fae folk of the sea. Jordon already knows me too well."

Aderyn nodded. Madoc had been spending a lot of time here with Naia once he'd learned of her love of the water. She wondered privately if there would be a problem between the two young men, friends since childhood, because of the girl. Aderyn was fond of them both and would not take sides one against the other, but hoped secretly that Naia would find favor with Jordon. The keeper of words had come to admire the young woman, with her swift intelligence and gentle ways. She wouldn't mind at all having Naia as part of her family.

It was late in the evening, after a shared dinner and Jordon's tale of his travels over the previous two weeks. He had found plenty of old books, which brought a flush of pleasure to Aderyn's face. There were parts of machines, all metal gears and plastic-coated wires. Jordon had found undamaged flashlights, but no batteries for them, which was disappointing. But the most incredible find was a small flat rectangle of battered plastic and metal. After finishing their food and clearing the dishes, Jordon presented this last find.

"It runs on batteries, but not like any of those I've found. I don't know how long they will last, or if I'll find replacements," he said as he touched a small lever on one edge. The top part of the rectangle swung upward on tiny hinges, revealing a glass panel in the top half. "I had to mess with it for a while, before I figured out how to work it." He touched a button on the lower half. There was a soft *whirr*ing sound and a red light blinked in the corner.

Then, like a portal to another world, a moving picture appeared in the dark glass. Clear blue sky with a few puffy clouds, and below that waves rushing onto the sand; in the foreground two children in brightly colored brief costumes ran along the closest edge of the surf. They shrieked laughter, and white birds with black-marked wings hovered above them shrieking their own calls.

Jordon looked at Naia with a smile on his face, expecting to see an expression of wonder. Instead, her eyes were filled with tears and her lips were pressed tight to keep from trembling.

"A recording of the times before the war," Aderyn guessed, her eyes sparkling. "Is there any way to date it?"

"There may be, but I haven't found it yet," Jordon answered, still looking at Naia.

"Don't go out too deep!" The voice was an adult's, coming from out of view on the screen.

"Come swim with us, Daddy!" The older of the two children, a girl with long blond hair, beckoned toward the screen.

"Go ahead, I'll keep recording." The woman's voice was

softer, and the tableau on the screen tipped and shuddered before becoming steady once more. A man wearing dark blue shorts and black lenses over his eyes appeared to one side and jogged away toward the water. "Give me a smile!"

The man and both children flashed bright grins at them, then began chasing each other through the shallow water, laughing and chirping like exotic birds.

low batt appeared at the bottom of the screen, and Jordon touched the button to turn it off.

"Amazing," Aderyn whispered, reaching to squeeze his arm for a moment. "I wonder if we could convert it to use the kind of batteries we already have? I would love to see the rest of the recording."

"I'm not sure; maybe." Jordon closed the screen, and glanced back at Naia who was as calm and composed as ever. Before he could say anything to her, she got to her feet and went to get another cup of tea from the kettle.

Madoc took his leave then, pausing only to speak softly to Naia for a moment before making his farewells. When he was gone, Aderyn made a point of giving them some privacy.

"A lot to go through tomorrow," she said, nodding as she got to her feet. "I'm for bed. No, you two don't need to hurry on my account. I'll see you in the morning," and she disappeared through the narrow doorway to her bedroom.

"I think I'd like a walk, to stretch my legs," Naia said, setting her steaming cup on the table. "Would you care to accompany me?"

Jordon nodded, following her out of the warm firelit room and into the breezy dusk outside. He noted that she no longer limped, her feet protected in soled leather shoes. The light wind pulled at her long hair, tossing it behind her; and then she had taken his hand to keep him beside her.

"It's not too far to the beach, if you're willing." She looked up at him, her pale face a ghost in the coming darkness. "I already know the path well."

He said nothing, just nodded and went with her. The feel of her hand in his was a touch of warmth that he hadn't known he was missing. The flowery scent of her hair filled his nose, and he admired the easy way she moved along the path. When they reached the sand she stopped, slipping her feet from the shoes, and turned to face him. The wind, still playing with her unbound hair, pushed it toward him so the ends tickled his face and throat.

"Isn't it beautiful?" she asked. She might have meant the stretch of untouched sand, the midnight blue waves touched with creamy foam, or the livid sky faintly touched with flickering stars. His answer was for her, though.

"Yes, beautiful."

He wanted to ask her why she'd been brought to tears by the sight of those long-dead children in the glass. He wanted to ask if she favored Madoc, who loved the sea as she did. But before he could ask her anything she was in his arms. Her slight form pressed against him, her hands caressing his face and then sliding into his tousled hair. Her lips touched his, warm and sweet, and Jordon forgot the barb of jealousy that had pierced his heart when he saw her with his friend. The wind blew her hair around them, curtaining their faces, and her sweetness filled him.

"I missed you," she whispered.

"I was afraid you'd chosen Madoc," he replied, unable to completely let go of that momentary glance, the two of them side by side at the table, with their heads leaned together.

"I chose you."

Although nothing was said, it became clear over the next few weeks that Naia and Jordon had reached some kind of understanding. Aderyn didn't ask, not wanting to pry, but she smiled when she saw them together. Invariably they touched hands, or brushed arm to arm. As they worked through the load of findings that Jordon had brought back from his latest foray, they began to finish each other's sentences, and quiet laughter became commonplace.

As it became more obvious that they were committed to each other, Madoc came less often. He still spoke to Naia about the ocean, and the best kind of boat to build for sailing on it, but he had lost some of the spark that had jumped between them in the beginning.

"You know that I love her," he said to Jordon one day after Naia had left the storage shed to return to the house, leaving the two men alone for a moment.

Jordon was silent, gazing at the face of the man who he had considered his closest friend. "I know. But you're not the only one to love her."

"We have more in common, she and I, than you do," Madoc went on, determined to have his say. "She loves the ocean as I always have. We spoke of building a boat together, to sail out into the open water, as our ancestors did long ago."

Jordon sighed. "You are the closest thing I've ever had to a brother. I don't want to lose your friendship, or your respect. But I cannot give her up. She chose me, and I won't let her go."

The silence held for a long time, and at last Madoc nodded once—not in agreement, but in understanding. He left the shed, not bothering to close the door behind him, and Jordon sighed again. He meant what he'd said. He didn't want to lose their friendship, but he would not give up what he had with Naia.

Jordon turned, catching movement out the open door, and saw Madoc standing just past Aderyn's garden. Naia stood with him, close but not touching as they spoke. The air was still, but he could not hear what was said. After a while, Naia reached up to touch the dark-haired man's face gently. Madoc put his hand over hers, leaning closer, but she pulled away. Finally, the other man turned and left, with Naia watching after him.

Late that night after Aderyn had gone to her bed, they retired to the room where Jordon stayed when he was home. Beneath the blankets required now that the season was winding toward winter, Naia lay with her head pillowed on Jordon's chest. She listened to the steady thud of his heart, fingertips drawing cryptic designs over his skin.

"Is everything all right?" Jordon asked, wondering if she would tell him what Madoc had said to her.

"I think we should go on one more gathering journey before the season ends," she said, surprising him. "You told me there was nothing to the north, but I passed at least two fair-sized ruins on my way here. I could show you where they are."

"You—you want to go on a trip with me?" he asked, cocking his head so he could see her face.

"Yes." She sat up, leaning on one arm so she could look squarely into his face. "By next spring, I will be too big to travel. I want to go once before the cold comes and we must stay close to shelter."

He gazed at her, brows crooked together as he tried to make out what she was saying. "Too big?"

Naia didn't smile, but her deep eyes were filled with a mix of emotions. She reached to take his hand and placed it on her belly. "Too big," she repeated.

Jordon's eyes widened as he understood, but she shook her head.

"Say nothing to Aderyn. I will tell her when we get back, but I don't want her to try and talk me out of going. I want to take a journey with you, Jordon; I don't want anything to stop it."

He held her close then, as close as they could be without becoming one person. He thought about the old customs he had read about in Aderyn's books, when people in the times before the war had bound themselves to each other with vows and symbolic rings. People didn't do that now. When two people wanted to be together, they just were, combining their lives and possessions with no fanfare. But Jordon found himself wishing he could give Naia vows and physical symbols of what he felt right now. He would be a father soon, and would pass on all that he had learned in life along with his genes and heritage. It seemed there should be fanfare.

They traveled north in blustering fall winds and the salt scent of the sea. The cart was light, and the horse made good time without having to hurry. Sometimes they walked, and sometimes rode on the narrow seat with Naia's head on Jordon's shoulder. Her dark eyes sparkled and she smiled often, with one hand resting on her belly.

In the evenings they would camp with a fire for light and to heat their dinner, a simple canvas cloth on stakes to protect them from the weather. Jordon would consult his maps, trying to determine where these ruins might be that Naia had passed on her trek. They skirted the burned remains of the ancient redwood forests, and Jordon was surprised to find saplings rising among the blackened stumps and fallen trunks. Rust-colored ferns carpeted the ash-enriched soil, turning the place into an autumn wonderland of bronze, umber, and burnt sienna.

A week had passed before they found the first abandoned town. Because of the change in the coastline and no sign of any highway, Jordon was unable to determine what it might have been.

"It could be Orick," he said, his expression confounded. "I don't think we've gone far enough north to be at Klamath."

"Does it matter?" Naia asked, looking around at the tumbled remains of old buildings and buckled pavement.

"It helps to mark on the map, for future reference. If we find some good things, we'll know how to get back and how long it will take to make the trip."

"We'll have to look for signs, then," she responded, "but we haven't reached the bigger town yet, the one I wanted to show you. It's still a couple of days ahead."

Jordon glanced up at the sky. Clouds had moved in, darkening the day so it was hard to determine what time it was. "You walked a very long way."

"Yes." Naia turned her head to the west. They were within sight of the sea, a blue-grey waste that stretched to the horizon.

"I only brought enough food for two weeks. Maybe we should look around here tomorrow, and then head back to Yurka the next day."

"Not yet," she said, putting her hand on his arm. "The larger ruin will be worth the extra days. There's plenty of food to last us until we get back." She leaned closer, putting her head on his shoulder once more. "I'm not ready to go back, Jordon. Just a few more days?"

He put his cheek against the crown of her head and stroked her soft auburn hair where it cascaded down his chest. "A few more days," he agreed, and kissed her when she raised her face to him.

Two more days brought them out of the remains of the

redwoods and into regenerating pine and deciduous trees. None of them were very tall or robust, but they were there interspersed amongst lichen-crusted granite and acres of dead grass. The groaning skeleton of a bridge crossed a river too deep to wade, and Jordon almost turned back there. But Naia slipped down off the seat of the cart and walked across, unconcerned at openings in the surface.

"I crossed this on my way south," she said, reaching the other side without incident and turned to beckon him forward. "It's stronger than it looks."

Teeth worrying his bottom lip, Jordon acquiesced and led the horse across the expanse on foot. Once on solid ground again, he shook his head at her. "You need to be more careful, Naia. What if you had fallen, or the bridge collapsed?"

She just smiled and climbed back into the cart.

As the sun dropped toward the horizon, they came to the large town she had told him of. Like all the old cities he'd found, this one was piles of collapsed masonry, rusted metal, and broken concrete paving mostly overgrown with vines or weeds. They made camp near one of the few structures still standing, a brick and mortar single story building with a steel framed portcullis along one side. Jordon unharnessed the horse and put down some oats as a treat while Naia started a fire.

"I'll get some more wood," she said while Jordon unloaded their groundsheet and blankets for sleeping.

He spread the heavy canvas and blankets beside the cart, then stretched the tent cloth as a lean-to from cart to ground for shelter. The fire was crackling merrily, and he added another branch to it. The breeze from the west was cool and tangy with salt, and he could hear sea birds calling. He put a kettle with water beside the fire to heat, and sat down with his map, trying to locate the rickety bridge that they'd crossed to get here.

After a while, as the lowering sun cast shadows over the map, Jordon looked up. Fog had appeared, sliding in over the water, and scant rags of mist swept through the open streets between ruins. "Naia?" he called, realizing suddenly that she'd been gone for a while. "Naia, where are you?"

He hadn't paid attention to which direction she'd gone, and

the humped asphalt before the building took no tracks. Worried, he folded the map to replace inside his pack. Fluttering from beneath the pack were the pages of an open book.

With a frown, Jordon pulled it out, recognizing the book that he'd given to Naia weeks before. *The Sea-Maiden, and other tales of Mermaids, Selkies and Merrows* was written in faded gold leaf across the cover. The book was open to a story about a Selkie woman who fell in love with a human man. A folded piece of paper protruded from the smoke-stained pages.

Jordon pulled it out, tucking the book back beneath his pack, and opened it. Naia's spare handwriting caught his eye. *"I came here to start a new life, although not in the way you might have expected my dearest Jordon. Poisoned by human refuse and the destruction of your wars, my people have perished until only a handful survives. I and my two sisters agreed to try the old way, to bring new life to our kind. And so we have each taken human form, and come to land to find mates.*

"I saw this as a duty. I never thought to lose my heart. I wish I could tell you everything, my love. But all I can do is leave you this letter to explain. Before the first day of Winter, I must return. I will don my sealskin and return to the depths, and there I will bear and raise our child in the ways of my people.

"I am sorry, Jordon. I never meant to hurt you. But I promise, our child will know of you from his very first day."

It was a terrible joke, too much to believe. And yet he remembered her odd ignorance of things that everyone knew, and her inordinate love of the sea. She had been gone too long. She wasn't coming back.

He picked up the flashlight he'd brought along for extra light. Switching it on, he scowled at the dim yellow glow. He hadn't brought any more batteries, as they were in such short supply. Even though the sky was still bright, it wouldn't be long before the sun dropped below the sea and then darkness would come swiftly. Leaving the flashlight behind, he took instead the glass-sided lantern with a candle fixed inside, hanging it from a loop at his belt.

Then he went searching for Naia, calling her name into the wind and stopping at every shift of windblown mist that caught his eye. There was no point in searching for her among the ruins. Her letter had said where she'd gone. He hurried toward the foggy beach and swift sunset, praying under his breath only that he might find her before she disappeared.

Spring finally arrived after a particularly harsh winter. The storms had been merciless, lashing the coast and covering everything in sheets of glistening ice. Now that it was finally warming up, Madoc spent as much time at the beach as he could. He had spent the winter in the cramped shop behind his dugout shelter, working on the boat he had dreamed of sailing all his life. After speaking with Naia last year, and taking her surprisingly sound advice regarding changes to his plans, he had at last completed his first seaworthy vessel.

It was small, only twenty feet in length with a single mast. He didn't expect to make a long voyage in it. But if it worked as well as he hoped, then he was sure he could get some of the other men in Yurka to help him build something bigger. With the help of Randon, the tanner's son, they loaded the wooden boat onto a long two-wheeled cart and transported it down the winding narrow path to the beach.

Madoc spent all his free time there, finishing the process of sealing the wood and smoothing the joints. He had tried to get Jordon to come down and see it, but his oldest friend refused to come near the water. After losing Naia last fall, he had become morose and monosyllabic.

Now, on the first truly warm day after winter had passed, Madoc prepared to launch the boat for the first time. He arrived early in the morning, with oars and sail in place, and bottles of water and a basket of food in case he should be gone for the day. When he reached the boat, he was surprised to find it wasn't alone.

A girl with long reddish-blond hair stood beside the prow, her fingertips tracing the smooth wood. She wore ragged clothing and her feet were bare, but she was lovely nonetheless.

"Hello?" Madoc called, halting a few feet away.

She turned toward him, her dark liquid eyes filled with warmth. "Hello."

"My name is Madoc," he said, rather at a loss. He had never seen her before, and yet she seemed so familiar. "Who are you?"

"Madoc." A smile touched her lips, changing her from merely pretty to beautiful. "I am Maris."

"Do I know you?" he asked, puzzled.

"My sister told me about you. And your love for the sea." She held a hand out toward him. "You're going out onto the water. Could I go with you?"

Dedication—
To Brandi, for all the reasons you know… and probably some that you don't.
To Sam, the best dad a girl never had. I still miss you every day.

BENEATH THE SHADOWS
OF THE RED-LEAFED MAPLE

Iflit, I skim, I float—like a leaf on smooth water, I glide sound-less through darkened backyards and along deserted sub-urban streets. I am a moth drawn to flame, as single-minded and as desperate, going from window to window of each quiet house. It is late, and many homes are dark, their occupants already dreaming in the safety of their beds. But here and there I see what I am seeking. Sometimes one or two, sometimes a family involved in watching movies or eating a late supper. I come to a house I have known before. The light in the window shifts and flashes, in shades of blue that reveal their faces. A father and mother, and two children below the age of ten. They sit on soft over-stuffed couches, their faces all angled to the big-screen TV mounted on the wall opposite. I cannot see the pic-ture, and the volume has been turned low enough I can barely hear the soundtrack.

As I watch the mother turns, looking down a hallway, one hand extended. After a moment a child appears, younger than the other two, a stuffed animal clutched in one hand, the thumb of the other planted firmly in his mouth. The mother gestures, wiggles her fingers, and the boy comes round the end of the couch and into her arms. She holds him cuddled in her lap and whispers into his hair. The father pulls a blanket from the back of the couch, spreads it gently over the child, then smiles and blows a kiss at the youngest of his brood.

"You've been here before." The voice is soft from behind me, the sound of silk or water. She gazes over my shoulder into the living room. "Not just since I've been here."

I try to ignore her. Even when she seems to be polite, or gentle, she is an irritation. A grain of sand in my shoe.

"You never knock," she says, not quite a question.

"They used to be my cousins," I reply without thinking, and scowl because she has made me break my silence. "They're nothing to me now. I'm nothing to them."

"They would recognize you," she says, but I turn away from the inviting window, like a big-screen TV showing something that is no longer real to me.

Without looking back, without another word, I drift away. I move through the darkness like a shred of mist—but no, there is no mist in this desert air. Smoke, perhaps—a ragged scarf of smoke that has not yet been dissipated by the breeze. If she follows me, I don't hear her, and I don't turn my head to look.

It is not long before I reach another window I have visited before. The light here is not blue, but golden. Not the white of the overhead lights, but the mellow tone of the floor lamp. The old linen shade with the beaded rim casts light the color of faded sunshine. My father sits in a recliner beside the lamp, a multi-colored afghan pulled over his knees. His face is pale, eyes sunk deep with sleeplessness and pain. He is alone in the room without the TV on, no stereo playing. Everyone else in the house must be sleeping, and he would not want to wake them.

I feel an ache in my chest, a stinging in my eyes at the sight of him. He was once so tall and strong, so easy in everything he did. But now, after months of suffering, he is diminished. His broad shoulders are rounded, his skin as dry and fragile as old parchment. The disease from which he suffers has nearly run its course, and he will not be long for this world. I do not knock. I do not enter. He would welcome me if I did, if only as a pleasant dream. But I do not know if I could control myself in his presence. I would convince myself that what I can give him is a gift, when for him it would be only a curse.

"Why don't you go in?" she asks. She is not close, not like before. She stands at the other end of the yard, beneath the dense foliage of the red-leafed maple that shades the back of the house. Her long hair, the color of shadows, covers her shoulders in darkness, and leaves only her pale face to glimmer in the dimness. "You know he must miss you."

I don't answer, still gazing in at him. He is a family man. His children and grandchildren mean more to him than his own life. If I took him away from them, it would be the same as death. Worse, for me he would never forgive.

"And you miss him," she whispers, her voice sibilant and wondering.

"Don't you miss anyone?" I finally ask, my vision trembling like a mirage as tears threaten to overflow. The yellow window ripples, sags sideways, then solidifies as the drops slide down, hot against my cool cheeks.

"I missed you," she says, that same detached wonder coloring her silken voice.

I turn sharply, to see her standing now only an arm's length away. Her skin is pale, slightly translucent like fine marble. The freckles she had always detested have faded to shadowed dapples across her nose. Golden-brown eyes are black in the darkness, and slightly crooked teeth are sharper than they once were. Her tongue is sharper. As is mine. "If you'd cared at all for me, you'd have left me alone."

Her eyelids tighten, lips thinning; her only reaction to my words. When she speaks again, her voice caresses the night air. "You are my best friend, always."

I can't listen to her, not in my father's backyard. Listening to her is a trap. She can make anything sound reasonable. She always could. So I slip sideways, moving like cloud-shadow through the darkness. I have mastered the art of movement, my wordless attempt at evading her. I drift, I glide, I waft, and not even the ghosts of my anger can follow me. But she can.

"Beth." Her cool chamomile-scented breath would raise gooseflesh on my neck, if my body was still capable of such a display. Her slender hands, cold and cautious, brush my bare arms and slide slowly down until her fingers encircle my wrists like stone bracelets. Her dark head rests against my back. She seems a trusting child. It is an artful lie.

"I love him," I say, feeling as though I must explain to her, before she does something even more monstrous. "But if I do to him what you did to me, he'll hate me forever."

"And do you hate me, my sweet Beth?" She moves even closer as she speaks, pressing her slender form against my back. She joked once, years ago in the first flush of our friendship, that if one of us had been a man we'd have married and lived happily ever after.

"I always have," is my soft reply, but I can feel her smiling against my shoulder.

"If I thought it would make you happy, I'd save him for you," she offers, and I pull away, gazing down at the slab of granite before us.

Elizabeth M Warden, the stone states in carved letters. *Beloved daughter, sister, friend.*

"If you did that, it would kill me."

She reaches out, smoothing loose strands of hair away from my face. I am alabaster in the starlight, opaque ice. Once I had rosy cheeks, a penchant for blushing, and a soft and yielding nature that matched my physical form. Now I am stone, much like her. "Nothing can kill you," she says.

I close my eyes, letting her caress my face. Years ago, before I knew her as well as I do now, we agreed—we would be friends forever.

"What do you want, Beth?" she asks, her voice so smooth and lilting, more beautiful than it had ever been when we'd both been human.

"I'll watch over him," I say, gazing at her once more. She is so lovely, now. The paleness, the otherworldliness suits her. "When he is finally gone, I'll mourn him. And then I don't care."

She smiles, shaking her head just a little. "You care," she says, stepping forward and leaning in to touch her lips to my cheek. "That's what I've always loved about you."

Then she turns away, walking much as any woman might

across the dew-wet grass of the cemetery.

"Mara," I call, and she glances over her shoulder at me. There is the slightest note of despair in my voice. This is the first time since my death that she has left me.

"I'll wait," she replies, her dark eyes sparkling. She knows she has won. "I have time to wait for you, now."

I am a vulture. I crouch, I skulk, I tarry; like a rat in the shadows I anticipate the coming end. He is my father, but I do not go to him. To him, I am dead and buried. I cannot be a ghost for him. I cannot comfort him. I cannot save him. His last agonizing breath might as well be my own. His sunken eyes close, clenched hands relax, and at last he is gone.

But I am not alone. Mara waits for me beneath the shadows of the red-leafed maple.

IN THE DARK

The sun had set and in a remarkably short time the ambient light in the sky had faded. As soon as it really got dark, that's when the ruckus started. The two dogs ran back and forth along the back fence, barking—barking—barking. They lived in a rural area, and there were no houses to be seen beyond the back fence; just fields with weeds and trees, and eventually another fence off in the distance.

"What do you think is out there?" Tristan asked. She tried to sound nonchalant and slightly disinterested, but there was a low current of unease in her voice. They'd only lived here for a month, and she wasn't used to the quiet or the lack of other people.

"Could be a lot of things," her father Jim replied as he put the last of the washed and dried dinner dishes away in the cupboard. "Rabbits or raccoons. Even birds." He closed the cabinet door and cocked his head, listening to the ongoing barrage of sound. "Although, it could be coyotes, too. Maybe we should call them back in here."

Tristan nodded and went to the back screen door. There was a light switch on the wall beside it, and she flipped it on. The bulb outside wasn't very bright, so the light didn't quite reach all the way to the fence. "Blue!" she called through the screen, then, "Brutus! Come on, you two. Time for bed."

The dogs must have looked back at the house to where she stood silhouetted in the doorway, because she saw eerie reflections from their eyes. Blue was bigger, so her eyes were higher and a little farther apart. Brutus was a terrier mix, only ten or twelve pounds, but his eye-shine was almost as high as the bitch's because he was standing on his back feet, front paws braced on the chain-link fence.

"Come on, time to come in!" she called again, and clapped her hands together sharply, making her palms sting. But they just turned away from her and went on with their barking, dashing back and forth along the length of the fence as though looking for a way through to the dark fields beyond.

"Stubborn little shits," Jim said, but he was smiling. He went to the little hidden closet tucked inside the laundry room just off the kitchen, and came back with a BB gun. He had put the gun there, making sure it was loaded, just in case they had any problems with wild animals getting inside the fence. Now he pumped it a couple of times, and told Tristan, "Open the door, T."

When she did, he stepped out on the patio and whistled, a sharp piercing sound that silenced the dogs. "Come on, dogs. Now," he called, and the authoritative tone in his voice did the trick. Reluctantly, they left the fence and trotted across the yard. "Get in the house," he added when they hesitated at the edge of the patio. Blue tucked her tail, and scooted through the open door. Brutus, true to his feisty nature, yipped once in canine defiance, then raced into the house. "Shut the door. I'm going to go take a look."

"Okay." She pulled the screen door shut, but watched as her dad walked across the lumpy back lawn and onto the bare earth and gravel that paralleled the fence.

Jim pulled a mini-mag light out of his pocket, and shined it through the fence into the field. A light breeze was tripping through the yard, catching the corners of his eyes as weeds shifted and moved. He heard bats squeaking from somewhere to the west, but couldn't see them. Crickets chirped and frogs croaked in an unpracticed but measured orchestra. After a couple of minutes, he decided there must have been a rabbit hopping through the field that caught the dogs' attention.

Something glinted and he turned his head, the flashlight following. In a stand of cottonwood and poplar near the northern fence line a pair of what had to be animal eyes glowed back at him. Even with the flashlight he couldn't see anything but the eye-shine. The animal, whatever it was, was too well camouflaged among the trees and high weeds.

The little hairs on the back of his neck stood up, straining away from his skin, and a chill skittered down his spine with little insect feet. The animal—coyote? or even a cougar?—stood taller, only its reflective eyes showing its movement as the breeze shook the tree branches and the June grass shuddered in waves. Jim turned the gun, sliding the barrel through the fence, and pulled the trigger twice. He didn't aim for the intruder, as he didn't know for sure what it was. He shot several feet to the left, wishing he'd brought out the .22 instead. At least then there would have been the sound of a gunshot instead of the wimpy *phut phut* sound that the BB gun produced.

The animal snarled, but so quietly it was almost lost among the other night sounds. Then the thing melted into the darkness and disappeared.

When he went back to the house, Tristan was still standing at the screen door, both dogs at her feet waiting for him. "Some kind of animal out there," Jim said, "but it's gone now." He pushed the wooden door shut behind him, double checking that it latched, and flipped off the outside light. "We'll just have to keep an eye on the dogs. If a coyote or bobcat got into the yard with them, they might get hurt."

"We're okay though, right?" Tristan asked, picking up Brutus and cuddling him against her side while she watched her dad put the BB gun back in its hiding place. "A coyote couldn't get in the house?"

"No worries, sweetheart," Jim said, and put his arm around her comfortingly. The last few months had been difficult for him, but infinitely harder on his daughter. There had been the bad break-up and then divorce, followed by Tristan's mother Sylvia announcing that she didn't want custody—in fact, she refused it. Although Jim had tried to explain to Tristan about her mother's mental illness and ongoing substance abuse problems, there was no good way to tell a teenage girl that her mom just didn't want her around anymore.

Dinner was finished and the dishes put away, but it was still too early for bed. Jim sat on the couch and turned on the

TV, scanning through the list of channels to find something interesting to watch. Tristan curled up in her favorite oversize chair with Brutus in her lap and pulled up the internet on her tablet. Blue lay on the floor near Jim's feet, her muzzle resting on her front paws and her brown eyes shifting back and forth between her two people.

Tristan pulled up a search engine, and typed in 'scary animals in Uintah County Utah'. Her dad had said their intruder was probably just a raccoon, or at worst a coyote; in either case no threat to them inside the house. But she wanted to know what else it might have been. She wasn't used to living in such a desolate area, and imagined bears or mountain lions stalking the unincorporated county in search of a canine snack. She laid the tablet on one overstuffed arm of the chair and watched as the search page populated with links to websites. She scrolled down the list with one hand, rubbing the terrier's soft floppy ears with her other. Brutus, having apparently forgotten all about the incident in the backyard, was nearly asleep and only turned his head a little to give her better access. Links came up for sites with tag lines like 'Animal Control', 'Division of Wildlife', and 'Utah furbearer guidebook'. Then there were the ones that really caught her eye: 'Bigfoot sightings in Utah', 'UFO Hunters', and 'Is Utah ranch the strangest place on Earth?'

Tristan glanced up at her dad. He was kicked back on the couch, engrossed in the latest episode of his favorite detective drama. She chewed on the inside of her bottom lip for a moment, then clicked on the last link.

There were photographs of scenery almost exactly like what she could see from their yard; red rock and tawny sandstone, dry areas with sagebrush and sparse weeds, greener spots with cottonwood trees and willow stands. There were maps as well, some just line-drawn with names of the highways and rural routes, and some that were satellite images showing elevations and the contours of the land. One map had little pushpins scattered across it, and when she moved the cursor onto one, an info-bubble appeared.

The pushpins marked where sightings and strange occurrences had been documented over the last four decades.

Unexplained lights in the sky, cattle mutilations, and sightings of odd unclassified animals made up most of these. Tristan didn't realize that her mouth had dropped open while she went through them, but she wasn't sure whether she should laugh at all this or start to worry. The center of all the phenomena was a ranch only a few miles northeast of their new house. It was close enough she would be able to ride her bike there, if she wanted.

"T, did you hear me?"

She jumped, waking Brutus up. The little dog scrambled to his feet and jumped down from the chair.

"Time to hit the sack," Jim said, reaching down to stroke Blue's head affectionately.

"Oh, okay," she replied rather breathlessly. She'd become so engrossed in the website, she hadn't noticed her dad's show had ended, or that he'd turned off the TV, let alone that he'd been talking to her.

"Are you all right?" he asked, thinking she looked a little dazed, as though she'd fallen asleep without realizing it.

Tristan nodded, and put on a smile for him. "Yeah, I'm fine."

He pursed his lips thoughtfully, then just nodded back. "I'm going to let the dogs out one more time for a potty break. You go ahead and get ready for bed."

She had bookmarked the website and was turning off the tablet when he said this, and she glanced back up at him quickly. "Are you sure?"

He cocked his head at her question. "I don't want to clean up a mess in the morning, so yeah."

"You should take the gun out with you," she added, standing up with the tablet tucked under her arm.

So that's what's wrong, he thought to himself. He came to her and gave her a hug. "We're safe here, sweetheart. You don't have anything to worry about. We'll just have to keep an eye on the dogs, to make sure they don't get out of the yard."

"I still think you should take the gun," she said under her breath, but returned his hug.

"Come on, dogs," he called when he pulled away from her. Blue and Brutus raced each other to the back door, the smaller male dancing on his back feet in impatience to get outside. When he glanced back, Tristan was still standing in the kitchen doorway, her tablet held against her chest and a troubled expression on her face. Jim sighed, but sidestepped to the laundry room. When he opened the back door, the BB gun held in his other hand, he looked to see that his daughter was smiling at him. "Go get ready for bed," he repeated, then followed the dogs out into the pitch-black backyard.

Tristan didn't get a lot of sleep that night. Once in bed with her covers tucked around her, she got back online to check her email. She had a cell phone, but had limited minutes, so most of her conversations with her friends were via email or social media. She had several emails from her best friend Leigh, most of them notifications of posts on Facebook. One was just a simple sentence that stated "I miss you, T!" Just reading that simple, four word statement was enough to make tears sting her eyes.

"I miss you too, Leigh."

She spent some time checking out her friends' posts, smiling at pictures of camping trips or shopping at the mall. When Brutus whimpered, she realized that tears were sliding down her cheeks. She tried her best not to let her dad see how much she missed her friends and her old life; the move from the city and his new position had been a big change for him, too. But sometimes she wished her parents had managed to just stay together until she was eighteen, then she wouldn't have had to move out here to the middle of nowhere. She wouldn't have had to give up her entire life.

Brutus whined softly, and belly-crawled over the blanket until he was cuddled up against her. His button-bright eyes looked up into her face as he nudged his cold nose against her hand.

"It's okay, Monster-boy," she whispered, using the nickname that told him how glad she was to have him. "I just miss my friends, that's all. At least I still have you." She set the tablet on her bedside table, and turned on her side, curling herself around the little dog. She sniffed, and smiled when he wiggled to get his tummy under her hand, then rubbed his belly until he drifted into sleep. Outside, the wind was blowing, invisible fingers plucking at her window and thrumming beneath the eaves. But Tristan just kept rubbing the dog's stomach, and reminded herself that Dad was right there in the next room, and he had bigger guns than the one hidden in the laundry room closet.

Tristan walked around the backyard with the poop-scoop, looking for doggie landmines. The sun shone hot from a cloudless cyan sky, and the wind from the night before was nowhere in evidence. Blue lay in the narrow slice of shade cast by the overhanging roof of the house, panting lightly in the dry air. Brutus followed behind Tristan, little black nose busily sniffing through the grass.

Her dad had gone to work this morning as usual, but until school started she pretty much just hung around the house. She had a list of chores that needed to be completed each week. One or two items were taken care of each morning, shortening the list and allowing her the rest of the day to do whatever she wanted. When she finished cleaning up after the dogs, she went back into the house and put the breakfast dishes into the dishwasher. The load of towels in the dryer needed folding, and once they were put away in the linen closet she had the rest of the day to herself. Dad had promised to bring home pizza for dinner, so she didn't have to worry about taking anything out of the freezer to thaw.

Eventually, she found herself back on the website she'd been looking through the night before. The list of incidents documented there were just as unbelievable now as they'd seemed the first time. Yet, she couldn't just close the web page and forget about it. She didn't know that she believed in UFO's or aliens, but even if she did, why would they come to a backwater area like this?

When she came upon a section of cryptozoological evidence in photographs documenting the tracks and traces left behind by what were claimed to be alien or unclassified creatures, she had an idea. She set the tablet aside, and went to get her digital camera out of her closet. She turned it on, checked to be sure the battery was charged, and went back outside.

The dogs followed her, but when she went to the side gate, she made them stay behind. "I'll be right back, guys," she said, latching the gate. "You can watch me through the fence." Then she followed the fence around their landscaped backyard until she was directly behind the house again.

This was where the dogs had been barking so stridently the night before. This was where her dad had stopped for so long to gaze through the fence, his little flashlight attempting to cut through the darkness with little result. Tristan gazed out across the field, looking for anything that seemed out of the ordinary. But it was just sandy ground covered sparsely with weeds and knee-high June grass. A few clumps of sagebrush were scattered haphazardly, until at the end of the field several trees grew near a rusted barbwire fence.

There was nothing moving out here now, except for the occasional flicker of butterfly wings or the rapid leap of sand-colored grasshoppers. She checked to see that her camera was still on, then slowly walked toward the trees, eyes scanning the ground for tracks or anything odd she could take a picture of.

Inside the chain-link fence, Blue whimpered and Brutus yipped, but she ignored them. She saw some bird tracks, little three-toed scratches in the sand, and then what looked like the wavy marks left by a snake. Round black pellets in a pile confirmed that there were rabbits in the area, whether or not they'd been out here last night when the dogs were freaking out. As she got closer to the shaded area of the trees, she saw a line of cloven hoof tracks that must have been from deer of some kind. She took pictures of all of these, to at least show her dad when he got home. But none of this was out of the ordinary. *He must have been right,* she thought; *it must have just been some local wildlife moving through the field that caught the dogs' attention.*

Tristan sighed, letting the camera fall to dangle from its lanyard around her wrist, and walked between the trees. There was still no breeze, the air so motionless and hot it had weight, and the shade felt several degrees cooler. She reached up to brush one hand across her forehead, grimacing at the glaze of sweat, and wiped her palm against her shorts to dry it. From behind her, Brutus was still barking, and she turned to glance back at him.

"You can see me right here," she called, exasperated but affectionate. She waved her arms, knowing by his reaction that the terrier could see her amongst the branches. "I'm not going anywhere, Noisy. Now pipe down—I'll be back in a minute." She turned back, ducking under the lowest limbs while she checked the mostly-bare earth near the tree trunks. Behind her, inside the fenced-in yard, Brutus kept barking, and now Blue was whining and jumping up on the fence. That was when she saw the tracks. She cocked her head to one side, trying to decide what they were.

"Dog tracks?" she whispered, brows drawn together as she lifted the camera again. "That's a big damn dog," she muttered softly, then snapped several pictures of the tracks. "That would explain why our dogs were so upset last night," she continued to herself, and followed the line of clearly visible tracks that paralleled the tree trunks. One particularly clear print gave her an idea. She squatted down on her heels, and put her left hand on the ground beside the track. Pulling the camera back as far as she could while still keeping her hand in the photo, she snapped several more shots, the flash like a strobe in the deep shade. She looked down at her hand beside the paw print, and felt a little shiver ripple up her spine. The main foot pad was nearly four inches wide; with the four toe pads and the clearly impressed claw marks, the track was as big as her hand.

"Honestly, it would have to be a Great Dane, or a Mastiff," she said, wondering how a dog that size could have been back here last night and not be seen except for its eyes. An insomniac cricket chirped somewhere close by, and insects buzzed and droned. Absentmindedly, she waved a pair of flies away from her face. Still crouched down on her haunches, she looked up at the tree trunk directly before her, and felt all the little hairs on her arms stand straight. The shade now seemed icy, and when she exhaled she expected to see her breath as a cloud of mist. Slowly, making as little sound as she could, she raised her camera and took some more shots. Then, suddenly glad to hear her dogs barking and yipping from within the fenced yard, she carefully backed out of the low shady branches and into the open field.

For a long moment she stood in the hot sun, waiting for her goosebumps to diminish. Nothing moved, except the feasting insects that she could now hear so clearly. But she felt as though she was being watched. She wanted to be brave and stand her ground, but she didn't know what was watching her. And her dogs couldn't do anything to help her if something did happen.

Quickly she hurried back to the side gate, not caring if she looked like a coward to whatever watched her. The dogs met her with whimpers and wet kisses, and she gratefully petted them and told them what good dogs they were. Then she went back into the house and locked the back door. One last glance out the window showed the same mundane and unthreatening view. But all she had to do was look at the last few photos on her camera to know there was more out there than she could see.

When Jim got home from work, presenting a box of hot pizza with a flourish, he found his daughter intent on internet research. She sat in her usual place, the soft oversized chair, with the terrier curled up against her. Blue, other than raising her head to look at him and swishing her tail a couple times in greeting, did not move from her spot right in front of Tristan's seat.

"Well there's no school, so I know you're not doing homework," he said as he continued on into the kitchen. "What's so important?"

"Daddy, I think it was more than just a raccoon, or even a coyote," Tristan called to him.

He sighed softly, closing his eyes for a moment. She was still worrying about what had happened last night. He should have expected it. She was a smart, creative girl; because of that she had quite an active imagination. He guessed he should count himself lucky she hadn't awakened with nightmares.

"There's a lot of information on the net, about weird things happening around here," Tristan went on as he came back into the living room. "Strange lights in the sky, and sightings of big animals that no one can identify for sure—"

"Sweetheart, I think you're getting a little carried away," he said, wanting to put a stop to this before it became serious.

"Have you heard of this ranch?" she said, turning the tablet so he could see the screen. "It's just a couple miles from here. It's had a bunch of different names, but the Utes that live in the area always called it Skinwalker Ranch. Do you know what that means?"

He realized then that she really was scared. Her blue eyes were shadowed, and her bottom lip inflamed as though she'd been chewing on it—which she only did when she was upset. "T, wait. Just slow down. What are you talking about?"

She held up the tablet wordlessly, her pale expression only asking him to look.

Jim leaned against the arm of her chair and took the tablet from her, glancing at the lurid red title at the top of the page, "*Unexplained Phenomena Rampant at Skinwalker Ranch*". As he scrolled through the site, Tristan continued.

"This says there are all kinds of weird things going on, not just on the ranch but in the surrounding area. I don't care about little green men or unexplained lights in the sky," she said as she stroked the little dog in her lap. "But I do care when strange things go wandering around outside our house, and scare the dogs. What if one of these skinwalker things decides to hop the fence?"

"Tristan," he said, setting the tablet aside and kneeling beside her chair so he could meet her eyes levelly. "Sweetie, you are getting way too worked up about this. We had a wild animal in the field behind our house. We're out in the country now, that's going to happen. It doesn't mean we're not safe. I would never let anything happen to you, or to the dogs. You know that, don't you?"

She stared at him for a long time, her lips pressed together as though holding back her objections. For one disconcerting moment, she looked just like her mother back when Jim had asked her to marry him—pretty, but a little shy, and completely unaware of her importance to him. Then Tristan pulled out her little point-n-click digital camera and handed it to him. "Just look," she said, and nothing more.

He sighed softly, and turned the camera to look at the screen on the back. As soon as he turned it on, a picture labeled "0001" was cued up. It was a picture of a bird track in dry hard-packed sand. Several more like it followed the first. Then a couple with soft wavy lines drawn on the ground. A pile of rabbit scat, which almost made him smile. Deer tracks going through the weeds and sagebrush. Then he got to the paw prints. He slowed, carefully perusing each photo to be sure he wasn't missing anything. The prints were well defined, as though whatever had made them had been taking its time, in no hurry to move along. The picture of his daughter's hand next to the print, giving sudden scale to the size of it, made his bowels tighten as though in preparation of a hard blow.

"Where did you take these?" he breathed, still gazing at the camera's screen.

"Straight behind the house, in the trees," she answered. "Keep going."

There were a couple more shots of Tristan's hand beside the track, and then the images changed to the trunk of a tree. The bark was thick and rippled with age, color ranging from dark grey to almost silver. Claw marks marred the bark for what appeared to be several feet, the wounds passing through the outer bark and into the gold-tinted wood beneath. There was also what appeared to be blood.

"What the hell?" he said, staring at the small impossible images.

Some kind of carcass was hanging on the tree, the fur gobbed with blood and viscera, and Jim realized that the odd black lumps he was looking at were hundreds of flies feasting on the remains.

"Who would do something like this?" Jim said, setting the camera down, and gazing at his daughter once more. No wonder she was so upset. He was upset too, and had only seen the photographic evidence. She had seen the remains of violence with her own innocent eyes.

"I think we should leave," she whispered, still gently stroking the enraptured dog on her lap, "before something bad happens."

"I'm going to go out and take a look," he started, quickly putting his hands over hers and continuing in a calm tone of voice when she began to protest, "I want to see this myself. It's too hard to really get an idea of what is there on the small screen of your camera."

"The sun is going down!" she protested, glancing toward the front window which showed long shadows cast across the road from the lowering light. "It could be out there waiting for you!"

"That's why I want to go now, before it gets dark." He leaned forward to put his arms around her, worried as he felt her trembling. She had been through so much already in her life, and this kind of ugliness and violence was more than she should have to endure. "I need to take a look at it myself. Then I'll come in and make some calls—to the Sheriff's office, or animal control."

Tristan just shook her head, clutching at his shoulder with one hand. "I don't think you should go out there," she whispered, remembering the greedy buzzing of the flies, the heavy weight of the hot air, and the feeling that something was watching her... and smiling.

Finally, he managed to disengage himself from the frightened girl. He went back to his bedroom, and opened the gun safe tucked into the corner. There were several options ranging from the .22 rifle to the break-action double-barreled shotgun. In considering the possible close quarters, and the fact that he intended to take a good flashlight with him to see better in the growing shadows, he chose a Colt .45 handgun with a full magazine, plus an extra that he stashed in his jeans pocket.

When he returned to the living room, he found Tristan standing in the kitchen doorway with Brutus in her arms. If anything, she looked more frightened now than she had when he'd gotten home. "Tristan," he said, and put his arm around her comfortingly. "I will never let anything bad happen to you. Do you believe me?"

She was silent for a moment, but finally nodded. Brutus wiggled as her grip on him tightened, and Blue whined at the back door. She had kept the dogs in the house since her foray into the field earlier in the day.

"You can stand right here and watch through the door," he said, as he crossed the kitchen with her to where Blue waited impatiently. The Aussie-mix stood, her fanned tail swishing against Tristan's bare legs. "I'll only be a few minutes. Just long enough to look at what you found, and to see if I can determine where the tracks were heading. Then I'll come back in the house and call the authorities."

Tristan nodded again, wanting to tell him again that they should just leave. When he opened the back door, Blue darted out at once and Brutus struggled to get down. Against her better judgment she let him go, and watched as the dogs raced around the yard sniffing and marking their territory yet again.

"I'll be okay," Jim added, waiting until she met his eyes. Then he picked up the big flashlight that he'd grabbed from under the sink, and followed the dogs out into the yard.

Rather than staying in the house, Tristan walked out on the patio and watched while her father went around the corner of the house. A few seconds later he reappeared outside the chain-link, walking with a measured stride on the same path she'd used earlier in the day. The dogs trailed him on the inside of the fence, and Tristan finally joined them. With Blue sitting relaxed on one side of her, and Brutus standing on the other peering through the wire, the three of them watched Jim as he cautiously approached the line of trees.

Tristan put her hands on the fence, fingers curling around the crossed wires, and watched intently as her dad turned on the flashlight and ducked under the first trailing branches. The sun was down, a thick bank of clouds scattering the last rays of light across the sky. Crickets were already chirping loudly, making it hard for her to hear if anything was moving across the field where her dad stood. As if on cue, a soft wind began to blow, tossing leaves and branches on the trees, and scattering sand and other detritus along the ground.

Soon, she could barely make him out except as a dim figure moving among the trees. The beam of his flashlight was bright and somewhat dizzying as it swept back and forth. Beside her, Blue began to make a soft rumbling sound deep in her chest. It was so low, Tristan would not have been able to hear it if she'd been any farther away. She glanced down at the dog, noting that the bitch's hackles were standing up, and then gazed back through the fence.

In the moving darkness beneath the trees, it appeared that her father had halted. The flashlight glow was still, perhaps shining on the desecrated tree trunk that she'd photographed earlier.

When Blue began to bark in earnest, Brutus joining her immediately, Tristan strained to see through the gathering dusk what had triggered their protective reflexes. The flashlight was still not moving, and she couldn't tell now if her dad was holding the light or had set it down to shine on its own. After a few seconds, she realized the dogs were not looking at the light; they were focused farther to the north, to something that was moving there.

Blue barked so viciously that foam flew from her bared teeth, and Brutus was putting so much effort into his vocalizations that he literally bounced off his feet with every snap and snarl. Tristan squinted, trying to look where the dogs were looking, but all she could see were moving branches and tangled shadows.

"Dad!" she called, unable to hold quiet any longer. "Dad, come back!"

Blue jumped, racing away from Tristan to the corner then back, still barking madly. The terrier matched her, jumping up on the fence every couple of steps as though he would climb it and run to his master's aid. There was a crashing sound, sounding like a branch had fallen in the rising wind, and Tristan looked just in time to see two glowing orbs apparently looking back at her. They were high, at least as high as the eyes of a tall man.

"It's in the tree," she whispered, heart hammering against her breastbone almost painfully. "It climbed up in the tree. Dad!" she shrieked, shaking the chain-link with her hands, fingers curled so tightly around the wires that they ached. It never occurred to her to wonder how a massive dog could have climbed into the trees. "It's in the tree!"

Something big moved along the tree line, pushing branches out of the way. Whatever it was seemed almost to glide, rather than lumber heavily. With the dogs barking and growling beside her, Tristan could hear nothing else. Then the flashlight beam spun, flickering with chiaroscuro shadows. The .45 fired, a muted muzzle-flash visible in the darkness. Then it fired a second time, and a third, in quick succession. Tristan was screaming, the dogs momentarily startled into silence by the sharp cracks of gunfire.

A bellow of rage, or agony, rang through the sudden quiet. Tristan had dropped to the ground and wrapped her arms around the dogs to keep them by her. Brutus struggled to free himself, whimpering quietly, but Blue submitted to her hold. Beyond the open fencing, June grass rippled in the breeze. Sagebrush tossed back and forth, and dead leaves skittered across the open spaces. The sky was a pale strengthless blue rapidly fading to black, stars already beginning to peer through the dark fabric. Across the field, hidden by intervening vegetation, the flashlight shone steady and unmoving.

"Dad?" Tristan whispered, unable to force any more volume into her voice. Her heartbeat raced those of the dogs she clutched against her.

Something moved, passing before the beam of light, and Tristan swallowed, her eyes wide as saucers as she tried to make out who—or what—was walking around out there. The light rose as it was picked up, and swung back and forth as though the holder were attempting to gain his bearings. The figure ducked, coming out from beneath the low hanging branches, and headed toward the house with a noticeable limp.

"Dad?" she tried again, managing to get a little more oomph behind the single plaintive word.

"It's okay, T," Jim called, sounding as breathless as she felt. He shone the light into her face, then quickly away when she winced. "Everything's okay, sweetheart."

She got to her feet, fighting not to sob at her relief that he was alright, and tried to blink away the tears that suddenly flooded her vision. "I was so scared," she called, hanging onto the fence again to keep from falling.

"I'm okay, we're all okay," he said, coming directly to meet her at the fence rather than walking around to the gate. He stuck the pistol into the waist of his jeans, and put the flashlight under his arm so he could slide his fingers through the chain-link and entwine them with hers. "The worst is over now," he added, favoring his right leg. In the dark and moving shadows and disorientation, he had stepped wrong and twisted his knee painfully. It would barely hold his weight now.

"What was it?" she asked, beginning to shiver in reaction. The dogs danced around her feet, vying for attention from both their people.

Jim shook his head wearily. "I don't know, sweetheart. But I shot it, and it's dead. The Sheriff's office can come out and determine what it is. I've had enough for one night."

"Okay," she agreed, suddenly so tired all she wanted was to lie down and fall asleep.

"I'll meet you at the gate," he said with a slight smile, and squeezed her fingers lightly through the chain-link. As he pulled back and turned away from her, the beam from the flashlight tucked under his arm passed over the figure crouched just a few feet behind him. Its eyes glowed as though with an inner illumination, and the long muzzle wrinkled, lips pulled back to bare long curving fangs.

The night was filled with screaming. Tristan screamed in warning, the beast screamed in anger, and Jim screamed in throat-tearing agony as he was borne back onto the hard earth. The dogs seemed to be screaming as well, clawing at the fence as they tried to get through. Jim twisted, trying to reach the pistol he'd stuck into his waist band, but the weight of the creature was too heavy and he could get no purchase. Jim screamed again, wanting to tell Tristan to run, to get into the house and lock the doors, to call 911 and get to the guns. Then the beast's wide maw closed on his shoulder and neck, and hot blood flooded from him in a torrent. He pushed ineffectually at the thing, trying to free himself. His head fell to the side weakly, and his last sight was of Brutus biting at the chain-link as he tried to get through the fence to defend his master.

Two days later, Warren Thomas pulled into the driveway and parked next to Jim's late-model pick-up truck. He got out of his car, glanced around at the quiet house and yard, then went up to knock on the front door. After several minutes with no response, he turned around and stared across the road.

This house was the only one for several hundred yards in either direction, and there were no buildings in sight across the asphalt lane. Sagebrush and weeds dotted the landscape, and a little more than a mile away the sandstone ridgeline rose into the sky. Warren let his eyes trace the ridge, looking for but unable to see the notorious ranch house from here. He knew where it was, however. He had been there before, although it had been years.

He remembered two days prior when Jim had come in to the construction shack/office and told him about the goings-on the night before. How there had been strange glowing eyes in the back field, and his dogs going ballistic over something hiding out there. About how much it had scared his daughter, Tristan. Maybe he should have warned Jim then. But it had been years since anyone this far from the ranch property had had any real problems. And it was hard trying to explain some of the weirdness associated with the location to someone who hadn't already been privy to it, without coming across as a gullible fool.

Warren glanced back at the house. No signs of movement, and the drapes in the front window were closed tight. He scratched his head thoughtfully, then walked around to the gate in the chain-link fence. It was hanging open, shifting back and forth a couple of inches in the fitful breeze.

"Jim? You back here?" he called, and went into the landscaped backyard. The grass was a little long, due for a mowing. A few flowers bloomed in a bed along the back of the house. The stone patio swept out in a semi-circle with a couple of wrought-iron chairs and a small table at one side. The back door was open, the screen gaping as it hung half off its hinges. "Jim?" he said again, wishing suddenly that he had brought his gun.

A small furry face peeked timidly around the edge of the wooden door, button-bright eyes half hidden beneath tousled hair. The dog's pink tongue hung from its open mouth as it panted.

"Hey there, little guy," Warren said gently, and crouched down to seem less threatening, holding one hand out in invitation. "Where's Jim? Is he in there with you?"

The dog whined, but didn't retreat.

"It's okay, little guy. I won't hurt you." He wiggled his fingers, and smiled when the dog hesitantly came out of hiding. He waited patiently while it cautiously approached him, and held still to let his fingers be sniffed. When he was able to pick up the little dog, he deftly rubbed its ears with one hand while he turned the tag on the collar so he could read it. "Brutus, huh? Does the name fit you, little guy?"

He stood then, still holding the dog in one arm, and went into the house. A quick search revealed a pretty substantial amount of blood on the floor in the kitchen, down the hallway and apparently originating in a bedroom. Judging by the décor, and the open gun safe in the corner, Warren guessed this was Jim's room. The other bedroom, painted pale violet and with posters of teenage boys on the walls, obviously belonged to Jim's daughter. There was no sign of her. Warren hadn't found the other dog, either.

He went back out into the back yard, still carrying Brutus who seemed to have no desire to get down. There appeared to be quite a bit of disturbed earth on the other side of the fence, so he went over to look.

Blood, and lots of it. Drag marks through the blood-muddied sand leading back toward a stand of trees. By now, he was pretty sure he was too late. Judging by what he'd seen, he probably would have been too late if he'd come over yesterday, when Jim did a no-call no-show at work.

Warren pulled out his cell phone, and called 911. As he spoke to the operator, he stared back through the warped chain-link which had been pulled away from the supporting posts and drooped down toward the ground. He gave his name, and the address of the house, by rote. Back among the trees, twisting and swinging slightly in the breeze, was something long and pale. He couldn't really tell from here what it was, and was suddenly certain that he didn't want to know.

"I've dispatched a Deputy as well as an ambulance to your

location, Mr. Thomas. Please remain there until they arrive," the operator said.

"Yes, tell them to hurry," he said, and hung up. Then he carried Brutus with him out to his car, and sat in the air-conditioned interior while he waited for the authorities. The dog curled up in his lap, apparently content to stay there forever.

SKRAELINGS

There were eyes on them, as they travelled southward through mature forest. The land here wasn't so different from home, miles and months away to the east. Virgin woodland with the scent of sea air borne on the wind led into lush thigh-high grass or stands of bushes thick with ripening berries. Thorfeld walked with one hand on his dagger, but he enjoyed the beauty of this place.

Behind him were three others; Tofi, Sigurd, and the old man Gunnarr. The old warrior, like Thorfeld, kept a sharp watch and one hand on a weapon. The two other men seemed bewitched by the new land, gazing about wide-eyed and with mouths hanging open. But none of them felt the weight of the eyes on them. This land was too empty, especially after weeks at sea shoulder to shoulder with the crew of their dragon ship.

At mid-day they stopped to rest and eat, pulling dried meat and dense dark bread from their packs. A nearby stream supplied water to drink. Tofi, being the youngest of the group and just lately out of childhood, asked questions none of them could answer.

"How can a land so large and plentiful be so empty?" he started, chewing energetically on his portion of dried meat. "There are trees and sod aplenty to build good housing. The river we crossed was full of fish. The wheat grows naturally, with no one to tend it. Berries cover every bush. Birds fill the sky, and deer roam the woods with no fear of us. Why are there no people here to partake of this bounty?"

"Perhaps they're hiding in fear of us," Sigurd said wryly. As Tofi's elder brother, he considered it his place to point out the younger man's folly.

Tofi gave it thought, but shook his head, apparently unaware Sigurd was mocking him. "We should have seen some sign of people, even if they are hiding."

"It's good that we've found no one here," Thorfeld said. "If there are none to lay claim to this land, then we can claim it for ourselves."

"I hear than Leif intends a settlement here, under his name and protection," Gunnarr added, his grizzled old voice matching his aged face. The puckered length of scar that crossed the empty socket of his right eye showed like a blaze of lightning against his sun- and wind-burned face.

Thorfeld shrugged. "That may be. I've heard that he won't be leaving Eiriksfjord any time soon. His wife Thorgunna is tired of his traveling, and wants him to stay closer to home. Since his brother Thorvald was killed in Vinland, and especially now that he's chieftain, I would be surprised if he didn't stay." He finished the last of his meal and stood. When the others made to get to their feet, he waved them off. "Finish your food and rest a bit. I'll be back."

The two young brothers continued their conversation about this strange empty land while Gunnarr chewed and kept his still-sharp left eye on anything that moved. Thorfeld walked into the trees, looking for a place to relieve himself in privacy. All was silent here, he could barely even hear the boys' voices. Birds chirped and whistled, but off in the distance. They were far enough now from the sea that he could not hear the waves, though he could still smell the salt on the air. Ragged remnants of the morning's mist hung in the damp shadows, and there was the occasional drip of condensed moisture falling from leaf or twig. Thorfeld made his own water against the trunk of a tree, then turned to head back to the meadow where his crewmates waited.

He froze, eyes wide as he looked back at the woman who watched him. She perched on the lower limb of a tree just a few feet away from where he stood. Her hair was dark and glossy as a raven's wing, her clothing made from leather that blended with the colors of tree bark and sewn with intricate skill. She stared at him, meeting his gaze with eyes as black as her hair, and she did not move.

"Lady, you startled me," Thorfeld said, heart pounding in his chest. He arrested his instinctual urge to reach for his dagger, not wanting to appear threatening. "Please, come down."

She remained perfectly still, her gaze direct as though she strove to read his soul.

A thought occurred, and he nodded. "Of course, you do not understand me." He reached up then with both arms, hands curled back towards him, and beckoned. "Please Lady, come down. I will not hurt you," and he lifted his palms to her, to show he held no weapon.

The tableau held for a long moment, but before Thorfeld could think of any other way to reassure her, she leaned forward and dropped six feet to the ground below. Gracefully she stood and faced him, her black eyes enigmatic in their strangeness.

"I have never seen such dark eyes," he mused softly, dropping his arms but keeping his hands open. "My name," he said slowly, "is Thorfeld Hallrson." He placed his hands on his chest, repeating his name, "Thorfeld Hallrson." Then he pointed toward her.

She tilted her head, an almost birdlike pose, and blinked.

"Thorfeld Hallrson," he said yet again, more slowly, as he touched his chest. Then he pointed to her once more.

For a long moment she just looked at him. Then, with no gestures of her own, she said, "Rayna."

"Your name is Rayna?" he asked.

She took a step toward him, lifting one slender hand to point at him. "Thorfeld," she said, her voice low and melodious. Her accent was odd, giving the simple recitation of his name a strange lilt that he found appealing. Then she placed her hand on her chest and said again, "Rayna."

"Where are your people, Rayna?" he asked, not moving as she took another step toward him, and then another. "You can't be here in this wild place all alone."

When she was barely arm's length away she stopped again. She was tall, only a few inches shorter than he, and she gazed steadily up into his sky blue eyes. Then dropped her eyes, staring at the cloak-pin on his shoulder.

It had been a gift from his wife's family. The brooch was

made of silver with bronze accents, shaped like a nearly-closed crescent with the long pin attached to the curve. The ends of the crescent were cast into the stylized rendering of the ravens Huginn and Muninn, the servants of Odin the All-Father. The end of the pin where it attached to the crescent had been made to look like a feather. Each raven's eye was inset with carefully shaped garnets that blazed a deep red against the silver.

"Rayna," he said, and she raised her eyes to his once more. "Where are your people?" he asked again, and gestured broadly around the empty forest.

Her only answer was to step closer and reach up to touch the silver brooch with light fingertips.

He caught his breath, suddenly aware of her scent. She was a beautiful woman, exotic and strange in this vast empty land. And he had not been with a woman since his wife had died in childbirth more than a year ago. His heart was pounding, and suddenly all he could think of was making this woman his own.

"Thorfeld!" The voice was young and strong, but he couldn't tell if it was Tofi or Sigurd who called for him.

He turned his head to call in reply, "I am here." When he turned back, she was gone. There had been no sound of her passage, and there was no sign of footprints in the soft earth except where she had walked toward him. Now, he clutched the hilt of his dagger as he rapidly scanned the surroundings. "Rayna!" he called, "You don't need to fear, Lady. They will not hurt you."

When Sigurd appeared, Thorfeld had already crossed to the tree where the woman had perched, and checked between the mature trunks for footprints or other signs of passage. He found nothing. It was as if she had dissolved into mist and blew away.

"Are you ill?" Sigurd asked, watching as Thorfeld checked the last possible way out of the small clearing in the trees. "We began to get worried."

"No, there was someone here. A woman."

Sigurd raised an eyebrow and rubbed his scraggly beard. "A woman."

Thorfeld sighed and nodded, not caring that the story

seemed far-fetched. "Her name was Rayna. When you called she disappeared into the wood."

"A woman by herself?" the younger man asked, his tone of voice changing from skepticism to avidity. "You spoke to her?"

Thorfeld nodded again. "Yes, but I don't think she understood me. I was unable to find out where her people are." He released his dagger, and started back toward where the others waited. "We'll have to keep a sharp eye out. I don't know if she'll bring her people to us. But either way we are not alone here, as we thought."

His explanation of his extended absence to Gunnarr and Tofi was short. While all he could think about was Rayna's lovely face, her silken black hair, and the way she had said his name, he only made clear to the others his concern. They had all heard of the last expedition of Vikings to the new world, where Leif's brother had been killed by the native people. Although that had happened in Vinland, and they were in Markland, there was still the danger of hostile natives. Thorfeld did not think Rayna was of those people in Vinland, for the reports had been that the natives had skin the color of dry earth, and the woman he'd met had been as fair-skinned as he. But while she had come to him peacefully enough, that did not mean the chieftain and warriors of her clan would react the same.

"We will travel as far south as we can today, camp and then travel one more day south," he said at last. These were the orders he'd been given before leaving the encampment at Hoyetrær, the camp of the Tall Trees. "Then we will go back with news of what we've seen. I had hoped we would find no one. But since we have, pray they are peaceful and willing to trade. If they are warlike, the coming winter will be uncomfortable."

The two younger men might have argued that fact, being young and sure of their own immortality. But even they realized that a crew of thirty-two men would be hard pressed to defend themselves against an entire village of enemies.

"Which direction did the woman come from?" Gunnarr asked.

Thorfeld shook his head. "I don't know. She was perched

in a tree when I met her. And I did not see which direction she went when she left."

The old man gazed at him steadily with his one pale blue eye.

"The trees grow dense, Gunnarr," he said in his own defense. "She could have changed direction within ten feet and I would not have seen."

"We will go on then," the one-eyed man said. "Keep south until nightfall. No more flower picking for you boys," he added to the two youngest. "Time to keep your wits sharp, and your senses sharper."

"We haven't been picking flowers," Tofi grumbled under his breath. But as they continued their journey the brothers made a point of being more alert.

Thorfeld kept cautious watch as well, but found his mind going back again and again to the short meeting with the woman. Other than her black eyes, she had looked much like a Danish noblewoman with her dark hair and fair skin. He wondered how her people had come to be here, and if they knew of the lands across the wide sea full of people who looked so much like them. As the day wore down, and the air became more chilled, they began to look for a place to make camp.

"We'll have to keep watch," Gunnarr said to Thorfeld, who was in charge of this expedition.

"Yes," he agreed.

They found a sheltered spot among the trees, and stretched oiled cloth between the trunks as a roof to sleep beneath. The brothers went off to find downed wood for a fire, while Thorfeld scouted the immediate area. Gunnarr, as a mark of honor, started the journey-fire and fed it twigs and small branches until the boys came back with larger fuel.

Dinner was more dried meat and heavy bread from their packs. Sigurd caught a couple fish from a nearby stream, and Tofi found some edible greens to add flavor. A handful of early berries were a sweet finish to the simple meal. Gunnarr stood for first watch. He would wake the brothers to watch together. A few hours before dawn they would wake Thorfeld for last watch.

Thorfeld walked the outskirts of their campsite once more before lying down near the fire. The air was cold now that the sun had set, and a dazzling array of stars filled the velvet black expanse of sky. Behind him firelight flickered, and Sigurd and Tofi talked softly, bickering over who should do what when it was their turn to stand guard.

For a long time he was unable to close his eyes and court sleep. Knowing they were not alone here made him scan the blackness for anyone creeping close. He saw glinting eyes reflecting the firelight, twice low to the ground and close together—most likely rodents of some kind. The last pair of eyes were high up in the shadowed branches of overhanging trees. A bird, or maybe a small wildcat. Off in the distance wolves howled, but this sound only put Thorfeld at ease. He had grown up with such nighttime music to put him to sleep, and at last he relaxed enough to ease into slumber.

When the boys finally stopped their arguing and dropped off into soft snores, Gunnarr found a spot to sit comfortably for his watch. Three huge boulders covered in moss tumbled against one another in a dance that had ended centuries ago. The old man leaned his aching back against the stone, and scanned the surrounding darkness. Aged he might be, but his mind and hearing were both still sharp, and he had the wisdom of his years to keep him attentive.

Well back in the shadows beneath the trees, Rayna crouched motionless in the darkness. She had found a place where she could see the big man, the one who wore ravens on his breast. He was asleep now, his back to his companions, the flickering fire-light picking bright strands of gold in his long hair, glints of copper from his rufous beard. He was tall and broad, a mountain of a man. But it had not been his coloring or his size that had drawn her to him. It had been the flash of something like recognition in his brilliant blue eyes when he'd turned to see her, as though he knew her from a past life. That, and the ravens on his breast.

There was movement beside her, and she turned her head. She lifted one hand, pressing the back of her first two fingers against her lips, requesting silence.

There was a white grin, easily visible to her even in the dense darkness. She shook her head, looking back at the strangers.

"We could kill them now," her companion whispered, his voice so low no one would hear it a stride away. "Drink their red blood and eat of their flesh, and burn their bones to placate the land."

"They are not alone, Aqissiaq," she replied, just as softly; but she did not take her eyes from the raven-man. "They explore, but will return to the rest of their kind in three days."

Again came the white smug smile, and he turned to watch the strangers as well. "Then we shall wait," he agreed. "Maiara and Nahuel are nearly here, and the rest follow. Plenty for all."

"That one is mine," she stated. She had never made a claim before, but did not hesitate now that her mind was made up.

Aqissiaq raised one eyebrow, the smile gone as he looked at her profile in the darkness. He had long desired her, and more than once had tried to press his suit. But she was a favorite of the chieftain, and so was allowed to go her own way. Now she had developed an infatuation for a stranger, an interloper who was not even their kind. He ground his teeth, but softly, and said nothing more.

The moon was dropping toward the horizon when Sigurd woke Thorfeld for his turn at watch. His younger brother, Tofi, was already wrapped in cloak and blanket beneath the oil-cloth roof.

"Anything?" Thorfeld asked softly as he rolled to his feet.

Sigurd yawned and shook his head. "Silent as the grave, even the breeze died down. The wolves stopped howling not long after Gunnarr woke us."

Thorfeld nodded, and clasped the younger man's shoulder for a moment. "Back to your dreams, then."

Sigurd smiled, teeth glinting beneath his mustache. "I'll dream of buxom blond barmaids, and save one for you."

Thorfeld shook his head, but smiled. He added another branch to the fire, stirring the embers to be sure it caught flame. When the light leapt up, sparks flying into the sky, he left the camp. He stood facing away from the fire until his night-vision returned, then slowly walked the outskirts. As Sigurd had said, it was quiet. There were no more wolf-cries from the distance, not even the soft hooting of an owl. The night might have caught them in a frozen moment, and Thorfeld took a deep breath just to be sure he could.

As he turned to continue his walk around the camp, he caught movement from the corner of his eye. He halted, right hand grasping the heavy sword hilt at his left hip, and scanned the unrelieved blackness for what had caught his attention.

Silent as a dream, graceful as smoke, a shadow moved toward him. A dim flicker of light from the campfire through intervening trees revealed the slender dark-haired woman.

"Rayna," he breathed, unsure if he should believe his eyes.

She tilted her head, eyes dropping to his hand gripping the sword.

He lifted his hand, palm out toward her and fingers spread. "You startled me yet again, Lady," he whispered.

She came closer, her feet making no sound. With no fear she came to him, one slender hand rising to trace the cloak-pin at his shoulder.

"I wish you understood me," Thorfeld said, looking down into her lovely face. She was not beautiful in the usual sense; her cheekbones were too high, her nose too long to be considered beautiful. But her black eyes were large and deep, and the shape of her lips made him want to kiss her.

"I understand," she returned, her low voice going through him like a knife, painful yet effortless.

"Who are you?" he asked, putting his hands at her waist when she made no attempt to move away. She was solid, not a ghost as he had wondered after her earlier inexplicable disappearance. "Where are your people? Are you from across the sea as well?"

She reached up with her other hand, fingertips brushing his lips to silence him. "My people are there, in the dark," she said, her accent so strange. "We have been across the sea, long ago. Not anymore."

He pulled her closer. Her silken hair fell over his hands like warm shadows, and her scent was of amber and lilac. He closed his eyes, breathing her in, feeling her melt against him.

"I dreamed of you," he said, and then his lips touched hers.

She tasted of honey and nettle, and something in him that had shriveled and paled since the death of his wife and child awoke.

"You, I will keep," she said, her tone fierce, and pulled back from him. In the darkness there was a rustling and low growling, but she seemed unworried.

"Rayna," he called.

She held up one hand, silver flashing on her palm. Then she turned and faded into the shadows, gone as though she'd never been there.

He tried to follow her, but had brought no torch and the darkness beneath the trees was too dense. Finally, he went back to where she'd come to him, and picked his cloak up off the ground. She had taken his cloak-pin with her.

In the morning, it was found that some kind of animal had been in camp during the night. Tofi's pack had been dragged away, the remains of it found in the forest half hidden beneath dense underbrush. All of the food it had contained was gone, the leather pack itself ripped and chewed to pieces.

Sigurd's dagger was missing as well.

A quick check around the area found wolf prints, crossing over Thorfeld's prints when he'd patrolled the outskirts of the camp.

"Did you see anything?" Gunnarr asked when they'd all returned to the embers of the fire.

"No," Thorfeld answered, having already decided not to say anything about his secretive visitor. They had barely believed him about meeting her yesterday; he was sure they would think him mad if he told them that she had come to him again, and seemed to understand their language. He wondered privately if perhaps he wasn't going mad after all. "Although I did hear some rustling about in the underbrush. We might be better to get started. It seems this animal was being playful; hopefully it will enjoy its joke and bother us no more."

They ate a cold breakfast, double-checking their food

supplies now that Tofi's portion was gone. Then the brothers took down the oil-cloth and refolded it, while Gunnarr buried the fire after saving the journey-ember. Thorfeld searched through his pack until he found an old plain cloak-pin which he fastened in place wordlessly.

"What happened to your fancy pin?" Gunnarr asked; one-eyed, he still rarely missed anything.

"I lost it," Thorfeld replied shortly, and turned away to shoulder his pack. "Let's get going. I want to make it as far south today as we can before camping. The more we can report to Ketill when we return, the better."

The day was good for traveling. The sun shone down from a cloud-free sky, the smell of salt was borne to them on the cooling breeze, and the land they traveled through became only more lush and desirable. They walked through meadows filled with tall grass that was beginning to turn yellow as summer made way for autumn. Thickets of spiked canes protected a rich harvest of ripening berries. Birds sang, and wildlife was abundant. Still there was no sign of human habitation. There were no buildings of either stone or wood, no trace of campfires. The trails that they followed had been worn by animals, not people. Water was abundant, and they crossed several streams and small rivers as they continued south.

As they traveled, Thorfeld looked for any trace of Rayna's people. She had said they were there in the dark; from her grooming and the intricacy of her clothing, they had to be at least as advanced as his own people. So where were their villages? Why would they not make use of the bounty of this beautiful land?

"Enough, I say," Gunnarr called, and Thorfeld pulled himself from his own worried thoughts to turn and look at the old man. "Perhaps you mean to walk until we find another sea. But the sun is low in the sky, and these old bones are ready for night's rest. How much further do you mean to go?"

Thorfeld looked around, bewildered to see that the old man was right. The sun was falling below the treetops, and long shadows painted dark stripes along the ground. The two younger men said nothing, but they looked weary as well.

Gunnarr stood his ground, leaning tiredly on a walking stick he'd cut earlier in the day. He was the eldest, but not the one in charge. Thorfeld could order them to go on all night, and there would be no challenge. But the one-eyed man had known Thorfeld since he'd been a child, and so spoke more openly to him than others might.

"There is a clearing ahead, we will camp there." He would apologize to Gunnarr later, but not in front of the boys.

As on the night before, the young brothers went to gather wood while Gunnarr prepared to start the journey-fire. This evening however, Thorfeld tarried until the boys were out of earshot.

"My apologies, Gunnarr," he said softly, knowing the old man had been waiting for it.

Gunnarr nodded perfunctorily, keeping his attention on the nest of tinder he was building. "You've been walking as though lost in a dream half the day, Thorfeld. Should I worry?"

Thorfeld crouched, watching as the other man's skilled hands shaved small curls of wood from a stick onto the base of weed fuzz. Above that would go small twigs and then slightly larger sticks. Once the ember from last night's fire had been taken from the hollow horn Gunnarr carried at his belt, and had well and truly caught the small kindling, larger branches would be added to feed the fire. "I've been in a dream," he breathed, closing his eyes and seeing the black-haired woman in his memory. "I think I am bewitched."

"By the woman you spoke of."

Thorfeld rubbed his face, trying to scrub away the image of her black eyes. "She took my cloak-pin, Gunn. She has something of meaning to me. Can she not cast a spell with that?"

The old man gave it serious thought, letting his gnarled old hands fall still. "I do not know the way of magic, son. But it seems to me she had hold of you before your brooch went missing."

Thorfeld stood with a sigh, knowing the old man was right. "I'll scout for any sign," he said softly. "Get the fire started, and tell the boys to stay close to camp."

Gunnarr nodded once more, and returned to the task at hand. But when the troubled younger man left the clearing, Gunnarr paused to watch him go. "Walk carefully son," he muttered under his breath, and cast a sharp glance around to see if anything spied upon him. There was nothing but the tall trees standing silent witness.

Not far away from the small encampment, a gathering had begun. Shadows moved, not drifting but with purpose. Some hugged the earth, while others rode the darkening air. All was silent, but a beat of power brought these phantoms together. As the last light left the dome of sky and stars began to sparkle, the half-seen apparitions solidified, taking what forms they chose. Most were wolves, thick-furred and sharp-toothed with golden eyes. There was a wolverine, low and sleek with a bushy tail and viciously clawed paws. There were weasels, foxes and coyotes, and a cougar sprawled bonelessly on a low-hanging limb with amber eyes glowing in the gloaming. In the trees were birds of several species. Owls, eagles, hawks and falcons perched wherever there was space and a good view of those on the ground. A single raven, large and sleek, sat alone.

The alpha wolf, dark grey with a grizzled muzzle, stood in the center of the gathering. Glancing around with eyes still sharp, he nodded once and shifted into his human countenance. As a man he was tall and broad shouldered with long dark hair liberally streaked with silver. He carried no weapon, but did not need one to command the respect of his people. His name was Tyr, and he was the eldest of them.

When he was sure all were present, he turned to look at the raven. He raised one hand, and at that gesture the raven flew down to land amongst the wolves. Her shift to human guise was smooth, and Rayna stood straight before the chieftain.

"Tell us of the strangers," he said simply.

She inclined her head just slightly, and answered. "They are from across the sea, where we came from so long ago. They are here seeking new lands and wealth, to take back in trade with their countrymen. Their chieftain sent them to establish a settlement, and intends to send more in the spring. In the mind of Thorfeld Hallrson who leads the scouting party, I have seen all of this. There may be no end to them, once the trickle becomes a flood."

"We can kill them," Aqissiaq offered softly, still wearing the guise of the wolf. "There is no profit in death." He lay quietly not far from the chief, head up but in an attitude of submission.

Rayna's expression did not change, but she only shrugged. "We could kill them, but there will always be more."

Tyr shook his head. "And yet if we leave them alone, soon they will overrun this land. There are not so many places left for us to live away from men."

Rayna looked down, hearing the sorrow and the resolve in the chief's voice. Once she and he had lived in the northlands among the Scandinavians, before this clan of skinwalkers and shapeshifters had banded together on this new continent. "We have kept the native tribes at bay," she said softly. "There must be a way."

When Sigurd woke Thorfeld for his watch that night, clouds had come to obscure the sky, and neither starlight nor moonlight cut through the gloom. Thorfeld stirred up the fire again, then lit the end of a small limb to use as a torch while he walked the outskirts of their small camp. Everywhere he went, he saw the reflection of eyes from the darkness, both low to the ground and above in the limbs of the trees. The eerie sight sent gooseflesh down his back. The night was silent, no cries from birds or animals. Even the insects were quiet. Nothing approached him, nothing moved at all; but glittering eyes watched him everywhere he went, and he walked with his sword unsheathed.

When he'd completely encircled the campsite, he found Rayna waiting for him. Glimmering at her throat, hung on a leather thong, was his raven cloak-pin.

"You do not need that with me," she said, looking at his naked blade.

"We are surrounded by something—something dark and deadly," he replied, making no move to sheath the sword. "They aren't animals like I've known before. They make no sound, they do nothing but watch. But I can feel..." he trailed off, unsure how to explain. "And how can you understand me at all?" he asked, going back to the thought that had been on his mind.

"Once, I lived across the sea," she said softly, making no move to approach him. "The language was different then, but not so different after all. I only needed to listen, to learn your way of speaking."

"In two conversations, you learned my language," he retorted bitterly. He was so drawn to her, so enthralled by her beauty; yet he knew he and his men were not safe. Somehow, he knew her people would not welcome them.

Finally, she stepped forward, ignoring the way his grip tightened on his weapon. "There is magic in the world you know nothing about. Your legends are full of tales of magic, of gods and monsters who are not as you are." She moved forward as she spoke, her eyes on his face now, disregarding both the burning brand and the sword. "I cannot tell you all, Thorfeld, but I can tell you this. I mean you no harm." She stressed "I" and "you" just slightly, and he closed his eyes.

"But your people do," he whispered, and opened his eyes again when he felt her gentle touch. She stood with her hands on his chest, gazing up at him steadily.

"Your people would come here and take what they can, and there would be no peace between us."

"We will leave and not return." There was conviction in his voice, but Rayna shook her head.

"You cannot speak for your chieftain."

"I can convince him." He didn't know if he could. He didn't know if he could stand the thought of leaving here and never seeing her again. Magic or something else, she was coiled within his heart.

"What must be done, will be done," she whispered, "But I have made my vow. You, I will keep." She kissed him then, her lips warm and sweet.

Thorfeld dropped both brand and sword to hold her, all thoughts of the men behind him gone, no more consideration for the larger group of shipmates two days travel to the north. He had little in the way of ties to anyone across the sea. His own family was long dead, and his wife's family while kind, had no use for him now that their favored daughter was in the ground. The woman in his arms was strange, but she wanted him. He found he wanted her in return.

He held her while the torch guttered and went out. Still, eyes glittered in the darkness, watching them. Most were little more than twin mirrors turning toward them and then away. But one set blazed with jealousy and never turned aside.

In the morning, they found that animals had been through the camp again. Sigurd's pack was gone this time, as was Gunnarr's walking stick and the belt that held the horn he used to carry the journey-ember. The ground was scuffed and marked with footprints of wolves and what appeared to be foxes. One of these unwelcome visitors had urinated on Thorfeld's pack, and he grimaced at the musky stench.

None of them had heard anything moving during the night. Even though Thorfeld had spent most of his watch away from the fire, he had been close enough to note if anything was moving in the camp.

Tofi and Sigurd searched for the missing pack and Gunnarr's belt, while the old man checked to see what food was left. Thorfeld dumped out the contents of his pack and took the soaked leather pouch to the stream. The water would make the leather stiff, but he couldn't use it as it was. He wet it and beat it on the rocks until the worst of the smell was gone, then twisted the leather to wring out all the water he could.

When he returned, the brothers had come back. They had not found Sigurd's pack, but brought back Gunnarr's chewed and torn belt. The horn was still attached, but scored with deep tooth-marks and the upper curve was cracked.

"It's time to go," Thorfeld said evenly, not wanting to take time to break their fast. They were running low on traveling food because of the thefts, and he wanted to be away from this place where bold but silent beasts prowled while they slept. They struck camp in haste and traveled back the way they'd come, going more quickly now that they knew their route. The brothers were more subdued than usual, but excited to get back to the main camp. Gunnarr, ever watchful, noticed the way Thorfeld walked with jaw clenched and one hand on a weapon at all times.

When they stopped at midday to eat and rest, the one-eyed man pulled Thorfeld aside.

"You've been sullen and silent all morning," he said softly, back turned to the boys who were busy devouring their food. "What happened?"

Thorfeld didn't want to say anything, but wouldn't lie to the old man he respected. "I spoke to Rayna again last night," he said. "Her people do not want us here. There is a chance it could get ugly."

"You spoke to her again," Gunnarr said, his voice troubled.

"I fear that if we don't leave this land, and quickly, they will attack us. I am sure there are enough of them to cause us great damage," Thorfeld went on.

Gunnarr was silent for a long time, thinking. Finally, he said, "Son, I have great respect for you. You are cousin to Leif, nephew of the great Erik the Red, and come from a long line of warriors and leaders. But as highly as I regard you, I am worried that—that your recent losses have affected your judgment."

Thorfeld stared at him, taken aback at these words.

"Neither I nor the boys have seen any sign of any people at all. Not roads or buildings, not a fence or a tool or even a footprint," the old man went on as gently as he could. "You say you've encountered a native woman who can understand your words, and warns that her people mean us harm. Why have you not brought her to us? So that we can verify what you say?"

"She is no native," Thorfeld returned hoarsely."

Gunnarr sighed. "We'll speak to Ketill on our return. But without some proof of your claims, son, I can't stand for you. Not when so much is at stake."

Thorfeld stepped back, offended and hurt by the old man's words. "Do what you feel you must. I will do the same," he said shortly, and walked away to sit by the nearby stream. He stayed there, keeping his own counsel, until the others were ready to carry on.

The shapeshifters called themselves Ketanteket, a word that meant "hunters" in the language of one of the local human tribes. They split into two parties, and the larger group went north to the foreigners' main encampment, flying or running in animal form to get there quickly. The smaller group of Rayna, Aqissiaq, Tyr, his mate Maiara and her brother Nahuel stayed behind to follow the four scouts. During the daylight hours, at Tyr's command, all were to remain out of sight of the men.

When day drew down into night once more, and the explorers prepared for sleep, then would come more fun. Aqissiaq and Nahuel especially looked forward to tormenting their prey. Neither they nor Maiara had ever lived among humans. Tyr and Rayna had both lived among men, many lifetimes in fact. Once, Tyr had considered himself a Viking and had fought beside men like Thorfeld. But he was not a man, and although his name had found its way into the Norse sagas, he would never live among them again. Nor would he allow them to take the land he had chosen for his home. His only concern was Rayna, who had become fixated on the blond leader of the scouting party.

Once they had all come together in the Viking settlement called Hoyetrær, the Ketanteket would let their inherent savagery break free. Truly they had little opportunity to indulge such blood-lust, as the native peoples had learned to shun this part of the coast.

That night, Thorfeld and his companions camped in familiar territory. Their travel had been much quicker on the return, and they had passed their previous campsite well before the sun dropped below the trees. As Gunnarr built the journey-fire and the young brothers went about their usual duties of gathering firewood and looking for edible plants, Thorfeld strung his bow and went in search of fresh meat.

The sky was still bright, and long skeins of amber sunlight streamed through the tall trees. Birds chirped and sang, and a cool breeze came into the forest from the east. Thorfeld had seen rabbit tracks, but lost them in the dense undergrowth. He walked quietly, hoping for sight of a deer or elk.

When he passed between two large trees and heard a low angry growling, he halted. There, barely visible in the dappled shadows, was a wolf. Its hackles were raised, fangs bared as it snarled at him in warning. He only thought for a moment. He was not inclined to favor wolf meat, but they needed to eat, and the animal's thick fur would be a welcome addition to winter clothing.

Thorfeld drew back the bowstring, arrow already in place. The wolf crouched, heavy muscles bunched as it prepared to leap—not away but toward him—when the raucous cry of a bird stopped both of them. The raven shrieked again, dropping through the branches in a streak of dark feathers, and dove at the wolf.

The wolf snarled again, and snapped at beating black wings before disappearing into the underbrush.

Without thinking, Thorfeld aimed the nocked arrow toward the bird. It landed on the ground, and turned to look back at him with black lightless eyes. It was the largest raven he had ever seen, with a wingspan of at least five feet. Hanging from a thong around its neck was a silver crescent-shaped cloak-pin.

He released the tension on the bow, dropping it and the arrow to the ground. The raven just stared at him, making no sound now that the wolf was gone. Knowing it was mad, he whispered, "Rayna?"

The bird stalked forward two steps, tilted its head to one side, then leapt into the air and disappeared among the shadowed branches.

"Perhaps Gunnarr is right after all," he said aloud, "and I am going crazy." He stooped to pick up the dropped bow and arrow. With a wolf in the area, there was little chance of finding deer or elk nearby. Thorfeld was practical by nature, and regardless of the unexplained and unsettling events of the last few minutes, he refused to let it get to him. "No fresh meat. Maybe Sigurd caught some fish for dinner," he said, and headed back for camp.

In the shadowed canopy above, the raven watched until he was out of sight.

Thorfeld had little to say that evening as he sat with the others around the fire. Instead, he ate his share of food and went to lie down beneath their oil-cloth roof. Tofi seemed unaware that anything was going on, but Sigurd gave Gunnarr a quizzical look when Thorfeld went to bed so early.

Gunnarr simply shook his head, and went to stand his shift at guard.

Not long after the brothers went to their rest, there came the sound of wolves howling, then snarling and snapping as though not too far away the pack were fighting amongst themselves. Thorfeld heard them, but did nothing except tighten his grip on his sword. Tofi and Sigurd got up and went out to the fire, adding more wood to bring light to the darkness. Gunnarr chided them for being children, but kept a sharp eye out. The sound of the battle had not been far away, and seemed to have involved several wolves. Gunnarr thought perhaps a pack was ousting one of their members, or maybe an ambitious youngling had challenged the pack leader. Either way, it was unlikely the wild canines would come anywhere near their fire.

When it abruptly quieted down, the brothers waited to be certain there was no danger, then returned to their places to sleep.

Tired as he was, Thorfeld did not sleep that night. Every time he closed his eyes, he saw the raven drive off the wolf, then turn to reveal his cloak-pin dangling round its neck.

It was mid-afternoon when the scouting party reached the main encampment called Hoyetræer. In their absence enough trees had been downed to build a sizable longhouse. Once the earthen floor had been dug out and leveled, the logs would be placed and strips of sod stacked to make the walls. Smaller branches would be laid across the roof beams, dried sod placed on top, then soil and more sod with the grass still growing. Judging by the size of the house under construction, it would be close-quarters for the crew of thirty-two, but it would be warm and sturdy.

When Thorfeld and the others came into view, the work came to a halt. Ketill, captain of the ship and commander of the expedition, came to meet them.

An older man, with grey at his temples and liberally peppered through his beard, Ketill was still imposing. He clasped hands with Thorfeld, and asked simply, "What did you find?"

"Forest, field and stream," Thorfeld replied, feeling the weight of Gunnarr's gaze upon his back. "Plenty of fish and game, but no sign of human habitation at all."

"Good," Ketill said with a nod.

"Still, I have reason to believe we are in danger," Thorfeld said, knowing that Gunnarr still stood beside him. The young brothers had already gone to join those working on the longhouse.

"Why?"

"I met a woman, not native to this land. She came here from across the sea as we did, and recognized my speech. She has made it known to me that her people do not welcome us, or any strangers."

"Thorfeld," Gunnarr said softly, but was ignored.

"They are not like us. I fear if we stay, they will attack us. I don't know their number, Ketill, but I think it best to change our plans."

Ketill looked from one to the other, from Thorfeld's set expression of duty to Gunnarr's of almost fatherly concern. When he spoke, his words were calm but bleak. "Last night during the deep watch, four men were killed. They gave no alarm. This morning their bodies were found, savaged almost beyond recognition, and so we believed it was an animal attack."

Thorfeld exchanged a glance with Gunnarr.

"Ivar cast the bones. He said there are skrælings here, dark and angry spirits. Perhaps they are of these people."

"When do we leave?" Thorfeld asked resignedly.

Ketill shook his head. "We don't. Until I've seen the threat with my own eyes, I'll do as commanded by Leif, our chieftain. We have much to do before winter."

Thorfeld gritted his teeth, but nodded.

"You can help with the construction, or volunteer for night guard. The choice is yours."

When Ketill walked away, Thorfeld watched him go.

"What will you do?" Gunnarr asked.

"I'll stand for guard," he replied. "Rayna will come to me again."

Gunnarr sighed, but did not argue it. Together, the two men joined the rest at the rising longhouse.

Guard duty fell to four men at a time, one at each quarter outside the meadow encampment named Hoyetrær. Thorfeld took the post farthest inland which fell within the edge of the forest.

When the moon rose, waxing now toward full, it lit the clearing where the longhouse was being built. Thorfeld could look across the camp and see the three other guardsmen silhouetted in moonlight. He himself was hidden within the shadows of the encroaching trees. All was silent, save for the soughing of the sea breeze in the long grass. The grasslands rippled in waves under the moonlight, reminding Thorfeld of open water. Behind him, tree limbs creaked, and leaves whispered riddles to each other. There was no sound of insects or birds. Several times he saw eye-shine, and thought perhaps the skrælings Ketill had spoken of approached. All he wanted was to see the woman who had stolen his heart along with his cloak-pin.

Shadows grew from beneath the trees, extending toward the encampment. A couple of men moved around the fire at the center, unable to sleep perhaps. Thorfeld, feeling as though an immense storm approached, pulled sword from scabbard and waited.

When the attack came, it was sudden and silent. The shadows separated into animals that leapt among the helpless sleeping men. Wolves they were, swift and merciless. By the time the men were aware of what was happening, it was already too late. Thorfeld bellowed warning at the top of his lungs, and ran out of the trees toward the half-erected longhouse, sword brandished above his head. Birds fell out of the sky, dark as cloud-shadow with glowing eyes; they shrieked as they dove, adding to the death-toll and the nightmare quality of the spectacle.

Those men who were still able came up with weapons in

hand; half-dressed or tangled in blankets they fought to defend themselves and their fellows. Fire spread from the central pit to the longhouse, and dried sod smoldered adding acrid smoke to the terrible scene.

Something leapt at Thorfeld, furred and fanged with requisite fiery eyes, and he swung the sword down as though chopping wood. Whatever it was—wolf or mountain cat— dodged his blade with fluid ease and lunged again.

As before, a fury of black feathers intervened, driving off the beast and Thorfeld raised his sword again. The bird swooped round, wind whining through its feathers, and the huge raven with the silver crescent at its throat *changed* before his eyes. Like black smoke it swept toward the ground in a slender column, and Rayna stood before him.

"Stop!" she called, holding her hands toward him.

He staggered, heart pounding and ears ringing with the sounds of combat and men dying. "What are you," he hissed, conflicted by the pull of duty against his own desire.

"There is nothing you can do for them," she said. "If you join the fight, you will be killed."

"They are my people," he cried.

She stood aside as though to let him pass, but she was right. Already the sounds of battle were fading. Wolves howled, and there was a wailing bubbling song from the throat of the great cat. Crows swirled in the air like black leaves in a maelstrom, then dropped down again to feast.

A tall man with dark hair and grey beard approached, dressed in the same style of clothing that Rayna wore. He carried no weapon, yet strode forward like a king. His eyes, like a wolf's, flashed gold in the darkness.

"And yet, one still lives," he said, speaking Thorfeld's language with a heavy accent.

Rayna said nothing, but turned to face him, placing herself between him and Thorfeld.

"He cannot stay with us," he said, and while his accent made it hard for Thorfeld to understand his words, he had no difficulty understanding the sympathy in the man's tone. "He is not our kind. If he stays, he will die."

"Once, we lived among men," Rayna replied, holding her ground. "You lived with them for so long, in so many guises, that they made you a god in their legends and histories. Tyr, god of war, giver of law; and here, among our own kind, still you are a warrior and lawgiver. If you give him safe passage, who will stand against you?"

Thorfeld stared at the other man now. Rayna had called him Tyr. Could it be true?

"You stand against me," Tyr said gently, and Rayna dropped her eyes, but did not give way.

"I have made my vow. He is mine, I have claimed him."

Tyr looked over her shoulder at the bone of their contention. "And what say you? Have you chosen her as well?"

Thorfeld was silent, closing his eyes when Rayna turned to face him once more. Oddly beautiful and strange beyond his comprehension, she had done nothing to help his closest companions, not Gunnarr who had been like a father, nor even Tofi who was barely more than a child. Yet still he had only one answer. "She is in my heart."

"Then it is already done."

"No!" A wolf, large and dark with muzzle painted in blood charged in, hackles raised and fangs bared. Thorfeld stumbled back, raising his sword once more. Rayna and Tyr both blurred, black smoke reformed into wolf and raven. The wolf that had been Tyr lunged for the other wolf's throat, as the raven dove for its eyes. It was fast, so fast that all Thorfeld could do was steel himself.

He fell, bracing his long sword before him, and the raging animal drove itself onto his blade, jaws snapping as it attempted to reach his throat. Blood sprayed, blinding Thorfeld, and his head struck a rock. Rayna screamed, the sound of an eagle more than the rough croak of a raven. The air went black and thin, and then there was nothing at all.

The longhouse took a long time to catch, as the wood was still green and the sod walls thick. But in the end it burned, coughing great billows of smoke into the late summer sky. The remains of the Viking explorers, what little was left, burned with it. With no ceremony, the carcass of Aqissiaq was also thrown onto the pile.

The dragon ship burned also, pulled up onto the sandy beach, and Thorfeld watched from the high ground blinking back tears at what felt like a desecration. The dragonhead carved at the prow had been removed before the ship was set fire. In a moment of nostalgia, Tyr had decided to keep it.

When all that was left of the graceful boat was a smoldering pile of embers and ash, Thorfeld turned to find Rayna behind him. She gazed across the water, black hair pulled gently by the sea breeze.

"Where do we go now?" he asked. He was still sickened by the carnage of last night, but knew his life depended now on the skræling woman who had chosen him.

"We will travel south and west, following the water," she said. "Once we are out of the range of my people, then we can do as we wish."

"So you are banished."

"It was my choice."

For a long time he was silent, wanting to ask but not wanting to offend. At last he said, "Why?"

"I have been alone for so long. When I saw you, I knew my loneliness was over." Her eyes were steady, her voice emotionless.

"And if I had chosen differently?" he asked.

She smiled slowly, and although he was captivated by her, he felt gooseflesh rise and chills skittered down his spine. "As soon choose not to breathe," she said. She was exotic and beguiling, but not, in the end, what she appeared to be. Clearly, had he chosen his people, he would be only ash now.

When she reached out her hand to him, he took it.

"Come with me, my warrior," she said softly, "And you will live a life of legend."

They left without speaking to Tyr, heading south along the trail on which they'd met. The old god, leader of the Ketanteket in this new world, watched them go from the shelter of the trees. His mate Maiara stood beside him.

"Will she return?" Maiara asked.

"I do not know," he replied. In the shapes of wolf, cougar, hawk and crow the Ketanteket slipped into the forest, sated by the night's slaughter.

The smoke from the fires had finally begun to dissipate, shredded by the sea wind. Perhaps the funeral pyres would be seen by Vikings to the east, and they would stay away. Chipped into the foundation stone of the burnt longhouse, a warning left for any Norsemen who ever came this way again, was the rune for Tyr, "↑"; Thorfeld's final message.

HARVEST OF NIGHT SEEDS

Crickets chirped beyond the garden, their repetitive symphony so common that Tracy barely noticed it anymore. The night air was cool, and stars sparkled in a clear sky like glitter thrown haphazardly across dark water. Behind her, the house sat plain and unassuming, an occasional creak coming from settling beams and supports. A dim light glowed through the kitchen window, and bluish-white flashes from a TV showed in the upstairs bedroom window where her parents slept. She was supposed to be in bed, too; dawn came early and she had to help with the milking. But this was her favorite time of day—after the sun had set, and she was alone on the back porch. The animals were quiet, lost in their own dreaming, and on this late spring evening she could almost hear her seedlings growing.

A few yards from where she sat, tucked between the old weathered barn and the clothes lines, was her little vegetable garden. Her daddy grew corn for profit, and her momma made goat's-milk soap to sell at a little boutique in town. Tracy had started the vegetable patch on her own, between school and helping with the chores around the farm. She was the one who had tilled the ground with an old gas-engine tiller older than she was. She had bought the seeds out of her allowance that she'd saved since last year. She was the one who made sure the rows of seedlings got watered, and checked daily for any offending weeds that had taken root where they weren't welcome. Daddy had no time for it, and Momma no inclination. In fact, when she'd told them that she wanted to grow her own garden, they had exchanged a knowing look and Daddy grunted while Momma rolled her eyes.

"If you want to waste half your summer taking care of a garden, that's your choice," Momma had said. "Just keep in mind it's your project. I'm not pulling weeds, or getting after you to water it. Is that clear?"

"Yes ma'am," Tracy had said, glancing at her father.

Daddy just grunted again, and went back to thumbing through the farm equipment catalogue that rested on his lap.

So Tracy spent all her free time in that little patch of dirt. She had found a website that sold all kinds of seeds, things she'd never eaten before, and some things she'd never even heard of. She had sent in her order, and got back a box filled with seeds for cowpeas, eggplant, finocchio, minutina, and scorzonea. There was chicory, banana cantaloupe, strawberry spinach, purple carrots, glass gem corn, tepary beans, marbled amaranth, and several different kinds of exotic squash. But the seeds she was most curious about had come as a 'special gift' tucked in amongst the others. The packet of black crescent shaped seeds had simply been labeled "oíche seeds". There was no other description, and she didn't know if they were vegetables, fruits or herbs. She'd gone back to the website to look them up, but they weren't in the list of available seeds.

Finally, she decided just to plant them, and see what grew. The seeds, like tiny glass sickles, clicked against each other in her damp palm as she carefully placed one in each prepared divot. She covered them with dirt, and watered them by hand. Last, she pushed a pointed stake into the ground beside them, the envelope with their name stapled to the top.

Over the next few days her seeds began to sprout. Some were thin and fine, like pale green whiskers. Some immediately put out bright green leaves that spread wide and strained upward toward the sun. But the oíche seeds didn't do anything. Tracy frowned, but figured maybe they were defective and wouldn't grow at all.

She made sure to water and weed the little garden patch, ignoring the way her mother shook her head and rolled her eyes. It didn't matter that everything Tracy had planted was edible, and that they would have fresh vegetables in the summer. All Momma cared about was that Tracy got up to milk the cow and two nanny goats they kept in the barn. She fed them and the chickens every day, and checked for eggs in the afternoon. Daddy spent from morning till night out in the corn fields with their two hired hands Billy and Russ, or in town bullshitting with the other farmers in the area. Momma went into town to have her hair and nails done, and to gossip with the other farm wives. She also made and sold her little oval bars of goat's-milk soap with the dried lavender or marigold petals infused in them. The only person who gave Tracy any encouragement at all was Billy. He would stand outside the fence and watch as she bent to pull the little pervasive weeds, or reformed the small earthen dams around the plants.

"Lookin' real good, Tracy," he would say with a crooked smile, a piece of straw hanging off his bottom lip. "Can't wait to taste some of what you got growin' there."

Tracy would just nod and go on about her work. Billy was twenty years old, and had worked for her daddy for two years. But he'd only started showing interest in her for the last few months, since her fourteenth birthday. He might be okay according to Daddy, but he gave her the creeps.

Almost a month after planting Tracy saw the slender shoots coming up from the oíche seeds, and she grinned from ear to ear. She had kept watering them, but hadn't expected anything would come of it. Now there were dark green stems pushing up through the earth, straight and sharp as hat pins. She had bought some plant food from the nursery in town, and sprayed a little on the newcomers to celebrate their late arrival.

The other plants were already well established, stretching up and out to greedily receive the light from the early summer sun. Back in the corner, the oíche seedlings seemed set apart from the rest of the garden. They had shade from the barn in the morning and from the trees along the fence in the afternoon. The lack of full sun didn't seem to bother them, although they just kept getting taller without putting out any leaves. In another week they were almost a foot high, still thin and shiny like long pins, and colored a deep green that was almost black.

Billy came by before dinner, and helped Tracy feed the chickens and check for fresh eggs. He was sweaty from working in the fields all day, but unapologetic when he brushed against her while she cast dried corn for the birds.

She was a quiet girl, but not shy. "You stink," she said and moved away from him. But Billy just laughed, that devil-may-care glint in his blue eyes that he thought made him look sexy.

"Well you smell good," he said, and put the last of the eggs in a basket. "Got anything good to taste yet, out of that garden of yours?"

"Not yet," she said and picked up the basket, leaving him behind with the chickens pecking at his feet.

When she tried to tell her parents about it, and how uncomfortable Billy made her feel, Daddy grunted and Momma let out an exasperated sigh.

"Billy's a good worker," Daddy said, taking a pull from his beer bottle. "He's a good boy. Been here more'n two years, and never caused a problem. You best not be making trouble for him."

"You're still a little girl, Tracy," Momma said when Daddy stopped. "He looks at you like a little sister, and has told me so before. Don't fault him for offering to help you with your chores, when he's got plenty of his own work to do."

So Tracy said nothing more about it.

Another week went by, and the temperature stayed high. The glass gem corn was up to her shoulders, the beans and cowpeas reached to her knees. The squash was sending runners through the rows, and many of the plants were flowering. The oíche stems were as tall as her hips, off in their own little corner of the garden. They stood perfectly straight and as slim as knitting needles. But when she went back there to check for weeds and to be sure they were well watered, she felt as though they leaned toward her. They appeared to be hard and glossy, but when she gently stroked her fingers along their smooth lengths they felt silky against her skin. She still didn't know what they were, really; but she felt as though they liked her.

Crickets chirped in chorus, and the moon hung low in the sky, a narrow crescent that reminded Tracy of her little black oíche seeds. Stars glittered, and a warm breeze made the trees sigh;

soft green corn leaves whispered riddles to each other. In the garden there were little crackling sounds, reminiscent of flames eating through a log in a bonfire. Tracy sat on the back porch, leaning against the railing with a half empty glass of iced tea beside her. The remaining chips of ice clinked softly against the glass as they melted.

Footsteps on the gravel path beside the house caught Tracy's attention. Her parents were in bed already, their window flickering with its nightly show of TV backlight. She licked her lips and crept back into the shadows of the porch. The post on the left side by the steps was wide enough to hide her.

A tall figure came around the corner, moving stealthily but not silently. Even in the dim moonlight she recognized Billy. He wasn't watching where he was walking. Instead, his head was tipped back, face shadowed by the bill of his baseball cap, and he was looking up at the second story windows. When he got to her bedroom window, dark at this hour not because she was sleeping but because she hadn't yet gone to bed, he stopped and stared.

Tracy took slow shallow breaths, making sure not to draw his attention. He was less than six feet from her hiding place.

He stood for what seemed like a long time, gazing up at her empty window. Then two pieces of ice in her glass separated with a loud *clink*, and his head jerked toward the steps. "Who is that?" he asked, staring directly at where she hid in the shadows. "Tracy, is that you?"

There was nothing for it. Tracy stood and came out of the deep darkness, leaning over to pick up her glass. "You lookin' for Daddy? 'Cause he's already in bed."

He shook his head, teeth showing in his sudden grin. "No ma'am; I just found what I was lookin' for."

"It's late, and I got chores in the morning," she said, hoping her voice didn't sound as breathless to him as it did in her own ears. As she started toward the back door, he came up the steps onto the porch and blocked her path.

"Don't be in such a hurry, sweetheart," he said, pouring on all his charm. "I've been thinkin' about you a lot lately. I was hoping you were still up, so we could spend some time."

Her heart was pounding, so loud she was afraid he would hear it. From the barn came the sound of one of the nanny goats bleating, and the old chimes hanging at the edge of the porch tinkled in the warm breeze. "Not tonight, Billy. I'm tired," she said, trying to sound normal.

He moved closer, still smiling at her with all his teeth showing. "It won't take long, sweetheart," he said and took off his hat. "You do smell good," he added, dropping the hat on the porch as he reached out to smooth her hair.

Pretense done, she turned and hurried down the steps, nearly tripping on the last one. She dropped her iced tea on the grass, hoping the glass wouldn't break, and ran across the back lawn. The grass was wet and chilly under her bare feet.

"Tracy!" Billy didn't raise his voice, obviously not wanting to wake the house, and then he laughed. "Don't you hurt yourself girl, running around in the dark."

She glanced back, and saw him following. She thought for one second of screaming, but knew already that he'd play it off as an innocent misunderstanding. Her parents liked him, and it was clear they didn't want to hear anything bad about him, regardless of if it was true.

She had several choices, but some were bad simply because she wasn't wearing any shoes. For instance, she wouldn't be smart to circle the house and run down the driveway to the road. The drive was covered in gravel which would just hurt her feet and slow her down. She wouldn't do herself any favors by skinning through the fence into the corn fields either. She had no light, and could easily twist or break an ankle running through the rows. She considered going into the barn, and maybe climbing up into the hay loft—and immediately decided that would be a bad idea. If he cornered her in there, he might think it was some kind of backhanded invitation for his advances.

All this went through her mind in a couple of seconds. No, her best choice was to lead him away from the house, double back and get inside where she could lock the door. She headed straight for the back fence where a line of elms and maples cast shade over the yard in the afternoons. As soon as she was in the denser darkness beneath their limbs, she slowed and dropped to a crouch.

Another glance back showed Billy following her across the back lawn. He was still smiling, as though this was all a game.

From the little garden she'd worked in diligently all spring and early summer came that odd crackling sound again, reminding her of hungry flames eating through dry wood. Her row of glass gem corn swayed slightly, their still-soft leaves whispering secrets. But the crickets had fallen silent.

"Is it hide'n seek then?" Billy called softly, walking cautiously into the shadows of the trees.

Tracy kept low, not wanting him to see her silhouette between the trees, and cautiously duck-walked toward the clothes lines. The strange popping, crackling sound from the garden continued, and she kept expecting to see sparks glimmering between the maturing plants. Instead, light glowed from behind her.

Billy held the disposable lighter that he'd dug out of his pocket and spun the striker wheel with his thumb. Sparks jumped, glittering, from the flint but didn't catch into a flame. "Damn thing," he muttered, and tried again.

"Shit," Tracy breathed. There was no way to avoid him if he could see her. He was faster and stronger than she, and knew his way around the farm as well as she did. She scrambled on all fours, heading for her garden.

The crackling ahead of her got louder, and then stopped all at once. There were still no crickets singing, no frogs croaking or bats squeaking. But in the sudden silence, the cow Daisy mooed and kicked inside the barn, hooves hitting the side of her stall with a muffled thud. The goats both started bleating, the brass bells hanging at their necks ringing through the still night air.

"C'mon, Tracy," Billy called, still keeping his voice low, "I don't want to waste all night playin' games."

Gooseflesh rippled up her bare arms, and Tracy stopped where she was, putting her hands over her mouth. Something raced past her on both sides, something dark that she couldn't see, and she jumped, wide eyes straining to make them out.

"I just want us to be close, is all," Billy said, and spun the striker wheel again. This time, the spark caught the butane and a trembling flame appeared. "Where are you, sweetheart?"

Something flickered in the darkness, too quick for either of them to see, and then Billy grunted.

"Ow," he said, then "Ow!" He turned, swinging the lighter before him as he tried to see what was happening. Slender yard-high *things* surrounded him, jumping forward to *bite* him. "What the hell?!" he exclaimed, dancing clumsily as he tried to avoid whatever was attacking him. "Tracy!"

She was frozen, hands still on her mouth. In the barn, Daisy and the nannies were raising a ruckus, and now the chickens were adding to the noise, squawking and flapping inside their coop. In one fairly clear glimpse as Billy swung around with his lighter, she realized what it was. It made no sense—couldn't really be true!—but what else could it be?

Billy stumbled back toward the house, dropping the lighter as he swatted at his legs. "Damn, damn," he said, still ignorant of what was happening. Long needle-thin things leapt at him, stabbing and slicing, drawing blood with each touch. "Tracy, help me!" he called again.

Tracy got to her feet and slowly walked toward the house, panting for breath and eyes wide as she watched disbelieving.

Billy turned, caught a glimpse of her now away from the trees. "Tracy, help!" he called, then tripped and fell backward. The slender creatures were on him at once, cutting and slicing, and blood flowed black in the dim moonlight.

Tracy skirted around the carnage, wondering if they would come for her when they were done with Billy. Before she reached the porch, they left him and moved toward her. The oíche stems, having pulled themselves out of the ground, had split off narrow appendages in three pairs. They were quick and agile, and held the top set of limbs like the forelegs of a praying mantis. Tiny beads had appeared at the top of each stem, apparently their eyes for they could obviously see very well.

"What do you want?" she asked, glancing from Billy's still form to her strange seedlings.

They seemed to look at each other, communicating in some way she couldn't fathom. Then one by one they approached her.

Carefully and oh so gently, they stroked themselves against her. As she had done in the garden, she grazed her fingertips along their silky stems, feeling an odd sense of affection from them. Then, with no further attempt to communicate, they slipped past her again, scampering back to where Billy lay still on the lawn. Tracy felt that she had to watch, as though she owed it to them. In short order they had reduced the field-hand to little more than a wet spot on the grass. When they were done, they crossed the lawn and disappeared back into the garden.

Tracy bent to retrieve her glass, luckily still in one piece, and went up the steps onto the porch. In the barn Daisy and the goats had fallen quiet once more, and the chickens had gone back to roost. In her parents' second floor window, the TV continued to flicker. From the fields beyond the yard crickets began to chirp again, and the warm summer breeze soughed through the trees.

WATERLESS

First of all, welcome to the Preserve. Here are your room keys, and a map of our little settlement here. You can see there's an all-night café right next door, and we have an enclosed walkway between here and there so you don't even have to go outside. One of the services we offer is a little oral introduction to the Preserve presented by yours truly. Some people don't seem all that interested, but I'd like to tell my story anyway, and if you don't mind I'll get to it right now.

My opinion? It all started with global warming. No one really believed it; I mean c'mon, the planet heating up until it started an ice age? That just makes no sense at all! But regardless of any of that, the winters were getting drier, at least around here. Not nearly as cold or long as they'd been when I was a kid. We didn't get as much snow in the winter. Used to be three or four feet of snow on the ground, sometimes more, from October on through April. Temperatures used to dip into the negatives and stay there for weeks at a time. Then, in the winter of '12, it never dropped below freezing. Still had a couple good snowstorms, but nothing like usual. The winter of '13 was so mild most folks didn't even call it winter. We never had more than two inches of snow on the lawn all season. Clear on into April, all the grass was dead, kind of a dried-up beige color lying flat against the soil, and not much rain either, so even the bulbs were late coming up.

The County sent out surveyors to see what could be done, when it was clear the reservoirs were likely as full as they were going to get. There was some snow in the mountains, but not enough to make up for what never fell in the valleys. This was farming country around here, despite what you might think driving through on the State Highway. A shortage of water was going to make life hard on everyone.

So those folks from the County (politicians every one of them, even those that had been born and bred in the county) decided the only thing to do was find a way to contain what water there was to be had. There were lots of canals and ditches, taking the water downhill from the mountains and foothills into the flat lands below. Some people still watered the old-fashioned way; they irrigated their land by blocking the ditches so the water would flood their fields. Some had invested in pumps and wheel-lines, and they'd just siphon the water out of the canals and spray it over the fields. Either way worked just fine. But the powers-that-be in the County seat decided that too much water was going to waste, traveling along those miles of canals and ditches. Water was seeping into the ground on its way to elsewhere, and never mind the fact that it was just going back into the aquifer.

There was a bit of a boom that year for construction workers. Every able man or woman who wanted a job had one, as crews headed out to lay concrete pipe where every open ditch had been. Enclose the water, those politicians said, so it can't seep into the ground, and can't evaporate into the air. There might not even be a water shortage at all, with this kind of conservation!

Just one thing they seemed to forget about. This is pretty good farm land around here, but it's dry. High-mountain desert is what I've heard it described as. From a high vantage point, you could tell where there was water by the trees. There's sagebrush, pinyon pine and scrub-oak all over the place, but the only place you'll see full-grown by-God trees is where there's water. Ponds, lakes, reservoirs, streams and rivers are all lined with lush growths of trees. Most of the canal banks are kept clear of growth, but there were too many ditches crisscrossing the landscape, and they developed their own stands of bushes, saplings and even mature trees.

So what happened when all those waterways were enclosed? It took a full year to pipe every waterway the surveyors could map. The winter of '14 was as dry and relatively warm as the previous one, but those politicians were smug.

The trees, however? They had a bit of a water-shortage crisis of their own.

Y'know, it's funny, for probably thousands of years people have taken trees for granted. They give shade on a hot day, block the wind when it gets to howling, and according to the scientists they actually make oxygen for us mobile creatures to breathe. You can burn their wood for warmth or to cook your dinner, or even to ward off some ornery critter that might want to take a bite of you. You can build your house from them, put a roof over your head, and fill your home with beautiful carved furniture made of them. And for a long time, I'm pretty sure if you made an effort to remove their regular water supply they would just eventually die, fall and then rot.

But this here high mountain desert with the good farmland isn't like anywhere else. We got one other thing going for us, and that's dead dinosaurs. You just about can't throw a rock around here without hitting an oil derrick or a natural gas drilling rig. Now the oil and the natural gas, that doesn't really figure into anything, except for this: when those companies started looking for better, more efficient and more cost effective ways of getting these resources out of the ground, they caused an unforeseen side-effect.

Now I never worked in the oil fields, so I'm just telling you what I been told; but they used this stuff they called "mud," made from water mixed with different chemicals. They would pump that mud down into their wells to help with the drilling, or to force pockets of natural gas to come up. That's all fine and good, but what it really meant was that a lot of that chemical soup ended up in the ground water. Since all the surface water in the county was enclosed so it couldn't seep down into the aquifer, the ground water began to get a bit...well, I won't say toxic. There were all kinds of government agencies supposedly keeping an eye on the water, what with us running short, to make sure it was safe for human and animal consumption. As for me and my family, we used filtration systems and bought bottled purified water for culinary uses. Because seeing that deepening red stain in every toilet, sink and bathtub made us none too interested in what might happen to our insides.

So that's what led up to it, in my opinion. The spring of '15 was just about bone dry. The temperatures of winter were cool but not cold, and we got barely any precipitation throughout the whole season. Everything was dying off, even in people's yards, because we were on a strict schedule for watering. All the trees in the area—the wild ones, I mean, that grew along those old defunct waterways—they were looking pretty sad. I wasn't the only one that shook my head and mourned the greenery of my youth. So when trees started disappearing, no one paid much mind. Unless you were to make your way over and verify that a tree had fallen, you'd just assume that's what happened.

It was around that time when ranchers in the area started filing complaints about missing livestock. Mostly it was larger, mature animals like adult cattle or sheep. The average number of deer and elk that always ended up road-kill declined dramatically. But again, that just could have been because they'd migrated elsewhere, what with there being little feed for them even in the higher pastures.

But then we started finding carcasses. They were left where the ditches and canals used to run open to the sky. Cows, goats, even dogs were found like they'd been mummified without the linen wrappings. Every bit of moisture had been sucked out of them, but not a mouthful of meat removed. Not even any teeth marks left behind to identify what had attacked them. The only mark on any of them was a few puncture wounds. Some were maybe the size of a number 2 pencil, but some were so small you couldn't see them with the naked eye. More and more animals came up missing, only to be found as dry desiccated husks a few days later. Those County politicians were in an uproar, calling the government for help. But it was already too late.

When a group of teenagers on a weekend camping trip never returned home, the powers-that-be called in the FBI. Their campsite was found, with their vehicles and all their supplies still ready for a campout. A week later all six seniors were found at the bottom of a dry well behind an abandoned cabin twenty miles from their camp. Everyone one of them was sucked as dry as a fly in a spider's web.

The National Guard came in. There was a curfew. There were town meetings. No one knew what to do, because no one knew where the danger originated. Surprising to some people but not to me, it was Old Man Boggess who had the right idea.

"I had a stand of cottonwoods," he said when he stood in the meeting at the high school, "Back behind my place about a hundred yards. They grew up along a little stream that trickled there since I was a boy. They ain't there no more. I don't mean they lost their rooting due to the drought and toppled over. I mean they're *gone.*"

A lot of people gave each other uneasy looks, and some outright laughed, but me and a few others just nodded.

"I went out there a few days ago at noon," he continued, leaning somewhat precariously on a gnarled varnished cane that he'd carried for as long as I could remember. "Those cottonwoods are gone. Judging by the state of the ground, I'd say they fairly yanked their roots out of that dry packed earth and went looking for more hospitable surroundings."

There was an uproar, angry people yelling and scared people crying, and the County Assessor banging her little wooden gavel on the table while she called for order. When the meeting was over, nothing was decided, and people were still scared and angry. But me and some other folks that lived in the same stretch as Old Man Boggess pulled him aside to find out if he knew any more.

"I found the start of a trail," he told us, pausing a moment to place a dip of chew inside his bottom lip. The man had never smoked a day in his life, but was proud to brag he'd been chewing tobacco since the age of five. "Ground's packed so hard, it might as well be rock, so I can't say where it was heading. But I believe those trees took off northward, maybe headin' toward the foothills."

"Trees don't move, lest they're blowin' in a wind," Dan Parker said with conviction. But there was a wild look in his eyes, as though he didn't believe his own self.

Gus Boggess just shrugged, then motioned with his head. "You've seen those trees on my property since you were a baby, Dan. You come on by and take a look for yourself, tell me what you think happened."

"Even if you're right, what do we do about it?" Doris Nelson asked, fluttering fingers rubbing across her lips in a nervous habit that had left them red and chapped.

Gus rubbed his chin thoughtfully, and the sound of his gnarled fingers moving across the stubble of beard rasped in the quiet evening air like some kind of unseen insect. "I haven't seen anything moving during daylight that shouldn't be," he mused, then turned his head and spat a line of brown saliva onto the ground. "So I figure they got to be moving at night. I don't go out after sundown, folks. Keep my dogs in the house with me, instead of letting 'em sleep in the lean-to like I always done. Lost my wife, and my kids all moved out of state. Those dogs are all I've got for company. I'll be damned if I find them sucked dry at the bottom of that old stream bed."

"What are you saying?" Dan asked, and there was a tone to his voice you don't often hear from men who've spent their whole life farming in a desert. Men like that don't have the imagination to get scared of things they can't see, because all they believe in is what they *can* see. "You think your missing trees have something to do with all the dead animals?"

Gus shrugged and spat again. "I'm an old man, Dan. In two years I'll see my century. And in my 98 years I have seen things you wouldn't believe, and I'm not takin' the time to tell you about them. But everything I've witnessed in my life, no matter how strange or confusing, in the end makes a kind of sense. The sense I'm gettin' from this is simple. We took away the water, and the trees went lookin' for it. Maybe by accident, and maybe on purpose, one of 'em stuck a root into a napping steer and tapped into blood instead of water. In my mind, I have to wonder if they didn't get a liking for the taste."

After that revelation, no one seemed to have much more to say. Dan Parker left pretty quickly, looking a little green around the mouth. Doris Nelson went to find her kids and drive them home. I offered a ride to Gus, but he just gestured with his cane to the old '54 GMC he'd driven. 98 years old, and still driving himself. His dogs, a blue healer named Tick and an Aussie cattle-dog named Flea were standing in the bed watching us. That old man had a funny sense of humor.

People talked about what they heard that night, and the rumors eventually made it back to the County seat. There was a lot of scoffing and derisive laughter that anyone would believe such a fairy-tale, but apparently someone must have put some credence to it. When the National Guard rolled into town with a flatbed load of freshly cut trees, there was a crowd on hand to watch. The reactions to the blood-red sap weeping from the trunks convinced most folks. The scientists brought in were disbelieving, then bewildered, and then alternately frightened or excited. Old Man Boggess had been right: the trees having lost their water supply, and metabolizing the chemical soup in the ground water, had become mobile. And when new water supplies hadn't been easily found, they'd tapped into the next best thing. Our trees had become vampires.

There were plans made for destroying the trees, burning them or hiring men to come in and free-clear whatever stands were found. That's when we found out the trees would fight back. It's bad enough dodging swinging branches, or evading thirsty taproots, but you do not want to go up against a pissed off Russian olive or honey locust. The thorns on their branches grow in excess of three inches long and are needle sharp. Russian olives have always thrived in this area, and they became the infantry of the tree army.

So, that's pretty much the story. Eventually, it just became too expensive to keep on. The government offered a settlement to every landowner in the area, with additional funds to aid in relocating. Pretty much the whole County has been added to the Preserve. They went through and opened up all the ditches and canals again, letting the water flow open to the sky. Some of the trees went back to the old ways, but a lot of them didn't. They move in herds through the daylight hours, picking off small mammals and reptiles, even birds. Deer, elk and antelope don't trust the shade anymore, for good reason; they sleep sheltered in the rocks now, or stay up in the hills where the trees never mutated. Most people are gone now, taking advantage of the government buy-out. Some died, Old Man Boggess among them. He never did see his century; Tick and Flea were out in his back pasture when they were cornered by a couple of globe willows and a Russian olive. By the time he made it out there, cane in one hand and thirty-ought-six in the other, it was too late. No one will ever know for sure, but I think he just decided he wasn't willing to go on alone anymore. The trees may have sucked him dry too, but not before he blew the back of his own head off.

Now me and a few other folks hang around. We run these little border motels so the tourists can come check out the Carnivorous Tree Preserve in safety. We run short little tours through the ghost town that used to be the County Seat. We point out the places where the National Guard had outright battles with one hundred foot tall poplars and ground-sweeping weeping willows. The cottonwoods with their sucker-roots devastated one group of soldiers, and the Russian olives and honey locusts finished them off. That kind of thing doesn't happen anymore, because we've surrendered the field. But that's not to say that it's safe, oh no. And we still keep a curfew. There's no wandering around inside the Preserve after sundown, and no one goes in there alone even in daylight.

So, here's my patented warning. Please make yourself to home. We've got cable TV, and the little café right next door that's open 24 hours. Enjoy your night, get some rest, and in the morning we'll take that tour into the Preserve. I know that you're young, and full of vinegar by the looks of it, but I'll say it one more time. Do not go out tonight, not even to peek through the gate. Because the trees are still restless, and they still get thirsty for something fresh that doesn't move on four legs. And there've been reports of a herd of Russian olives trolling the fence line.

You don't want to run into a gang of Russians in the dark.

HEARTWOOD

The sun was hot, like a weight on her shoulders. The wind was arid and she swallowed, grimacing at the dry click in her throat. Just a few feet away, past the jumbled boulders she hid among, was a trickle of water. It wasn't much, just a shallow runnel coming out of the rocks and slipping along for a few feet before disappearing again between dusty stones. It should be simple to creep forward and get a sweet, wet mouthful of it. There were weeds and scant bushes growing beside it, but it wasn't the brush that made her wary.

A few feet beyond, motionless except for long narrow leaves that fluttered in the wind, was a tree. She wasn't sure exactly what kind, *some kind of willow,* she thought. Behind it, nearly hidden by the spread of branches, was a second tree. This second one seemed to skulk, with pale greyish-green leaves and two-inch long spikes growing all along its rough branches.

Russian olive, she thought, but didn't say aloud. No one knew if they could hear, or just sensed vibrations somehow, but she couldn't afford to alert it to her presence. The sun continued to blaze down. She had started to sweat, which was bad. She couldn't afford to lose the moisture. Cautiously, she wiped her hand across her forehead, then touched her parched tongue to her dampened palm. The salt taste was strong, and her thirst clamored.

She closed her eyes, remembering the old days, when the trees were just trees. Back then they were rooted deep and stationary, a comfort of shade on hot summer days like today. Decades of pollution in the air and the ground water had wrought irreversible and unforeseen changes in them. Water shortages in wide swathes across the country, even around the world, had been the final straw. The trees had mutated, pulling their roots from the earth and hunting for new sustenance.

Something rustled, and she started. When she peeked around the granite curve, the willow was still where she'd last seen it. But the Russian olive was gone. Her heart pounded, and she touched the canteen hanging at her side. She had been without water for almost a full day. If she didn't get some soon, she would die. There was no one left to mourn her. She hadn't seen another person in weeks. Even alone and scared, she was unwilling to give up.

Quietly she removed the cap from the canteen, her other hand tight around her last defense. She came out of hiding, crouching to dunk the canteen under the flow of water. Shade blocked the glare of sunlight, and she flinched back as the olive reached for her, spikes sinking deep into her skin.

Ignoring the agony, she struck the head of her last flare and shoved the flame against the trunk, aiming for heartwood. As the mutated tree siphoned her blood with every thorn, its bark began to burn. And then it began to scream.

A THING OF BEAUTY

The sun would soon be setting. Gregory knew this because he kept meticulous track of the time. Gone were the days when one could just look up at the sky, and say, "Oh, the sun is just above the horizon. Soon it will be dusk, and then dark." No, now it was difficult to tell day from night, and so he kept careful count of the hours.

The ever-present cloud cover stretched from horizon to horizon, making the failing evening too warm and humid. Gregory could remember clear skies and fresh breezes, golden falls of sunlight and the scent of fresh-mown grass. He remembered—but not as clearly as he once had. It had been years since he had seen blue sky, or even a star through the polluted atmosphere.

"I'll just check one more time," he said aloud, mostly for his own benefit. His mother had told him, "People who talk to themselves are one step away from crazy." That was before the Alzheimer's had taken her memories, and many of her opinions. At the end, she'd talked to herself as much as to anyone else.

Following his daily routine, Gregory walked the wide path out to where a road had once been. He kept the path swept clean, and was glad there was no need to weed between the flat pieces of stone. For a while, he'd tried to keep the roadway clear as well, but had eventually given that up. There wasn't enough traffic to warrant it, and he had other uses for his time.

At the end of the path he stopped, looking right and then left, searching for any sign of life. As usual, there was nothing. A sluggish breeze moved the air, stirring dust and ash, but bringing no relief of the temperature or humidity. Gregory stood a bit slump-shouldered, the sweat-stained collar of his shirt turned up under his ears, and hummed tunelessly to himself. He waited for a while, knowing it was foolish to hope, but then as his mother had once told him, "Hope is a wellspring."

At last he turned and went back to the house. He walked slowly, keeping his back straight and strides even. He was tired, but his day's work was not yet done. He looked up one more time before going into the house. With the clouds above, the sky never went completely dark. Although dim, there was a phosphorescence, as though a huge glowing city just out of sight cast its light up to reflect back from the low-lying overcast. The temperature had cooled perhaps a degree or two, but the humidity was still oppressive. Gregory wiped his forehead with the back of his hand, then went into the house.

"I'm back, darling," he called, and pulled the door securely closed behind him.

Mikhaila trudged slowly down the road. She was tired, and wanted to shuffle; but that stirred up too much ash and dust into the air, making it hard to breathe. So, exhausted as she was, she picked her feet up for each step. Behind her she pulled a child's wagon heavily laden with all her possessions. At one time, the wagon had been bright red. Now, like everything else, it was dingy and grey. In the bottom of the wagon were two full cases of bottled water, worth more than their weight in gold these days. Stacked on top of that were canned goods; soup, vegetables and fruits, and spaghetti sauce. The cans were past their end date, but none of them bulged so she took the chance. On top of the cans were some dried goods including corn meal, sugar and salt, and white rice. Tucked in the end of the wagon was her cookware consisting of a small camp stove with fuel, two pans and a tea pot, and her dishes—dented metal plates and cups and some mismatched flatware.

Tied on top was a zippered bag that held her clothes. They were in a sad state, but she'd been unable to give them a proper washing in a long time. She remembered vaguely, such a long time ago, going to the laundromat with her mother. Sitting on the hard plastic chair and swinging her feet while she colored in a coloring book, and her mother gossiped with the other people there doing their laundry. The air had been moist and clean smelling, and had rumbled with the sound of washers and dryers spinning their loads of cloth. She could remember being bored, and wishing they were anywhere else, doing anything else. Now, she would have given a lot to spend a couple hours in a laundromat, smelling the bleach and spring-fresh scented fabric softeners with clean soft clothes to wear at the end.

According to the wind-up watch she wore strapped to one wrist, it was a few minutes after six pm. She didn't know if the time was right, it wasn't like she had any way to verify the exact hour and minute. But she'd set it to twelve noon on a particularly bright day when shadows fell directly below what cast them, and made sure to wind it every night before going to sleep. She could probably continue on for another hour or so, but much later than that she'd better have a safe place to spend the night. There wasn't a huge difference in the light between day and night, at least not as far as Mikhaila could tell. But the monsters that roamed the night hunting and killing could tell. Travel during day hours was marginally safe; traveling at night was definitely not.

She'd walked through the remains of a small village earlier in the day, and she'd thought about stopping to camp. But she'd been sure the buildings would last longer than they had. And now she was in a bit of a quandary. Continue on in hope of finding a suitable structure in which to spend the night, or turn back and retrace her steps?

She stopped, making sure the wagon wouldn't roll away, and lifted the plastic bottle that swung from a lanyard around her neck. She twisted off the cap and took a mouthful of stale tepid water, letting it sit on her tongue and slide between her teeth for a few seconds before swallowing. She could taste the ash that coated everything; she couldn't really remember what anything tasted like without that ash seasoning. After a moment, she took one more swallow then put the cap back on and let the bottle fall to the end of its leash. It sloshed softly before falling still. She had two full cases of water in her wagon, but did not know when—or if—she'd ever find any more. So she rationed herself strictly, and pretended that her face was clean. She dreamed of taking a shower or a bath, of rinsing dishes and tossing out the dirty dish water. She dreamed of rain.

With a sigh, she put thoughts of falling water out of her mind, grasped the handle of her laden wagon, and began walking again. She'd made up her mind; she would chance finding a safe place to spend the night rather than turning back.

Slowly, almost imperceptibly, the light dimmed as she walked. The wagon she dragged behind her seemed to gain in weight, as if she pulled a wagon full of metal bars stacked to her waist. The half empty bottle hanging from her neck swung back and forth as she went, a sloshing metronome that bumped her right side and then her left. Mikhaila looked up at the nicotine and soot stained sky, feeling sweat slowly bead from her pores until the droplets fell from their own weight and began to slide down her forehead and cheeks. She glanced at her watch; it said 6:45, and she had to wonder if she hadn't made a bad choice. She was running out of time, and soon the nocturnal oddities who hunted the night for fresh meat would be abroad. Her only weapon was a long curved sword she'd found buried in the back of a ransacked Asian market. It was sharp, the blade strong, but she didn't want to get close enough to the night-hunters to use it.

With renewed vigor born of her anxiety, she continued on with a quicker step. If she couldn't find a suitable building to hold up in overnight, she'd have to hide her wagon and find a tree to climb. There would be no sleeping if that happened. Fifteen minutes later, according to her watch, she topped a slight rise and saw something at the side of the road.

She slowed cautiously, eyes darting left and right as she checked for anything that might be a threat. There was nothing, no movement but for herself and the sluggish swirl of polluted clouds high above. She approached the object that had caught her attention, squinting her eyes in the lowering light.

It was a sign, the post only standing four feet tall. The sign itself, once painted white but now a dingy grey, had been hand lettered. The letters, perhaps faded from a bright brassy red, were now the color of old blood. It said:

Welcome to
The Rose Vine Arbor
Bed & Breakfast

Just past the sign was a pathway of flat stone blocks which looked to have been recently swept clean. Mikhaila followed the path with her eyes, seeing a dark two-storied building about a hundred yards off the dilapidated road. On one end was a glass room, like a greenhouse. A few trees, skeletal silhouettes without their leaves, surrounded the building. But what caught her eyes was a glimmer of light coming from a window on the ground floor. It was just a narrow slit of brightness, as though someone had not closed the drapes completely.

She glanced at her watch again. 7:08 pm, the second hand skimming in its prescribed circle with no regard for her concerns. She looked around again, but there were no other buildings in sight. She wiped her face with the back of her hand, smearing dust mixed with sweat along one cheekbone. Farther along the road, and back the way she'd come, there was nothing to see. With no other good options, she turned off the road and walked along the stone pathway, her wagon jerking and bumping along behind her.

When Mikhaila reached the wooden house, she dropped the handle of the wagon and pulled the sword from its hiding place amongst her possessions. She held it down at her side, parallel to her left leg, and slowly climbed the three shallow steps to the deep front porch. Latticework framed both sides of the porch, and dead vines still climbed the brittle slats, no leaves or flowers clinging to them, but an abundance of triangular thorns. She crossed the porch on soft feet, cringing when a loose board squeaked. At the front door, a heavy wooden slab bound with metal top and bottom, she tried the tarnished brass handle. It moved only a fraction of an inch, clicking slightly as she tried turning both directions. The door was locked.

Remembering the slit of light from the ground floor window, Mikhaila took a deep breath and knocked. Her knuckles barely made a sound on the heavy wood. Glancing over her shoulder nervously, she lifted the sword. She turned it, and used the end of the handle as a knocker.

In the distance, something called. When Mikhaila had been a child, her mother had taken her to the zoo. All of the animals had been in their cages with signs giving their names in English and Latin, and descriptions of their habitats and life-spans. All of the animals except for the pea-fowl. The hens were brown and nondescript wandering the walkways and flowerbeds, but the peacocks were fantastically colored and larger than life. All these years later, Mikhaila could still remember their royal blue and emerald green coloring, and their multicolored fanned tails with the repeating eye pattern at the end of each vane. She also remembered their cries. Half call, half scream, and it had made her cover her ears with her hands when they began sounding off. All those beautiful birds were dead now, long dead and no more than bones; but the night-hunters screamed that same peacock cry in the darkness, and Mikhaila wanted to cover her ears again.

For long seconds nothing happened, and she began to wonder if she should walk around the building, and perhaps peek into the window of the lighted room. There was a soft creak on the other side of the heavy door, and she stepped back, holding the sword low but in readiness. There was the sound of bolts being drawn back and chains disengaged. Then the tarnished doorknob twisted and the door swung inward revealing a shadowed figure holding a shuttered lantern. A candle set before a mirror inside the lantern flickered slightly, casting a single bright beam into Mikhaila's face.

"Can I help you?" a low male voice asked, as though a stranger on his doorstep was an everyday occurrence.

"I saw your sign," Mikhaila replied breathlessly. Another soulless, spine-weakening cry came from the near distance. "I need a place to spend the night. If—if you have room, and don't mind," she added awkwardly. She knew what a B&B was, from her childhood. Her mother had never had the money to take them on vacation, so she'd never even stayed in a motel, let alone a place like this.

"Do you have any luggage?" the man asked. He was still no

more than a silhouette in the doorway, his lantern shining into her eyes almost painfully.

"I have a wagon," she said, pointing behind her.

"Of course," he said, gesturing to her left. "There's a ramp, there. Feel free to bring your things inside."

When he turned the lantern, she could see the narrow rather rickety ramp at the far edge of the steps where some of the lattice had been broken out. She hurried down to her wagon and pulled it around, not wanting him to change his mind and lock her out. The cries from the desolate woods were beginning to sound nearer, and she knew what her chances of outrunning the beasts would be.

The ramp was barely wide enough for the wagon to fit, and steep enough to test her strength. The man at the door made no attempt to help her, just stood with the lantern in his hand as he waited. When she finally managed to muscle the wagon onto the porch, he stood back and pulled the door wide so she could pass inside.

The room within the front door was dim and slightly cooler than the air outside. She waited while her host closed the heavy door and shot home the three steel bolts and engaged the two heavy chains. When he finished, he opened the shutters on his lantern so that light bloomed beneath his hands. The floor and walls of the room were all made of blond colored wood, as were the chairs and tables set along the walls. Dark rugs, their colors disguised by the flickering candle, were scattered before the different seating areas. Another sign, a twin of the one out by the road, was hung on the wall to the right of the door. It again reiterated the name of the place: The Rose Vine Arbor Bed and Breakfast.

The man finally turned so Mikhaila could see him in the lantern light. He was older than she, but she wouldn't guess by how much. There were crow's feet around his eyes, and grey streaked his dark hair. But these days, that didn't mean so much. There was no grey yet in her red hair, and she didn't think she'd produced any wrinkles so far; but a glance into her eyes would show her older than her years accounted for.

"My name is Gregory," he said and nodded to her. He made

no attempt to shake her hand. Those kinds of pleasantries had died out long ago. "I have a room on the main floor, so you won't have to worry about taking your luggage up the stairs."

She glanced back at her wagon, the handle still clutched in her right hand. Her left hand still held the hilt of the sword.

"We don't accept money anymore, for obvious reasons," he went on serenely, and she noticed that he was clean-shaven. More than that, his face was clean, with no sign of the ash or dust that she knew was ingrained into her very pores. "But we have a very generous trade policy. Do you have anything to trade?"

"I—I'm not—" she stuttered, looking at her wagon again.

"I don't get out much," Gregory went on in that smooth, cultured voice that made the moment even more surreal to Mikhaila. "So there are some things we are low on. If you have any canned goods, that would be most welcome. Alcoholic beverages of any kind would certainly be acceptable. Antibiotics or painkillers would also be more than sufficient."

"I do have some canned stuff," she said when he fell silent. "I'm sorry, I don't have any alcohol, or that other stuff you mentioned. I do have a bottle of aspirin." She actually had two, but didn't want to give them both up.

He nodded thoughtfully, then said, "Very well, I think we can make a deal. Shall we say six cans? And the aspirin."

When it was clear he was waiting for payment, she turned and crouched beside her wagon, reaching beneath her clothes bag to pull out the items. She didn't want him to see her water, or how many cans she actually had. If he noticed her sword, he made no mention of it.

He took the cans from her one by one as she pulled them out, inspecting them carefully to be sure there was no outward sign of damage. Two cans of chicken noodle soup, two cans of French cut green beans, and two cans of sliced peaches in heavy syrup. When she handed him the bottle of 100 aspirin, he smiled, setting everything on the table beneath the B&B sign.

"Wonderful!" he said, showing the first real animation since he'd opened the door for her. "If you'll follow me, I'll show you to your room. I'm afraid you've come too late for dinner, but you're welcome to freshen up before bed. Breakfast is at eight in the morning, and you won't want to miss that."

That surreal quality had come back, and Mikhaila kept a tight hold on her weapon.

When he reached a particular door, Gregory opened it with a flourish. He stepped inside, pulled a lighter from his pocket, and lit candles in sconces on either side of the door, then another on the bedside table. In the flickering unreliable light, the room looked relatively clean. There was a large bed with real pillows and blankets, and a heavy overstuffed chair in the far corner. There was a narrow door open to reveal a small empty closet, and a coat tree in another corner made of shiny untarnished brass.

"You may leave your luggage here, and if you'll just follow me once more, I'll show you to the facilities."

Mikhaila frowned. The facilities? What on earth was he talking about? She left her wagon, but kept hold of the sword as she followed him out of the room and down the wide hallway to another door. When he pushed this door open, there were already candles lit inside. In a small alcove to one side was a low toilet. But that wasn't what caught her attention. Displayed grandly in the center of the tiled floor was a graceful porcelain claw-foot tub. Heavy terrycloth towels hung on a rack to one side, and narrow brass shelves held bottles with shampoo, conditioner, and soap.

"What is this?" Mikhaila breathed. She'd seen nothing like this in years.

"It's a bathroom," Gregory answered matter-of-factly. "I'm afraid there is just the one for the entire floor. But a bath before bedtime is included in the price of the room. There is a complimentary robe hanging on the back of the door."

"Where do you get the water?" she asked, feeling tears sting her eyes. She'd dreamed of bathing, and now… This place was a dream come true!

"We're very lucky," he said, nodding when he saw how moved she was. "We have a very deep well, and a huge stock of coal to heat water when we want it. Please, take as long as you like to bathe. There is nothing in the world like feeling clean, especially these days."

As he backed out of the room, pulling the door shut behind him, she reached out to catch the doorknob. "Wait, uh—Gregory?"

"Yes?" he replied, keeping his eyes averted, as though she were already stripped for her bath.

"You keep saying 'we'", she said, feeling awkward. "Are there other people here?"

"No, just me and my wife," he said. "You'll meet her at breakfast. I'm afraid she's already gone to bed."

"Oh, okay," Mikhaila said, letting him shut the door. "Thank you!" she called without opening it. She waited for a moment, then quietly turned the thumb-lock. She leaned her sword against the wall where it would be close to hand. When she was sure she wouldn't be disturbed, she went to the tub and slowly twisted the white-enameled knobs to turn on the water, a child-like smile curving her lips as it began to fill the tub. The water was clean, no trace of ash or other contaminants, and with some experimentation she could make it the temperature she wanted. As the tub filled, she stripped out of her grimy clothing, letting it fall to the floor in a grungy pile. Her hair was in as bad a state, so filthy the auburn color was changed to a dull brown, and stiff in the habitual braid she confined it to. She pulled the plait apart with her fingers, and climbed into the spacious tub with a groan of pure pleasure.

She slid down so that the water came up to her chin, only sitting up to turn off the water when the tub was completely filled. She lay in the tub for a long time, reveling in the feel of clean water against her skin. After a while, when her fingers started to prune, she began to wash. The soap felt like silk against her skin, the scent something light and flowery. Washing and conditioning her hair was very nearly an orgasmic experience, and she relished every moment.

Finally, after more than an hour, she climbed out of the tub. One soft fluffy towel was wrapped around her head to keep her hair from dripping, while she dried herself with another. The soft friction of the terrycloth against her clean skin was something she'd never thought to feel again.

When she looked at her castoff clothing, she felt tears prick her eyes once more. How could she possibly get dressed in them again now that she was clean? She put on the robe that Gregory had pointed out to her, and rubbed her hair with the towel. There was a large-toothed comb on the shelves, and she used that to pick the snarls out of her long hair. Clean and combed free of knots, it hung nearly to her waist; in the candle light it gleamed with copper highlights, and Mikhaila smiled at the feel of the silken strands beneath her fingers.

"The towels and this robe are clean," she whispered to herself, gazing into the steam-obscured mirror. "Maybe he would let me wash my clothes tomorrow? I could give him more cans for that." She watched her reflection as she slowly combed her hair until it was dry. "Maybe he could use some help around here, keeping up the place," she said to herself. She had nowhere she needed to be, wasn't heading to any particular place. She was just a nomad, trying to stay alive in a hostile world. Maybe this place could be her destination.

Gregory waited until he heard water start running, then went quietly down the hall. He had the lantern in one hand, but didn't need its dim light to find his way. At the end of the hall he turned right, following his often-trod path to the greenhouse. Double doors at the end of this shorter hall swung open soundlessly beneath his touch, and he set the lantern aside after snuffing the candle. It was not wise to use light where it could be seen from the dead forest. The high trilling calls and sharp hair-raising cries could be clearly heard through the glass panes that made up the walls and roof. Strange mutated creatures had been drawn to the B&B before, and he didn't have such a large store of glass that he wanted to have to replace any more of it tonight.

"We have a guest, darling," he said softly as he crossed the slate-tiled floor. Near the first planting bed his wife reclined on a chaise lounge, her dark eyes turned upward. If there had been stars, she might have been searching out constellations. Now, she just studied the slow monotonous roil of poisonous clouds that covered the sky. She didn't move her gaze from the heavens, but her right hand twitched at his approach.

"I know, my dear, it's been a long time," he said gently,

seating himself on the edge of the chaise. He touched her cheek with his fingertips lightly, frowning slightly when he felt how fragile she had become. "Don't worry, darling. She is bathing now, and then will sleep. You must rest. You can meet her in the morning."

Around the room there was a soft rustling, and the subtle suggestion of movement. But Gregory just sat with his wife, enjoying time spent with the woman he loved.

When Mikhaila awoke, for a moment she couldn't remember where she was. Her head rested on a pillow instead of her clothes bag, and she lay in an actual bed instead of on the floor of some abandoned building. For the first time in a long time she couldn't smell dirt or her own sweat. She stretched languorously, and reached to pick up her watch off the bedside table.

The watch said 4:27, but the second-hand was no longer making its prescribed sweep around the dial. It had stopped halfway between the 3 and 4.

"Shit," she sighed. She'd forgotten to wind it before going to sleep.

There was a soft knock at the door, and she called hesitantly, "Yes?"

"Breakfast is ready, you don't want to be late," came the muffled voice of her host.

She got out of bed, pulling the covers with her, and opened the door just a crack so she could see him. "Um, I wanted to ask you," she said a bit breathlessly, keeping the covers pulled up in front of her. "All of my clothes are really dirty, and I was wondering if I might be allowed to wash them today? I'll pay more."

Gregory pursed his lips in thought, and then nodded. "I don't see why not. We'll have to discuss the price, but we can do that after breakfast." He interpreted her glum expression correctly when he added, "We don't stand on ceremony around here. You can wear the robe to breakfast, Miss—I'm afraid I never got your name?"

"Mikhaila," she returned, and added, "Thank you." Her

smile changed her face from wan to pretty. Her green eyes smiled as well, and Gregory found himself smiling back. It had been a long time since he'd seen such a lovely young woman, and after her bath she really was attractive.

He suddenly realized what he was thinking, and backed up a step both physically and mentally. "Well," he said a bit brusquely, "Please do hurry, we don't want to start without you. Just follow this hallway," and he pointed farther into the house, "around the corner, and we'll be through the double-doors at the end.

Without waiting for a reply, he turned and followed his own directions. Mikhaila watched until he turned the corner, then closed her door.

"He's an odd bird," she said under her breath as she dropped the blanket she'd covered herself with back on the bed and reached for the robe. "I wonder what his wife is like?"

A few minutes later she walked barefoot down the hall, turning the corner cautiously when she reached it. There were no windows along here, and only two candles lit in sconces to show the way. At the end were the double-doors Gregory had told her about, each with high round stained-glass windows. They were beautifully colored in the design of red roses, and the brighter light from the other side made them glow softly. Mikhaila smiled as she pushed the right-side door open and looked into the next room.

She was surprised to see, instead of a dining room or even a kitchen, the glass room that she had noticed the night before. As she had thought last night, it was a greenhouse. Someone must have spent time every day brushing ash off the glass panels, and while they weren't sparkling clean they were clear. The nicotine-tinted sky stretched like a vault above them, a pale brownish-orange smear to the east all that could be seen of the sun.

"Ah, there she is!" Gregory exclaimed, more animation in his voice than Mikhaila had previously heard. He stood beside a table covered with a red cloth that hung almost to the floor. The table was oblong, already placed with plates, cups and glasses. There was the mouthwatering scent of cooked ham and toasted bread. At the far end of the table was a woman, ostensibly Gregory's wife. Her hair was black, lank and dull in the overcast light. She wore no makeup except for black kohl outlining her eyes, and her face was pale white with a slight greenish cast. She was wearing a red loose-fitting garment that matched the tablecloth, and sat slumped in her lounge-chair behind the table.

As amazing to Mikhaila as the woman's odd appearance was the lush growth of plants in the room. Green leaves crowded the windows more than halfway up to the angled ceiling panes. She had only a hazy recollection of seeing growing plants in her childhood, and didn't know if any of these were food. But she knew roses when she saw them. Huge blooms of scarlet, crimson and burgundy nestled between an abundance of dark glossy green leaves. There were leaves as far as she could see, but the blossoms were only near the table.

"Mikhaila, I'd like to introduce my wife, Rhosyn. As you can see, she has quite an ability with flowers, a veritable green thumb." As he spoke, Gregory rested one hand on the woman's shoulder, and now he leaned close to her. "Darling, this is the guest who came last night."

Mikhaila didn't know what to do. Gregory was dressed in button-up shirt and slacks, with shiny black shoes on his feet. The woman Rhosyn was wearing what might pass as a festive outfit, as though ready for a party. And she herself stood there in a borrowed bathrobe, with bare feet on the cool slate-tiled floor.

"Please, come and sit. Get acquainted. It's been a long time since we've had anyone for breakfast." Gregory pulled out a chair beside his wife, and gestured for Mikhaila to approach. Rhosyn did not move, except her head turned just slightly so she could watch Mikhaila walk self-consciously to the chair and sit down. "There is coffee and sugar, but we have no creamer," Gregory continued when Mikhaila was seated. "Or there is lemonade. Not real lemonade of course, it's made from a powder mix, but it tastes all right."

"Coffee would be great," Mikhaila said softly, feeling incredibly uncomfortable. As he lifted an insulated carafe to pour hot coffee into her cup, she noted that his wife was staring at her. Rhosyn's eyes were dark, as black and lackluster as her hair. The woman never blinked. There was no animation in her expression. She was like a life-sized doll propped up in the chaise lounge.

"For breakfast there is ham, toast made from bread I baked myself, and hot oatmeal." Gregory had walked around to sit across the table from Mikhaila, on the right side of his wife. He removed domed covers from the platters where the breakfast food waited. The smell of the meat made Mikhaila's mouth water, even if it was canned ham. "What would you like?"

"A little of each, please," she replied, suddenly worried that she would drool down her chin and embarrass herself even more.

As Gregory served Mikhaila, Rhosyn languidly lifted one hand from beneath the table. The arm and hand extending from the belled sleeve of her gown was exceedingly thin, pale skin stretched over bones and tendons. Her fingers were also long and thin, each fingertip ending in a long sharp nail painted a deep green that shaded to black at the pointed tip. She laid her hand on the red tablecloth, fingers relaxed and slightly curled toward the palm. It was an ordinary even commonplace gesture, but Gregory flinched, and tried to hide it.

Mikhaila swallowed her saliva, and said hesitantly, "I just wanted to thank you so much for letting me stay the night, and for the bath. I haven't had such a comfortable night's sleep in… well, in years I suppose." She directed her words to Rhosyn, not wanting to show bad manners before she stuffed herself with whatever amount of food Gregory would give her.

The woman said nothing, but her head moved slightly as though she nodded.

"Forgive my wife, Mikhaila. She has been ill for some time, and no longer speaks," Gregory said as he filled a plate and set it before her. "Please, eat. You look hungry."

Mikhaila didn't argue, and began to eat as quickly as she could without choking. She couldn't remember the last time she'd had meat, even canned meat. It was tender and moist, and tasted divine. The fresh bread was also a treat, and she savored the texture as well as the flavor. There was no milk or butter for the oatmeal, but it had been cooked with brown sugar and cinnamon. She could not remember the last time she'd had such a diverse and filling meal. She was so busy enjoying her own food, it wasn't until she'd cleaned her plate that she realized Rhosyn had eaten nothing. The other woman simply lay in her chair, one hand lying limp on the table, the other still hidden in her lap. She stared at Mikhaila, her thoughts inscrutable. Across the table, Gregory ate his own breakfast.

"So, how long have you been here?" she asked, trying self-consciously to be polite.

"Since the world changed," Gregory said, setting his fork down and picking up his glass of lemonade. "I go to the nearest town now and then, and bring things back that might be useful. But I haven't traveled more than a few miles since my darling became ill. Rhosyn is fragile, and I don't like leaving her alone for very long."

Rhosyn sighed almost soundlessly, but Gregory just smiled and patted her limp hand.

"Is there, I don't know, anything that can be done to help?" Mikhaila asked, looking at the other woman again. Behind the painful thinness and gothic complexion, she didn't look to be much older than Mikhaila herself. But again, it was always hard to tell.

"That's very sweet of you," Gregory said, and beamed a smile at her. "Would you like some more coffee? It's the house blend."

She picked up her cup. She'd only taken a couple of sips because she'd been so interested in the food. Now she drank some more, and her nose wrinkled a little at the burnt, bitter taste. Beggars couldn't be choosers, and she'd gone so long without coffee that she wasn't altogether sure this wasn't the normal flavor. She finished her cup and set it down, having decided not to take any more even though her host had offered. When she looked up she was startled by a sudden wave of dizziness that made her slump back into her chair. Beside her, Rhosyn had lifted her other hand onto the table. Like the first it was little more than skin-wrapped bones with long dark nails. It was strange, because the nails reminded Mikhaila of something. Something she'd just seen.

"There you go, Mikhaila. No worries, you don't have to be afraid," Gregory said, getting up from his chair and coming around the table to stand behind her. She was unable to turn her head or sit up in her chair. "This is just the effect of the drug in your coffee. It won't last very long, maybe half an hour. I'm sorry about the bitter taste it gives the coffee—almost sacrilegious, that. But from years of trial and error, I've found that mixing it with coffee is really the only guaranteed way to get guests to take it."

"Wha—" she tried to say, but her tongue felt too big for her mouth. She felt as though she was sliding out of her chair, like the cartoon rabbit she remembered from years ago when she'd sat in front of the TV on Saturday mornings. She had little control over her body, but when Gregory put his hands on her shoulders, she could feel them just fine.

"It was very sweet of you to ask if there was a way to help my lovely wife," he went on with the cheerful intonation of a man who regularly talked to himself. "Because that is exactly what you are going to do. I am afraid that it's a bit painful. I apologize for that but there's nothing to be done. I did ask if you had any painkillers, if you remember; but I doubt aspirin will really do anything to dull the pain. Although," he said thoughtfully as he pushed her forward and leaned down to put his arms around her. He lifted her out of her chair, his arms around her ribcage making it hard to breathe. "I don't think the aspirin will dull the pain, but it might thin the blood enough to make the ordeal easier."

He wasn't a particularly large man, but he had ample strength to man-handle Mikhaila. Once he'd gotten her out of her chair, he was able to hold her up with just one arm. With his other hand, he reached to lift the bright tablecloth up and away from his wife, revealing her mutated form.

Rhosyn was not entirely human. Extending from beneath the hem of her gown were not human legs, but thick thorny vines that trailed off the edge of her chaise and into the surrounding beds of roses. Drugged and unable to move, Mikhaila could still think and feel at maximum capacity. The other woman's dark pointed nails were not really nails; they were thorns, like the sharp dangerous thorns growing on the nearby rose stems.

"The world has changed so much," Gregory said gently, his breath warm against her cheek, and he reached up to stroke her soft auburn hair. "It even changed my beautiful wife. She is not like the monsters out there," and he gestured beyond the glass-paned walls, "She is still human. But she needs a special diet, one that is somewhat hard to procure. And so I'll thank you now, as there won't be any time later."

He turned her toward Rhosyn; the other woman had sat up in her chaise, and was watching this exchange avidly. Her eyes were still black, but her gaze had sharpened. She, not Gregory, was the one to see tears well in Mikhaila's green eyes.

To have traveled so far and for so long, Mikhaila thought, knowing that this place would be her destination after all.

"Here you go, my darling," Gregory said jovially as he stepped forward, Mikhaila's limp form in his arms. "As my mother used to say, don't let any go to waste. I don't know if there are any starving children in Africa these days, but waste-not want-not still applies."

Something moved; the roses rustled and shook. Mikhaila's head had dropped and so she saw her own tears fall and land on the heavy twisted vines that connected Rhosyn to the planting bed. The vines moved snake-like, shifting sideways and catching Gregory's feet. Unprepared, he tripped and fell forward landing across Rhosyn's 'legs' with Mikhaila trapped between them. Large thorns punctured Mikhaila's skin through the robe, drawing blood from multiple lacerations on her stomach and chest. The cuts burned and stung, and the rush of adrenaline gave her the only chance she might get.

Forcing her muscles to answer her commands, she pushed herself sideways and fell off the end of the chaise. She had enough control left to look up, and witnessed maybe the most horrifying thing she'd ever seen.

"Darling, wait!" Gregory called, trying to get his feet under him once more. Rhosyn, no longer weak and lethargic, darted forward. The thorn-tips on her fingers dug into his upper arms, and the thin spindly arms were stronger than Mikhaila had thought as she dragged her husband closer. "Wait!" he said again, no longer the cheerful B&B owner. He looked into his wife's black eyes and saw his own death.

Rhosyn opened her mouth, her jaw unhinging like some kind of reptile, revealing rows of needle-like thorns instead of teeth. She jerked forward, her lamprey mouth clamping down on his throat with an impact that shook his whole body.

Mikhaila strove to move backward, away from this terrible scene, and hopefully out of reach of the other woman before she finished. Her adrenaline had given out, and her muscles shook and shivered. There was still too much of the drug in her system. So she lay four feet from the end of the chaise lounge, not wanting to watch, but unable to close her eyes for fear she would miss Rhosyn coming for her.

The black-haired chimera held Gregory close, almost cradled against her. He was no longer moving. When she was finished with him, he was as pale and insubstantial as she had been. She dropped him, and took some time to lick her thorny fingertips clean of his blood. As he had admonished her before, she didn't let anything go to waste.

Mikhaila lay on the hard slate floor, her coppery hair spread around her like a nimbus, the puncture wounds on her torso burning. If she lived, would she turn into something like Rhosyn? She didn't know how the mutations worked, but couldn't imagine this would end well for her.

"You're welcome to stay." Rhosyn's voice was soft and breathy, reminding Mikhaila of the sound the wind made through dead leaves. "I won't hurt you."

"Like you didn't hurt him?" Mikhaila managed to whisper.

The other woman rose from the chaise lounge, balancing effortlessly on the twisted vines that were her legs. Behind her, the many blooms of red bobbed and moved as though trying to get a better view. "You are beautiful. I would never hurt a thing of beauty."

Mikhaila said nothing, just lay on floor.

Rhosyn moved closer, and leaned down gracefully. In one hand she held a stem with a red rosebud, three dark glossy leaves standing out beneath it. "Blood red roses. Aren't they even more beautiful now?" She pressed the stem into Mikhaila's slack hand, a tiny thorn stinging her palm. "All I wanted was beauty. He never brought me any, until you." She moved away, out of Mikhaila's line of sight. In the planting beds the leaves whispered, stems and vines moving of their own volition.

Mikhaila waited for the drug to wear off. She couldn't see, but it felt as though the rose stem had grown into her skin. And she was very, very thirsty.

~ FIN ~

fin: a membranous, wing-like or paddle-like organ attached to any of various parts of the body of fishes and certain other aquatic animals, used for propulsion, steering, or balancing.

fin: Latin word meaning 'end'

In the open Pacific, somewhere between Fiji and Hawaii, the Korean fishing vessel *Weibeu Daenseo* pulled in their second net of the day. The first haul had been large, and the captain might have called it a day, but he was not the owner of the boat. He would not head back for land until his fish holds were full.

Captain Seong ordered the crew to the deck. The winch began pulling in the nets, and all hands were available. Seong was lost in thought while he waited for the call that all the nets were in. As a child and then a young man, he had romanticized the idea of being a boat captain. However the open water was no longer an imagined wonderland. The reek of salt and the stench of blood and dead fish were no perfume to his nose. He grew tired of the crude, uneducated men he commanded and wished that he'd taken his father's advice and gone into business.

When cries of alarm from the deck registered on his wandering mind, he nearly fell out of his chair. Leaning forward to see what had caused the commotion, he could only stand and stare for several seconds. The nets had come in with only a few flopping fish in comparison to their earlier haul, but lying gasping on the deck amongst them was a woman.

Seong snapped an order, and his second in command Eun stepped up to take his place. Then, the captain hurried down to the main deck to find out what had happened.

"Daejang," one of the men called, his eyes wide with shock and something like fear, "She was in the net. We pulled her out like a fish."

"I can see that, Babo," Seong said. "Where did she come from?"

As the captain spoke with his crew, the woman watched them but did not respond to what was being said. When she had sufficiently caught her breath, she sat up.

Every man on deck took a step backward, except Seong.

"Who are you?" he asked in Korean. When she just shook her head, he tried heavily accented English. "Who are you?"

"You may call me Ka'ahu," she said, and coughed, covering her mouth with one hand.

"Water," Seong ordered, not looking to see which man jumped at his command.

Soon a crewman came back with a plastic bottle of water, which he handed to Seong. The captain twisted off the lid and knelt as he handed the bottle to the woman.

Her fair hair was long and tangled, her skin pale and smooth. Her eyes were dark, so dark he could not discern pupil from iris, and they seemed rather flat. She had nearly drowned, and was surely in a state of shock.

"How did you come to be here?" he asked slowly. It had been many months since he'd had reason to speak English, and he was sure she would be hard pressed to understand him.

"I fell," she replied after taking a long swallow from the bottle, "I've been in the water for a long time."

"You are safe," Seong assured her, touching her shoulder lightly.

She was wearing what appeared to be a body suit made of grey neoprene-like fabric that covered her from wrists to throat to ankles. It was dappled and striped with strange patterns that were familiar to him, although he couldn't place it.

"Come," he said to her, "you may rest in my cabin. If you're hungry, we will feed you. Then I will call the mainland for you."

He helped her up, letting her clutch his arm, while she freed her feet from the net. As he slowly escorted her across the deck, he gave clipped orders to reset the nets and prepare for another haul. Even in this instance, they could not return to the mainland if the holds were not full. Fishing was a cutthroat profession and there were plenty of men willing to take his place as the captain of the *Weibeu Daenseo.*

In his cabin, Seong immediately handed Ka'ahu a towel with which to dry herself. While she did so, he pulled a couple of blankets from a compartment to warm her.

She wrapped herself in one, not bothering to remove her damp clothing, and sat on the edge of his bed. Her face in the dim light of the cabin was very pale, almost iridescent, when she turned to look at him.

"What ship were you on, Ka'ahu?" he asked, sitting at the tiny desk at the end of the bed. He'd found a piece of paper, and waited to write down the name she gave him.

"A cruise ship, Sapphire Princess," she said, her dark eyes never leaving his face. She never blinked. "It passed by here. Two days ago, I think."

"You've been in the water for two days," he repeated, astonished that she'd survived. In the open ocean with no floatation device and completely alone, her survival was a miracle. "These waters are full of predators. You are lucky to be alive."

Slowly, she nodded. "Yes, I am lucky."

"Are you hungry?" he asked, getting to his feet again. He would need to contact the mainland to let them know about the castaway they'd found, and make arrangements for her safe return.

"No, thank you. I am tired." She continued to look directly at him in a way that made him uncomfortable. There was something about her level gaze that was almost predatory.

"Please, rest," he said politely. "I will check on you after I've talked to my superior. If you need anything, that button there," he pointed to the little intercom on the wall next to the bunk, "will connect you to the bridge. I am at your service."

She nodded, the barest smile curving her lips.

For a moment, the romance of the sea that he had imagined as a boy returned to him. A beautiful woman rescued from certain death, and who would most certainly fall in love with the dashing captain…

"Rest," he said again, feeling rather flushed. He quickly left the room, being sure the door was latched behind him.

A little more than three hours later, the intercom buzzed. "Captain?" Ka'ahu said, her soft voice sounding tinny through the speaker.

"Yes, what do you need?" he answered. The crew was preparing to pull in the nets from their third cast. Hopefully, it would contain more fish than the last one, and no more castaways.

"I'm feeling much better. I would like to come up onto the deck."

"We're about to bring in the nets, Ka'ahu. It would be better if you waited," he replied, not wanting to worry about a civilian when the carnage began.

"I understand," she replied, and said no more.

Seong had no time to continue the conversation as the nets appeared over the port side of the deck. He smiled and nodded to Eun when he saw the haul. Once the nets were cleared the holds would be full, and they could start back to the mainland. He hadn't had a reply about the woman pulled from the sea, but was sure there would be a response before they made port.

The crew, a degenerate group with no breeding and little education, was well trained in the task at hand. The faster they worked, the better the meat—the better the meat, the higher the price that would be split between them.

As usual, they separated the catch. Different types of fish were packed in the hold together and covered with ice. Though the real prize was sharks. Shark fin soup sold for 50,000 won per serving in Korea. The fins themselves sold from one hundred to five hundred dollars a pound in the international market, depending on the demand. Seong was pleased when he saw how many sharks had been caught in the nets.

As the crewmen who specialized in finning began their gruesome work, the strange castaway appeared on deck.

Babo had just finished slicing the last fin from the shark before him. He turned to throw the animal back into the water, as was the custom, where it would slowly sink without fins to propel it until it drowned or was eaten by another predator. He didn't know the woman was behind him until something cold and sharp slid into his back. He couldn't even cry out, the pain was so intense.

Seong heard the yelling from panicking crewmen before he understood what was going on. The deck was a mess of dying fish and blood, half the crewmen still working over the sharks that thrashed as they fought to escape. One man was down, no two—and then the captain realized that the castaway was in the midst of it. He was so shocked to see her there it took a moment for him to understand that she was pushing the sharks back toward the edge of the deck.

"Stop her, grab her!" he yelled over the PA system. When they did nothing, he realized that the men were afraid to approach her. "Eun, take over," he barked at his second and raced out of the small bridge and down the steps to the deck.

When he reached the killing floor, all was pandemonium. Half the crewmen were down now, some struggling to regain their footing while others were still. The rest of the men were giving the castaway a wide berth as she shoved struggling sharks over the side and back into the water.

"Ka'ahu, stop what you are doing!" Seong ordered, putting every bit of authority into his voice.

She was covered in blood, even her pale hair dyed in it. The expression on her face was cold fury.

"You must stop now or you'll be bound and confined," he added, coming close enough to touch her.

"You should be ashamed," she said, rounding on him. Two sharks, already deprived of their fins, had stopped struggling near her feet. Their mottled hides slicked with blood resembled the odd designs on the woman's clothing. The rest of the sharks had been returned to the sea. "You know this is wrong. No one should abuse the sea like this. Even the sharks only kill to survive. You kill and kill, wasting nearly all," she said, her voice grating. Her pain was so intense Seong expected to see tears on her face. But her dark, flat eyes simply stared at him, unblinking.

"This is not your concern," he said gently but firmly, hands held before him to show he was weaponless. "You are sick from being so long in the sea, alone—"

"Daejang," one of the men called, terror in his tone, "Look at Babo. Look at Yun!"

Seong glanced sideways, irritated that he should be interrupted. Of course, none of the men spoke English, so they had no idea what was being said. His eyes widened when he saw that not all of the blood on the deck came from the catch. Babo and Yun's arms had been removed, and were lying next to the opening into the hold.

"The killing, the waste will end. It is over," Ka'ahu said, raising the long bloody knife that she held. "Finished." She smiled slowly, revealing multiple rows of sharp, serrated teeth, like those of the shark.

When the Korean fishing vessel *Weibeu Daenseo* was found several days later, it was drifting with the tide. No one was found on board, not the captain or his crew, nor the unknown castaway with the strange name who had been pulled miraculously from the sea. All that was found was a hold full of fish. In the back hidden section, where the prized shark fins were usually stored, there were fourteen pairs of human arms, carefully packed in ice.

ABOUT THE AUTHOR

Rose Blackthorn lives in the high-mountain desert, but longs for the sea. She is a writer, dog-mom, jewelry-maker, avowed coffee drinker, and photographer. She has been writing steadily since high school, and her short fiction and poetry have appeared online and in print with a varied list of anthologies and magazines beginning in 2010.

More info can be found at:

http://roseblackthorn.wordpress.com/
http://www.facebook.com/RoseBlackthorn.Author
http://amazon.com/author/roseblackthorn
https://twitter.com/rose_blackthorn

Curious about other Crossroad Press books?
Stop by our site:
http://store.crossroadpress.com
We offer quality writing
in digital, audio, and print formats.

Enter the code FIRSTBOOK
to get 20% off your first order from our store!
Stop by today!